FUNNY MONEY

A Novel

T R SCHUMER

Funny Money
Copyright © 2018 by T. R. Schumer
All Rights Reserved Worldwide

Published by T. R. Schumer
ISBN-13: 978-976-96031-6-5
Printed Edition v1.1 - July 2018

Cover Design by Damonza
Editing by Scribendi

For Tony...

Paper money eventually returns to its intrinsic value: zero

– Voltaire

One

"A tallboy? That's all you want?" LJ held both hands on the wheel, your granny's perfect ten and two, just like always. "If I was the one who'd just been let out of the can? I'd be wanting a hell of a lot more than just a beer."

"I don't know what else to tell you, man." Sebo said.

"Well shit, if my man wants a tallboy? Then that's what he's gonna get."

From the front passenger seat Sebo stared out through the windshield of LJ's Impala, not looking at anything in particular, mostly just letting the glare of the outside world roll up against him, and taking it all in, because it'd been such a long time since the last time he'd been outside doing anything. Traffic rolled by him, and the parking lots too, the cheap stucco, and the loud plastic signs, all of it rolling up into view, before sliding by, and being replaced by more of the same. The world hadn't changed much.

"Where we goin' anyway?" Said Sebo.

His question wasn't getting an answer, so Sebo glanced across just as LJ smoothly spun the wheel for another turn,

1

tracking with the motion of LJ's hands, slender enough to slip into anything with ease and slip back out just as quick. Sebo was watching them change places, one over the other, and it was like a little dance just before the car straightened, and LJ let the steering wheel spin back freely beneath his fingertips. The way LJ drove always reminded Sebo of his mom's driving, but he'd never say that to a guy like him.

The steering wheel's fighter-wing-shaped bezel leveled out again, along with Chevrolet's, twin flags logo: red *fleur-de-lis* on the left, checkered flag to the right. Now Sebo could see that LJ was heading east on Cortez, so he decided to change the subject. "You still haven't filled me in on what's, what." Sebo caught LJ cracking a smile, and it made him feel a little queasy.

"What's what is that you're gonna chill."

That's the part Sebo never liked much, because it was like the guy could read minds or something—always seemed to know when you were getting antsy, and at this moment, he was feeling plenty antsy. "I'm not talking about that kinda shit," he said. "I just wanna know where we're going, that's all."

"No worries, my man," LJ said. "I got you all set up—just like I promised." LJ, still with both hands on the wheel and looking straight ahead with his eyes on the road, the Impala gliding along just under the limit, as always. "You don't have to worry about a single thing; it's all been taken care of."

"How about that beer?"

"You can't drink in the car, man, you know the rules."

"So, where're we going?"

"Jesus!" LJ glared at Sebo before returning his eyes to the road again. "You are worse than having a fucking kid in the car, you know that?"

Sebo slumped back against the rolled white Naugahyde, his legs spread across it like two thick roots of a rainforest tree. The AC was blowing ice-cold, and it felt good. The gaudy chrome details of the Impala's dash held his attention as he sulked, but he'd always liked how LJ kept his car perfect. He liked how smooth the vinyl felt too—wished they still made cars with front seats like sofas. Sebo waited a little longer for LJ to relax again before he said, "is it east of I-75, or west of I-75? That's all I'm asking."

"West of 75."

"That's good, thanks, man."

"I told you I'd have you all set up," LJ said, but just as he said it, Sebo could tell his attention was being pulled elsewhere. LJ straightened and then tapped at the hands-free stuck inside his right ear. "What the fuck you want?"

Sebo, listening, couldn't help but grin, because it was like old times—like nothing had changed at all in the past twenty-six months that he'd been away.

Sebo leaned back and relaxed while LJ continued to bark into his hands-free device. "I told you, man… What the fuck did I tell you? No, *you* listen you dumb fuck—*what the hell did I tell you?* Yeah… that's right, that's what I said—and did you do it? That's why you're in the spot you're in… I said to leave those wrestlers alone, didn't I? *Didn't I?* I told you *specifically* to leave those mother-fucking wrestlers, the fuck alone."

LJ ended the call, and just like that, not another word was said on the subject. Sebo knew better than to ask. The AC nice and cold on his face, he looked out again as they were approaching 14th Street West; big-box retail on all four corners, chain restaurants—everything surrounded by football fields worth of scorching hot asphalt and carved up on all sides by eight lanes at

3

street-level. LJ caught a solid green and coasted straight on through the intersection.

A minute or two later the Impala cruised by the dying and deserted, 1970's vintage, DeSoto Square Mall, and kept right on going, bleeding off onto 44th avenue East and into the low-rent side of town. LJ slowed a couple of blocks shy of Old Highway 301, before the Impala made a smooth entry into the parking lot of a Quick-Stop. The convenience store was a standalone, with two sets of pumps out front beneath a shade port. LJ, rolling up and stopping right in front of the store, clicked off the engine, and then said, "This is it."

"This mean I can get a beer now?"

LJ chuckled. "Yeah man, you can get a beer, but what I'm say'n is—*this is it.*"

Sebo sat quiet for a moment as he took another look around, then said, "You got me set up at a Quick-Stop?"

Cranking down his window, LJ shook his head. "Hell no—what kind of guy you think I am?" LJ pointed through the opened window, and out across the asphalt to his left. "I got you set up right over there."

Sebo shifted in his seat and then squinted out in the direction that LJ had been pointing. Beyond the gas pumps, and the vacant lot next door, he could just make out a faded sign: "Pelican Court Trailer Park?"

"That's right—got you a crib, got you a job, and I even got you a roommate."

Sebo, without another word, twisted back against the smooth vinyl. He reached into the back seat and grabbed the top handles of a cheap, nylon duffle. LJ, just looked on for a moment, and then he said, "I like you, man, you know that?"

Sebo had his duffel in his lap by now. It held a single change of clothes, a toothbrush, a pack of disposable razors, and not much else. He stared back at LJ and said, "Thanks for getting me a place to stay; I appreciate it."

Chuckling once more, LJ responded, "That's what I dig about you the most—you haven't even seen the place." Sebo opened the passenger side door and stepped outside. He closed the door easy, just the way LJ liked. Shouldering the duffle, he walked around to the driver's side window.

LJ had his car keys out of the ignition and was fumbling with the over-stuffed ring. He thumbed through a few more keys before unsnapping the right one. "It's number 114," he said. Sebo stuck out his free hand, and LJ dropped the key into his palm.

Slipping the key into the left front pocket of his jeans, Sebo said, "So what's the job?"

"Maintenance."

"Who am I sharing the place with?"

LJ grinned. "You'll like him; he's Italian like you."

"What's his name?"

"Alfonzo Lanzano, but everybody just calls him Alfi."

It took a moment for the familiar name to register, then Sebo said, "You mean the print shop dude? I thought that guy was still locked up."

"Got out a few months ago—good behavior or some shit like that."

Then Sebo saw LJ reaching for his wallet. "Here," he said. Sebo held out his left hand again and then closed it around a wad of fresh twenties. "There's a couple hundred to get you going," LJ said.

Sebo stuffed the cash into the same front pocket that held the key to his new home. He nodded his thanks, and LJ, turning over the Impala's V8, said, "I'd stick around, but I gotta bunch of shit to do. I'll check in on you later in the week."

Sebo nodded a response, didn't watch LJ drive off. He just turned away and walked across the convenience store's sun-baked asphalt. He felt a slight downward shift in temperature when he made it beneath the fuel island's shade port, then a much more pleasant drop when he swung open the glass front door, and the store's AC hit him full blast—felt good.

It was late morning, a Tuesday, and the place was empty. First thing to catch Sebo's eye was the wall of refrigerated display cases that lined the rear of the store. Sebo was tempted, but instead, he kept glancing around until he spotted what he was really hoping to find—two big plastic tubs full of slushy ice sitting on stands near the register. One would have sodas and energy drinks, the other would be filled with beer. Sebo walked over, slung his duffle down from his shoulder and dropped it on to the floor; he stared down at the 12- and 24-ounce cans floating around inside a frozen slurry.

"If you're looking for a cold one, you're in the right place."

Sebo looked up from the plastic tub and smiled at a tanned and freckled girl standing behind the counter and liked it when she smiled back. Then she said, "Anything else you need?" She gazed up at his timbered presence, thick at the top, narrow at the middle, with hands that said he could fight and a face that looked like it had seen the losing side. She liked what she saw, even though she knew better.

"No thanks," he said, "just a beer'll do for now." Sebo watched her little fingers tap at the register keys; she was wearing black nail polish.

"Regular or tallboy?"

"Tallboy."

"How about a quick pick to go with that?"

"They tell you to say that, huh?"

With half a shrug, she said, "Manager likes us to push it, but this week is a good one. I'd do it if I were you." Sebo, indifferent, was being honest when he said, "I'm just not into it." Her fingers tapped the keys some more. "That's cool," she said, "but don't you wanna know how much the Mega Millions jackpot is, this week?" A brief sigh left his lips. He wanted to say '*no thanks*', but he liked her smile, and wanted to see it again, so he played along. "Okay then," Sebo said, "how much?"

"One hundred and eighty-seven." She paused a beat, waited for his reaction—didn't get one, so she said, "Million."

"That much, huh?"

His answer got her to smile again, and it felt good to him. "Pretty cool, right?" She said. "It'll go higher too; always does when the pot gets this big." Sebo thought about it, then said, "I don't know, gambling's never interested me." Her smile stuck around for a bit longer, then she said, "I can't play on account of the fact that I sell the tickets, but if I could, I would, because it's a great rush."

"How's that?" He was staring at her face and enjoying the experience of talking to a woman, hearing a female voice—even though she was just a girl, really, but nicely put together all the same. Almost high-class pretty but not enough to keep her from where she was. She said, "Yeah, well, you get your numbers, right? And now you're in the drawing along with everybody else, and of course, the odds are like, stupid-ridiculous, but then you realize, the odds are the same for *everybody*, right?"

"I don't see what you're getting at."

"Okay," she said, "well, right up until the drawing, you have your ticket, right? And it's like this fun ride, because you have the same chance that anyone else has, and you get to fantasize about what you'd do if your numbers came up—know what I mean?"

"I guess so," said Sebo. Then he saw her smile again, and he reached into his pocket. "All right, you sold me." He watched her grin at him, then she giggled, and he figured it was worth a buck just to see her do that and to have a conversation with a real live girl. He peeled off one of the twenties LJ had just given him and tossed it onto the counter. He watched her little fingers, with their little specks of black nail polish skip over the keys on the register.

"That'll be five dollars even," she said. "You want a bag for your beer?"

"Sure, thanks."

Sebo pivoted on his heel, and then plunged his right hand down into the plastic tub full of slushy ice, his fingers burning numb as he fished around for the one he wanted—the one he'd been dreaming of for the past two years.

His hand came back out gripping his tallboy. Sebo rubbed the dripping wet can against his jeans, and she handed him a little paper bag that just fit it. He slipped the can inside and then set the beer on the counter. She printed out his receipt, and the lottery machine spit out his quick pick numbers. Then she handed it all back along with his fifteen bucks in change, and said, "Hope you have a nice day—enjoy the ride."

Two

Meeting the old lady…

S ebo stood just outside the front of the store with his single can of beer, and all that was left of his previous life zipped inside the duffle bag. The steaming heat of the day was already coming on strong; he breathed in the thickness of it. The subtropical humidity clung to his skin, but the ice-cold beer chilled his palm in a pleasant way.

By the time he had covered the few steps needed to reach the side of the building, the little paper bag had soaked through with condensation. Once there, Sebo ducked in behind a tangle of weeds and thick palmetto, overgrowth that was clustered beside the store's painted block, a wall layered with years' worth of tags left by punks and bangers.

A thick row of scrubby trees ran behind the building and marked the border of the trailer park. Its rumpled and rusted chain link perimeter fence, only marginally serving its purpose, struggled to contain it. Sebo moved closer to the fence and deeper into the shade before cracking open his tallboy. He listened closely to the sound it made when the tab popped, rewarding him with a whiff of fresh hops along with a bit of pure white froth that rose up through the opening and begged for his tongue.

He tilted the can into his mouth and drained it. The ice-cold beer poured down his throat like it was his first time, and he could feel it flowing all the way down into his gut. Seconds later the rush hit him as the alcohol his body no longer recognized came on full force.

Sebo held the can high until every last drop had drained away and the smooth tingle on his tongue faded until all he could taste was the aluminum. He let go a satisfied belch and straightened, crushed the empty in his hand, and smiled. Then Sebo glanced down at his feet, where dozens more crushed beer cans lay scattered and still wrapped inside their tattered little paper bags. The carelessly tossed empties littered the ground, stuck inside weeds, or in the branches of the overgrowth. Eyeing the mess with disgust, Sebo turned away, walked back around to the front of the store, and dropped his can in the trash.

* * *

"You must be Sebo."

"Yeah, that's right. You gotta be Alfi."

Sebo stood beneath the trailer's carport, and through his beer buzz, eyed a guy who couldn't fill a narrow doorway. The skinny little dude had a flowered apron tied around his waist, and his face had the typical look Sebo always got back whenever he met someone for the first time—the girl back at the Quick-Stop being a lone exception—an anomaly he was still puzzled about, but this little dude in front of him was following the standard script: surprise, followed by nervous, followed by trying hard not to look nervous. But other than the flowered apron, the guy looked normal enough, and straight-up Italian, in Sebo's opinion.

"Are you hungry?" Alfi said. "I was just cooking something for lunch."

"Sure, thanks," said Sebo. He followed Alfi in after first topping the trailer's three concrete front steps with a single stride. Sebo ducked through the doorway, and once inside, took a couple of quick glances around. "Who else lives here?" He said.

"Just us."

Alfi's voice came at a normal volume from the kitchen, on account of the trailer being only a single, and vintage at that. Sebo dropped his duffle bag on the gold shag carpet and near a brown velour couch before he reached up and briefly touched the ceiling just above his head. Judging the clearance to be sufficient, he crossed the rest of a neatly furnished living room that included a formal dining set. He could see Alfi shrouded in steam as he hovered over the stove in the kitchen.

"Place looks like Granny's still home," Sebo said.

"She was until she died," Alfi answered.

"So LJ must've paid for the whole package then, huh?"

Alfi, still stirring the boiling pot, said, "LJ has two-thirds of this park already. As soon as one of these old people dies, he makes a cash offer to the family; buys the lot, and everything on it, cheap."

Sebo, still looking around, said, "Yep, that's LJ's style all right."

Stepping back into the living room, Sebo noticed an upright piano sitting against the far wall, and next to a hallway that led

11

to the bedrooms. The upright was wedged in between two narrow bookcases packed with cheap paperbacks and a bunch of Time Life editions. The piano had lace doilies draped across its top. There were black and white family photos in little silver-plated frames. Sebo stared briefly at their ghostly faces before glancing again at the piano. He pressed down on a couple of the keys. The sound they made came off clear, and in tune. He heard Alfi call back from the kitchen: "Do you play?"

"Nope."

"It's a pity; neither do I." Then Alfi briefly appeared, the flowered apron still tied around his waist. "Do you like pasta?"

"You mean like spaghetti?"

"Spaghetti is one kind of pasta," said Alfi. "What I am cooking is called *penne*."

Sebo made a nod of agreement, and, sniffing at the air, said, "Whatever you're cooking smells fine by me, man." Alfi was already back in the kitchen. "This place gotta phone?" Sebo asked. Hearing Alfi call out the phone's location, Sebo went for his duffle. Unzipping the nylon bag, he fished around and came out with the card that had his PO's number on it.

Sebo dialed the number using the dead old lady's rotary landline, getting an answer on the second ring.

"This is Bill Mazurek. To whom am I speaking?"

"Sebastian Corrado, sir. I was told to call this number and report in as soon as I got home."

"All right then, Sebo, good to hear from you, and cut it with the *sir* crap, okay?"

"Yeah, uh, so is there anything else you need from me, Mr. Mazurek?"

12

"There's a lot of things I need from you, like calling me Bill for one thing."

"Sure, Bill, but—I mean today."

"I do mean today."

Bill bent over his desk with pen in hand, and inside an office he shared with two other POs; a portable building surplused from the county school board six years ago, although his superiors had assured him at the time that it would only be temporary: cheap paneling, kid-stained carpet, a smell that stuck to your clothes, and a noisy air conditioner bolted to one wall.

His county-issued phone held to his ear, Bill said, "So let's get started. What's your address? Yeah… got it. Phone? Okay, got that too, and you already have a job lined up, is that right? Good to hear…" Sebo waited, then he heard Bill say, "I'll be around your place this afternoon; let's say three o'clock."

After scribbling the last of the information into Sebo's file, Bill tossed the pen back onto his desk, and said, "Thank you for being prompt, Sebo, you're off to a good start—let's keep it that way, all right? Expect to see me around three then." Mazurek hung up his phone, and Elaine said, "Did I just hear right? You got Sebo?"

Leaning back in his chair, Bill said, "Uh huh, you heard right."

"You do know that guy works for Little Junior." Elaine set her coffee mug down on her desk, folded her chubby arms, and stared across the room at Bill. "If LJ's clean, then I'm a dead ringer for Beyoncé." Bill, taking her comment into consideration, said, "Well, I gotta say, from behind, and in the right light…"

"Shut the fuck up."

Then he saw her smile, and Elaine said, "You really think my ass looks like Beyoncé's?"

Bill, with a shrug, replied, "I'm no expert, but just say'n—it is pretty nice."

"You're a dirty old man you know that? I could write you up for saying shit like that, and you wouldn't get your pension. How does that strike you?" Bill didn't say anything further, he just smiled at her, and waited. A couple of seconds went by before Elaine finally let out a huff, and, serious this time, she said, "Promise me you'll be careful around Sebo, do you hear me? I honestly don't know why the parole board let a guy like that out on the street. He's a dangerous motherfucker who runs all-breezy-like with a whole pack of dangerous motherfuckers, and no matter what the guy tells you, I'll guarantee he's still rolling with LJ's crew."

Leaning back in his chair, still listening, still focused on Elaine's round face, Bill said, "I don't doubt it, but truth is, LJ's got no priors—as in zilch—so he's not my concern."

"He sure as hell oughta be," Elaine snapped back. Then she saw Bill grinning at her again, and she knew what it meant—the man didn't have to say another word. "You're right," she said, "you don't gotta say nothing—you're right. If I'd wanted to be a cop, I'd have stayed a full-blown cop instead of doing this shit."

Bill chuckled. "I'm glad you're not a cop," he said. "Anyways, this shit's not so bad once you give it a chance."

Three

Obviously not Italian…

S ebo placed the telephone's receiver in its cradle and turned back toward the kitchen, pausing at the old lady's dining table, which he noticed had been set for two. Alfi'd even laid out her vinyl lace placemats, her electroplated silverware, rose-printed paper napkins, and the dead old lady's fancy china plates. There were a pair of pressed glass iced teas that almost looked like they were made of crystal. The glasses dripped with condensation, chilled and waiting. Sebo put his left hand around one of them and lifted it to his lips for a sip. "So how come all this family stuff's still here?"

"The son came down from Ohio right after she died," Alfi said. "LJ told me if I wanted this trailer I had to work for it, so I helped the son go through the whole place and find everything he was looking for."

Sebo took another sip from his iced tea. "It doesn't look like he wanted much of anything."

"All he was interested in was his mother's car, her jewelry, and any old coins, stamps, or cash she had stashed around."

"So, he just looted the place then, huh?"

"The man even took her change jar—you believe that? I felt embarrassed for the woman—her son was disrespectful. No man in Italy would act that way after his mother had died."

Sebo thought the trailer's kitchen, just like the rest of the place, looked about as old as the Carter administration, but neat as a pin, and hospital clean. The aroma of Alfi's cooking drew Sebo in closer. "What's in the sauce?" he said, leaning in for a better look. Alfi, stirring gently, said, "It's pomodoro."

"What the hell is pomodoro?"

Alfi, still stirring, and gazing down at his simmering red sauce, said, "Your name is Sebastian Corrado, and you don't know what pomodoro is?" Still stirring his sauce, Alfi said, "It's the Italian word for tomato."

"Seriously?" Sebo questioned, and taking in another whiff, he said, "you mean like marinara sauce?" Alfi shook his head. "Marinara is not Italian," he said. "Sure it is, man, everybody knows marinara sauce is Italian." Still shaking his head, still stirring gently, Alfi said, "Marinara è dell'immigrato; it's not traditional."

"What does that mean?"

"Means that if you go to Italy, and you ask for spaghetti with marinara, the waiter is just going to look at you, and not know what the fuck you want." Using a slotted spoon, Alfi began scooping his pasta out from the boiling pot and into the pan of simmering sauce.

"Why do it like that?" Sebo said. "If it's done, don't you just drain it and then pour the sauce on top? That's what my mom always did."

"Nothing against your mother," Alfi said. "She was obviously not Italian." He spooned in the last of the penne, and then folded the pasta into his sauce, allowing the mixture to simmer on top of the stove. He stirred it until the olive oil and tomato, and the salty pasta water, had all emulsified with the starch in the pasta to form a thick, glistening red smoothness that coated every piece perfectly. "She is ready," Alfi said. "Now we eat, okay?"

"This shit's incredible," Sebo mumbled through his chewing before stuffing in another big mouthful. Alfi, just watching for a moment, said, "I'm glad you are enjoying. I love to cook; it is a passion many Italian men share. I could teach you." Sebo dragged a rose-printed paper napkin across his mouth, said, "I've never cooked anything other than toast."

"Women like it when a man can handle himself in the kitchen—lets her know he can handle himself in other ways. Where I come from? Cooking is not just about eating, it is a romantic endeavor." Sebo was listening to every word because the guy was interesting, and different. "So, what's really in this sauce anyway? It's gotta be more than just tomatoes."

"No, not just tomatoes," said Alfi, "tomatoes from my garden, and pure, imported olive oil of course, the real thing, not that supermarket garbage. A bit of sea salt, and the pasta must be quality, and it has to be cooked perfectly, or else the dish will be terrible."

Four

A bad motherfucker...

"How you doin' today, Trudy?" Bill could hear the baby crying before she'd even opened her front door. He said, "I can wait out here, go ahead and take care of little Derek."

In a tank top, no bra, cutoffs way too short for a woman her age, Trudy flashed a wide, yellow grin. "Thanks Bill," she said. "You're really sweet."

Bill stood just outside Trudy's ground floor apartment for a couple of minutes, using the spare time to answer an email from his supervisor about an upcoming court appearance. The door to her apartment hung open, and the AC was flowing out strong. The chilled air washed over Bill and it felt good, even if the place did smell like dog. When she came back, Bill said, "Your drug test is coming up, you gonna be okay?"

"Yeah Bill, I'll be fine," Trudy nodded an eager response.

"You been attending your meetings?"

She nodded again. "Yeah, I got the slips right here." She dug down into a front pocket of her cutoffs in a way that made it obvious she didn't have on any panties—Bill looked away. She handed him her NA slips. Bill folded the slips of paper and tucked them into his shirt pocket without looking at them. "What about Robby?"

"No sign of him."

"You sure about that?" Bill watched her for a moment, studied her face... waited. Then he saw her bony shoulders sink, which made the tendons in her neck stand out like ropes.

"Yeah, okay," she said, "he's come around, but only to see Derek."

"The restraining order doesn't mean shit if you willingly allow him to enter your home." Bill watched her wilt a bit more, and when she looked back, she seemed even more tired than before.

"Yeah, I understand Bill, thanks." Then she suddenly straightened, her eyes went bright, and, staring right at Bill, she said, "I hear through the grapevine Sebo's out on paper. Is that right?"

"You heard correct."

"He's a bad motherfucker. Why'd they let a guy like him out anyway?"

"You're the second person to tell me that today." Bill focused on her face again and didn't like what he saw. "You know anything I should know?"

Trudy folded her arms in close around her skeleton of a body as if she were freezing in the ninety-degree heat. "He'll be working for LJ, I know that much."

"Anything else?" Bill asked, and Trudy said, "I feel sorry for the PO that gets assigned to him."

* * *

Sebo picked up the spoon Alfi had used to stir his pomo-doro sauce and scraped the last of the tomato-coated pasta onto his plate. He finished it off while still standing at the sink. Alfi, washing dishes, said, "tomorrow I will cook for you some more, okay?"

"What about tonight?" Sebo handed Alfi his empty plate. "I'm sold on your cooking."

Alfi took the plate from Sebo, and let it disappear beneath the soapy water. "I work nights," he said, "but it would be my pleasure to cook lunch for you every day if you like."

"That's fine with me," answered Sebo. "Thanks." He paused a moment, thinking. "LJ said I'm supposed to be doing maintenance, but that's all he told me." Alfi remained quiet, still washing dishes, and Sebo said, "I mean, I got my PO coming by this afternoon. He's gonna need to know about my job, and I don't know shit about my job."

"Didn't, uh, didn't LJ say something to you about it?"

"No. I figured you might tell me." Sebo waited a few more seconds before he decided to leave it be, on account of the fact that he was making the little Italian dude nervous. "Hey, it's not your issue," he said. "It's mine, all right? Don't worry about it, you got your own problems."

"I do have a key to the maintenance shed," Alfi said.

* * *

Sebo lifted the rusted padlock chained to a set of double doors and let out a groan. He kicked at the weeds that crowded the shed's opposing doors until he was able to break one of them free. Once inside, he first discovered that the light didn't work, but there was a window. A quick recon revealed a fully stocked tool box, some yard tools, an old weed-whacker, a chainsaw, and some spare parts for a riding mower that he'd discovered hidden beneath a tarp. The mower had a flat. Sebo figured he could get that fixed pretty quick, but what he really needed, was gas.

"Hey, didn't expect to see you back so soon."

She was smiling again, and it was a nice thing to see—still fresh. Sebo gestured back over one shoulder and out toward the front where a red plastic gas can sat next to the lawnmower wheel with the flat. "I need five gallons of gas."

"You got it," she said. "Anything else?"

He was watching her face again. Her tan and her little nose covered in freckles that told him how much she liked the sun. His eyes shifted next to her round little tits, smooth and watery beneath her white tee-shirt like twin spoons of instant mashed potatoes. He said, "Oh uh, does your air compressor work?"

She nodded. "Sure does."

"I need a couple quarts of oil to go with that gas."

He dropped two twenties on the counter and watched her fingers dance over the register keys as she tallied up the five gallons of gas. He took one step back and grabbed two quarts of oil from a display under the counter, which she added to his total and bagged. "My name's Shelly," she said, handing over the bag along with his change and receipt. "Just in case you were wondering."

"Shelly's a nice name," he said. "Everybody just calls me Sebo."

"I kinda figured that's who you were."

Sebo folded the loose bills with his receipt, stuffed everything back into the left front pocket of his jeans, and said, "You know LJ?"

21

She put both elbows on the counter, rested her chin, and said, "No, I mean, not really, but I know his car. Everybody around here knows LJ's Impala."

* * *

The mower seemed to be running pretty solid so Sebo made another pass. It was an old, but sturdy, commercial model that had a catcher on the back. Which he liked, because he hated raking up clippings. Sebo cut a tidy swath along the single-lane of asphalt that looped through the trailer park. When he'd finished both sides, he headed for the front entrance.

Afternoon sun baked against the asphalt road and radiated heat like an oven on high. Sebo could feel sand grit mixing with the sweat rolling down his back. Bits of grass and dirt clung to his face and neck. It stuck in the back of his throat, too, but he liked the work—enjoyed it even, because he was outside, and he could stay as long as he wanted; no razor wire fences and not even a single guard with a gun anywhere in sight and it was a pretty damned amazing feeling being back on the outside.

The trailer park's entrance consisted of two narrow lanes separated by a strip of weed-infested median. There were two painted cement pedestals on either side, each with two painted pelicans also molded from concrete. A cinderblock sign in the middle of the median read: *Pelican Court Trailer Park*, with smaller letters beneath: *An Over Fifty-Five Community*...

The background was faded but still visible; a blue sky, a sunny beach with breaking surf, and a seagull flying overhead. All of which Sebo found kinda funny because the beach was at least ten miles away. He figured he'd finish up the mowing, and then break out the weed-whacker. The Bronco got his attention.

The Ford four-by-four, entirely vintage, was on the main road and slowing for the turn into the park. A two-door hard top with two-tone paint, white over blue, and with the old-style locking hubs. Sebo could tell whoever owned it took good care of it. The Bronco rolled to a stop beside his mower, and Sebo didn't even need to look at the guy who was driving; he figured he knew already. He shut down the mower, and then pulled his plastic earmuffs down around his neck, safety goggles too. Sebo stepped off the mower and stretched his back—waited...

The guy who got out of the Bronco was older, sparsely gray, but still in pretty good shape. The man left the driver's side door open, held a steady gait straight up until he was standing right in front of him and without a second's hesitation—without so much as a blink. Then he showed his badge, and said, "You must be Sebo, am I right?"

"Yeah, that's right—you a cop?"

"I'm not a cop," he said. "I'm your probation officer." Bill stuck out his hand. "We spoke on the phone this morning; I'm Bill Mazurek."

Sebo was still taking in his new PO's lack of reaction as he was shaking the guy's hand; nothing like Alfi's had been, but not oblivious like the girl's, either. This guy's take was more like how LJ had always looked at him, which was no different than any normal person. Then Sebo said, "You carry a badge, but you're not a cop? What's the difference?"

"A cop's job is to put you in jail. I'm a peace officer; my job is to see to it that you stay out."

"That's a pretty good difference."

"It is, but people like you make it difficult."

"Why's that?"

23

"Because most of you guys don't learn shit, that's why, and you wind up back in lockup anyway."

"You talk pretty tough for an old guy."

"Should I be worried?"

Shaking his head, Sebo said, "No man, you got nothing to worry about around me."

"Good to hear," Bill said. "So let's get down to business—that all right with you?" Sebo nodded his agreement through streaks of dirt and sweat, watched as Bill pivoted back toward his Bronco, saw him grab his notebook off the front seat, and then reach for something else.

Bill spun back to find Sebo waiting right where he'd left him, and watching close as Bill walked up to him, holding out an ice cold bottled water—Bill practically put it right into Sebo's hand. "Here, I just picked this up. I was about to crack it open, but I can see that you need it a hell of a lot more than I do."

Five

Pocket litter...

Sebo came through the front door of the old lady's trailer and spotted Alfi sorting his laundry into neat little piles on the living room carpet. "The AC in this place works pretty damn good," Sebo said. He proceeded to peel his sweat-soaked tee-shirt from his back, and without another word, dropped it onto one of Alfi's piles of dirty clothes.

"Hey, what the fuck?"

"You're doing laundry, right?"

"Laundry yes," Alfi said, "but that shit you just put in front of me is more like toxic waste."

"Sorry man, I apologize." Sebo, bending back down for his tee-shirt, hears Alfi tell him to leave it be. "Are you sure, man?"

"It's okay, don't worry about it."

"Cool, man, thanks." Sebo dug into the front pockets of his filthy jeans and pulled out the key to the maintenance shed. Next came his change, then his gas receipt, the receipt from his 10 AM beer, and finally, the Mega Millions ticket the cute chick at the Quick-Stop sold him. He pitched everything onto the dining table before fishing around some more and coming back out with the rest of the bills LJ gave him. Sebo pushed it all together into a tidy little stack before he stripped off his jeans and tossed them on top of his sweaty tee.

Alfi was just watching.

A few seconds of silence passed before Alfi stepped over to the dining table and stared down at the little pile of crumpled cash. Sebo heard him say something soft in Italian, but it didn't sound like anything nice. "What is it this time, man?" Sebo said. He was standing in his boxers, his hands on his hips, and now he sees Alfi has the twenties in his hands—thumbing through them like he's never seen cash before.

"Did LJ give you these?" Alfi asked.

"Yeah, what of it?"

Alfi, still eyeing the crumpled bills in his hands, fanned out the twenties between his fingers and then laid them out flat on the table. Sebo was still watching close, as Alfi lifted a single bill from the table and then held it up to the light.

"You shouldn't have these."

"Why not?"

"Because they're counterfeit, that's why."

"Fuck…"

That queasy feeling was coming back strong until the delay caught up to him, and the queasiness shifted to anger. "Fuck!" Sebo shouted. "Fuck an ever-loving, mother-fucking ass." Then Sebo sees the little Italian dude is getting pretty freaked, so he backed off. "Hey man, don't fall apart on me, okay? You don't have anything to be afraid of around me."

Alfi was already on the far side of the room by now, and, standing close to the door, he said, "LJ told you that your job was maintenance, right?"

Sebo, still standing in his boxers with his hands on his hips, and with all of the pieces coming together fast—cringed at his own stupidity. "So, this is the job?" He said. "I'm supposed to be guarding you? That's the fucking *maintenance*? Baby-sitting *you*?"

"I was really surprised when LJ didn't tell you."

"I'm sure as hell not." Sebo took in a breath, let it out. He stepped back over to the dining table and picked up one of the twenties. Alfi was still standing near the door but fully focused on the action, observing as Sebo slowly turned the note over in his hands, before softly rubbing his fingers across the bill's surface. The thickness and texture of the paper felt perfect, but the kicker was the raised, old-school printing technique. This feature more than anything else left the bill feeling so incredibly real that it made him blink. Even the smell was spot on. Next, he tipped the note back, and allowed its iridescent surface to catch the light. Sebo let out a soft chuckle. "This is the best work I've ever seen, man."

"Thank you."

Dropping the bill back onto the table, Sebo turned back toward Alfi. "I don't get it, man, you just got out, why go at it again?" Then he read the look from Alfi. "LJ's got you by the nuts too then, huh." Alfi remained quiet, and Sebo said, "Look, I'm cool, all right? If this is the gig, then I'm as stuck in it as you are." Seeing Alfi relax a bit, Sebo said, "what's your plan?"

Alfi moved away from the door and back over to the dining table where the slender Italian reached for one of his hand-crafted twenty-dollar bills. He held it up in front of Sebo, and said, "My plan is to be so fucking good that I don't get caught this time."

"How's that supposed to work?" Asked Sebo. "I mean, no offense, but you got caught last time, remember?"

"Last time was different."

"How so?"

"It was an accident."

"What's that supposed to mean? If I remember right, you're the guy who printed up forty-thousand bucks worth of silver certificates—how does anyone call something like that an *accident*?"

"What I am telling you is the truth, okay?"

Sebo, skeptical as hell, but needing to know more, said, "So what happened then?"

Alfi took in a breath. "For me, it's about currency—not money. I don't care about money. What I love is the physical form, the fine art of paper currency." Alfi paused a moment, then he said, "It is my passion."

"Your passion got you three-to-five," said Sebo. He dropped his hands from his waist. "Look, Alfi, you're still not telling me anything."

Alfi pulled out one of the dining chairs. "Take a seat," he said. "I will explain." Sebo sat down as Alfi went to the harvest gold Frigidaire. He swung open the door and grabbed two cold bottles of beer. Returning to the table, Alfi opened one; he set it down in front of Sebo, kept the other, and then sat down himself. "Salute," Alfi said as he raised the bottle in Sebo's direction. Sebo took a long pull from the chilled bottle and Alfi said, "Like many Italians, my dream was to come to the United States, but not to become rich. I've never cared about that." Alfi took another sip of his beer, then he said, "I came here because I wanted to create your money."

Lowering his half-finished beer, Sebo said, "That statement makes, like, no sense to me whatsoever."

Alfi took another sip of his beer and set the bottle down on a coaster. "In Italy, I worked as a master engraver—this was my trade. The men in my family have always been engravers. I am the fifth generation." Alfi drank a bit more, then said, "My grandfather worked for the Italian government; he created designs for the lira."

"What's the lira?"

"It was our currency in Italy before we joined with the European Union and adopted the euro—I hate the euro," Alfi said. "It's ugly—a currency designed by technocrats. It has no spirit. No life. All of the images are fake—meaningless. It represents nothing." Alfi took another sip of his beer. "But American currency is an example of classic beauty. The U.S. dollar is one of the last currencies in the world that is still being made using traditional intaglio methods. By the modern standard it is old-fashioned, but to me, this is what makes it so beautiful. Everything you see on an American bank note means something. For the engravers who create the plates, the designs are extremely challenging, but what they create is fine art that represents real history—real passion."

Alfi finished off his beer, and then leaned back in his chair. "All nations have a flag," he said, "but the most powerful national symbol people see every day is the one they carry around in their pockets—their nation's currency."

Sebo, still listening, drank down the last of his beer, but he took it slow, because now he was interested in hearing the rest of Alfi's story. "So what were you really trying to do?"

"I wanted to work for your Bureau of Engraving and Printing; I wanted to work as an engraver for your government. My dream was to create designs for the U.S. currency."

Sebo briefly scratched at the back of his head. "Well," he said, "the only two places that do that kinda stuff are in Washington DC, or Fort Worth. What the hell were you doing down here in Bradenton, Florida?" Then Sebo saw a familiar glimmer in Alfi's eyes, and the sight made him groan. "It was a woman, wasn't it?" The next look from Alfi said more than the guy's mouth ever could, and Sebo, reading the man's face, said, "I'm really sorry."

"It wasn't her fault; I created my own problems. I am the one who is responsible—she tried to convince me to go to the police, and to do the right thing, but I was too afraid."

Sebo got up and went back to the fridge. He grabbed two more bottles, but Alfi waved his off. "I have to work," he said.

Sebo only half-shrugged at the refusal before sitting down with both bottles in front of him, and after opening the first one, he said, "tell me the rest."

"Her name is Angela; we were living together, and it was wonderful."

Alfi's eyes took on a bit of a glow as the memories of her floated into his mind. "Her father owns a commercial print shop. I took a job there, but in my spare time, all I wanted to do was engrave. I knew I needed to create a perfect set of plates from which to print samples that would demonstrate my skill. I love the silver certificates from the 1960s; I think they are some of the most elegant of all the U.S. currency designs, so I chose the twenty-dollar note as my subject." His eyes fading into sadness now, Alfi said, "I thought, because the silver certificate was out of circulation—so long out of circulation—that it would be meaningless to reproduce it, but of course, I was mistaken."

"How'd you end up making forty-thousand bucks worth of the shit?"

"My samples fell into the wrong hands."

"LJ's hands?"

"Not at first."

"You mean, it was those two dick-weed wrestlers who forced you into it?" Sebo's voice sharpened as he spoke. "I never knew that; I always figured it'd been LJ's idea from the start."

"They came to the printshop to order flyers for LJ's car lot," Alfi said. "One of my samples was taped to the cash register—Angela's father liked showing it off to the customers. I think the wrestlers believed they could run an operation without LJ knowing, but somehow, LJ always seems to know everything."

"Did those two assholes threaten you?" Sebo said, and by now, he knew he was looking at a guy who was the closest thing to a genius he'd ever met, but who also made a lousy criminal—because honesty came too naturally. Alfi wasn't talking, so Sebo simply read the Italian's face instead, and what it told him made him even more angry. "Shit," Sebo said. "They threatened *her*, didn't they?" Alfi nodded and Sebo, shaking his head in disgust, said, "That really sucks, man."

"LJ keeps telling me he's protecting me, but he's just using me," Alfi said. "I have nine months left of my probation. The moment I am released, I will be deported back to Italy. Until then, I am LJ's bitch."

31

Six

The sound of his master's voice…

Next morning: 7:08AM to be exact, Sebo stood in the kitchen wearing his freshly laundered tee-shirt and jeans, and feeling much more civilized, as he watched the old lady's Mr. Coffee steadily drip into the machine's glass decanter. It was a pounding fist against the trailer's front door that woke him up. Sebo left the kitchen for the door and opened it. Outside, a stubby-looking guy with a surprised look on his face stood and stared up at him.

"Who are you?" The guy huffed.

On first impression, Sebo thought this guy looked like he'd gotten lost on his way to an early morning round of golf. A striped polo tucked into pressed chinos, soft shoes—soft around the middle too. Sebo recognized the badge when the guy flashed it in front of him. "You a peace officer?" Sebo asked.

"Answer my question."

"Sebastian Corrado."

The guy's face went flat for a moment, then turned pale, before he took a step back, and then three more as he reversed down the steps to the carport. After gaining a bit more distance he ordered Sebo, "Out of the house."

Sebo's only choice being to comply, so down the steps he went, the trailer's cool envelope of air-conditioning leaving him fast, and in its place, a steamy subtropical heat folded in around him like a warm damp towel. Sebo hit the carport and then walked to where he figured this freaked-out badge wanted him to be. All of this going on while a familiar, queasy feeling returned to his gut. It was somewhere around that moment when Sebo caught sight of the guy's right hand moving beneath the roll of his burger gut—a holstered sidearm visible for the first time. A lightweight nine by Sebo's guess—he lifted his hands.

"Turn around," the officer ordered. "Place your hands on the back of your head."

"What'd I do, man? What's this about?"

"Obey my order—I won't ask again." Sebo clasped his hands behind his head and turned around. He didn't move a muscle during the pat-down, but then he felt the PO grab ahold of his right wrist, and then his left. Sebo winced when the cuffs went on. "Am I under arrest?" He said.

"Not yet, but I'd say it's a strong possibility." Sebo felt the officer's grip on his arm, followed shortly by a sharp jerk, so he spun back to face him. And now Sebo was looking straight down at this guy, and it was obvious this armed badge in bad street clothes was edging toward panic. In Sebo's opinion, nothing was more dangerous than a panicky badge with a gun.

"Where's Alfi?"

"Inside sleeping."

"Wait here—don't move."

Sebo wasn't going anywhere with his hands cuffed behind his back—only freaked-out teens and tweakers pulled shit like that. He watched Alfi's PO lumber back up the three concrete steps like it was an effort. That queasy feeling in his gut was churning hard when the PO disappeared through the opened doorway of the old lady's trailer, this being the exact moment when Sebo remembered that the shit from his pockets was still sitting out on the dining table.

"Alfi!" The PO's loud voice rattled through the place. "Get out here!"

Stumbling inside his bedroom, Alfi struggled to rejoin with the living, trying to get dressed. This after the shock of his PO's voice had jolted him out of a dead sleep. Blurry-eyed, Alfi tripped pulling on his jeans and fell against the dresser, sending the lamp from the nightstand crashing to the floor before he was finally able to find his feet. By now, Alfi's PO was standing just outside his bedroom doorway. "Get some clothes on," he ordered. "I'll be in the living room."

Sebo, still standing outside in the carport as ordered, was wishing like hell he had a better view inside. The cuffs cutting into his wrists on account of the PO being so freaked when he clamped them on, which of course, was the whole reason he'd clamped them on. Sebo's gut was a full-on, twisted up knot, even if the expression on his face was a big, flat nothing—his only clear thought being Alfi's artisanal cash sitting out on the dining table.

Sebo caught a glimpse of Alfi's PO walking back out from Alfi's bedroom. By the time the guy had passed by the opening in front of him, Sebo was leaning hard to his left and straining for a better view. What he saw first was Alfi's PO searching around inside the living room, and then a second later, the guy was standing right in front of the dining table.

Alfi's PO raised his hands to his hips—still inspecting the room. Then Sebo saw something attract the PO's attention. The guy stepped closer to the dining table and stared down at the wad of crumpled cash. Sebo stopped breathing.

At first Alfi's PO only poked at the small pile of paper. By now, Sebo was sweating like hell, but still straining to see as the PO continued to push the bills around. He separated out the receipts from the cash and loose change with one finger before briefly examining the pair of receipts more closely. Then Alfi's PO picked up one of the twenties.

From the corner of his eye, Sebo caught Alfi's slender outline coming out from his bedroom. Alfi paused at the opened doorway when he spotted Sebo standing outside, stone-faced, dripping wet, and with his hands behind his back—Alfi froze in place.

Sebo twisted his body enough that Alfi could see the cuffs. When he looked back again, he caught a brief nod of acknowledgment from Alfi before the Italian turned in the direction of his PO—just as the officer was snapping one of his counterfeit twenties out straight between his hands.

Sebo was fully expecting the little Italian dude to fall apart at any moment. He let out a brief sigh before dropping his chin. At this point Sebo was just waiting for the inevitable. He briefly contemplated his 24 hours of street-time, his sloppy stupidity, and the fact that, because of him, Alfi would be going down hard this time. Sebo waited… then he waited some more…

When Sebo finally lifted his chin again, he realized Alfi still hadn't moved. Alfi was still standing in the exact same spot and still looking in the direction of his PO. His face looked calm, and Sebo wasn't reading any fear—nothing at all from the slim Italian. Alfi was just quietly watching. Then Sebo saw Alfi twist in place and stare right at him. A hint of a smile flashed across Alfi's face, and so Sebo looked back in the direction of the PO—just as the guy let the counterfeit twenty-dollar bill drop back down onto the table.

Then Alfi's PO picked up the Mega Millions quick-pick, and snickered... The officer then twisted back in Alfi's direction, and waving the lottery ticket in his hand, he said, "Hey, Alfi, don't you think you're over-estimating your luck?"

Seven

Third butt from the left…

"I thought we were fucked." Sebo lifted the carafe of hot coffee and filled two mugs. Handing one to Alfi, he said, "you sir, are one cool-headed criminal." Taking a sip from his steaming mug of joe, he said, "I'm impressed, man, I am really fucking impressed." Then he watched Alfi lift his mug to his lips, and he noticed his hand was shaking. Sebo chuckled, "Don't sweat it, man, I was freaked too, okay? When that cuck PO cuffed me? I was like… ah shit—I was just fucking freaked."

"I am not a cool-headed guy," Alfi said. "I was too afraid to move, that's all."

"I'm not buying that shit, man." Sebo pointed at Alfi's face. "I saw you smile, man—I saw it." Alfi grinned and Sebo said, "It was my fault, man. I was an idiot to leave that shit sitting out like that."

"I was the one who knew better," Alfi said. "The guy always comes by unannounced—he does it a lot, okay? I should have warned you."

Sebo set his mug down, folded his thickly muscled arms and leaned back against the Formica. "I owe you, man," he said. "And you need to know—from here on out? Anyone wants to give you any shit at all? They gotta get past me."

* * *

Shelly caught sight of Sebo just as she handed the old man back his change. "You have a nice day sir," she said, but her eyes were already elsewhere as she tracked Sebo's prominent profile striding past the Quick-Stop's front windows. His red plastic gas can swinging from his left hand. Sebo set it down outside by the door and made eye contact when he walked in.

"Back for more, huh?"

Sebo flashed a grin her way. "Yep, need five more gallons."

She eyed his sweat-soaked tee-shirt, and the bits of dirt and grass that clung to his neck. "Sure is a hot day to be working outside," she said. Sebo nodded his agreement just before he plunged his right hand down into the tub of slushy ice. This time his hand reemerged from the depths of the frozen slurry gripping a Gatorade. He cracked it open and gulped down the 24-ounce sports drink in a matter of seconds. Setting the empty on the counter, he said, "add that to my total, too, please ma'am."

He watched Shelly's fingers as she rang up his purchases— neon pink polish this time. "That'll be twenty-two eighty," she said. Sebo dug down into the front pocket of his jeans and pulled out the bills Alfi'd given him—real stuff this time. Dropping the cash on the counter, he said, "So what do you like to do when you're off work?" Shelly gave him his change. Smiling a little, she said, "Uh, the usual stuff, you know, go to the beach—I like to see a movie sometimes…"

"You like the beach, huh?"

"Yeah, my friends and I usually drive out to Anna Maria, sometimes Palma Sola, but I like Coquina Beach the best, you know, on account of the powder-white sand—I love the dunes."

"I haven't been out that way in a while but it's nice out there, I like it." Then he said, "You like to do anything else?"

"I do some modeling sometimes."

"No shit?"

She nodded. "Yeah, there's this photographer guy who lives out on Holmes Beach, but it's not like serious money or anything."

"You ever do calendars?"

Shaking her head this time. "No," she said. "Nothing that big—I model for postcards."

"Postcards, huh? What kind?"

"That kind." She pointed at a rack near the register stuffed with beach-themed postcards. The glossy images of risqué bikini-babes got Sebo's attention. "So which one's you?" He asked. Shelly reached over and plucked up one of the shiny cards. She handed it to Sebo—a tidy row of pert bottoms bathed in brilliant sunlight and clad only in Brazilian-styled thongs.

Reaching across the counter, she pointed again with one of her neon pink nails. "That's me right there," she said. "Third butt from the left."

Staring at the image a bit longer, he said, "You do have a beautiful bottom."

She smiled. "Thanks... I usually don't let guys know that card's got my ass on it, you know—for obvious reasons."

"I can see why." Sebo handed the card back. "You wanna get together some time?"

She flashed a grin before resting her elbows on the counter and staring up at him. "Sure... I get off work in a couple of hours, I mean, just say'n."

* * *

Alfi'd already left for his night job by the time Sebo heard the little knock on the door. She was wearing some tight black shorts and a matching sparkly tank top—smelled of a fresh shower... He liked it, thought she looked nice. Then he spotted a red Ford hatchback sitting out along the grass. "You can park inside the carport if you want," Sebo said. "I don't have a car yet."

"Maybe later," she responded, and eyeing the chilled bottle in his hand, "got one of those for me?"

Four hours later, and he was just watching her sit up in bed in front of him. He had a profile view and was admiring the way her breasts stood out like two solders at attention, fully armed and prepared to launch another assault at any moment. She sat cross-legged, bent over one of the old lady's flowered china plates—expertly rolling a joker blunt. When she'd finished, she set the plate aside and twisted back toward him with the fat joint lightly balanced in her hand. He still wasn't looking at her face. Sebo leaned forward and she placed the tip of the joint between his lips; a hand-blown Jack Skellington, apparently, but she'd been talking about her collection. He thought the glass felt smooth and classy. Then she said, "So you just got out of prison, is that right?"

"Yeah."

She stretched across him for the lighter on the night stand, her breasts brushing gently across his chest with her movement. She sat back next to him—held the flame as he drew in on the joint—a good long toke. She said, "Did you kill somebody?"

Coughing out smoke, Sebo said, "Fuck no." He handed the joint back to her and watched her take a nice deep hit for a girl. He continued to stare at her—puzzling over this cute little chick. "Why would you say something like that?"

Passing the joint back, she answered, "You're a really big guy. I mean, you look tough."

"You mean this?" Sebo reached up with his thumb and traced along the crooked path of a vicious scar that tumbled down the right side of his face from his temple to the tip of his chin. "I've had this since I was 14," he said. "It's been getting me into trouble ever since."

"Was it from fighting?"

"No. I grew up around here, mostly Samoset. There was this old rusty radio tower; it's not there anymore, they tore it down. Anyway, my friends and me, we used to hang out around there a lot. We were always talking about climbing it, so one day I did. I got all the way to the top, and I could hear those guys yelling up at me from the ground. I was feeling pretty cocky, and on my way back down I slipped on the ladder and fell through the metal framing for like, the last twenty feet or something—I don't really remember that part, but I remember it took 137 stitches to patch me up. My mom was so pissed; not just because it cost her money, but the doc did such a crappy job sewing me up."

She reached up and he felt the tips of her fingers lightly touching his scar. "So, you didn't kill anybody?"

"Beat up a bunch of guys, but I've never killed anybody."

"Drugs?" She took her hand back.

Shaking his head, feeling a nice rich buzz coming on, he drew in on another toke and then exhaled it slow. He handed the joint over to her. She lifted it to her lips for another hit before passing it back, and Sebo said, "It wasn't drugs, neither—it was car theft." He took in another hit, held on to this one for a bit longer. Then he said, "I took the plea deal—thirty-six months, but I got out early; I was only inside for twenty-six."

"You on paper?"

"Yeah," he answered, before passing the joint to her. He smiled at her through a pleasant haze and said, "you ever been arrested?"

Holding the slowly smoldering joint between her fingers for a moment, she replied, "I was in juvie once."

With a smile, he said, "You kill anybody?"

She busted out laughing—nearly lost the burning joint inside the rumpled sheets. "No!" She shrieked. Recovering control of their joint, she laughed some more, and Sebo, laughing along with her, said, "I don't know, girl—you look pretty dangerous to me."

With a relaxed sigh, Sebo folded his arms behind his head and leaned back against the pillows and the bed's carved oak headboard and comfortably into a fully stoned state of mind. It was a nice enough high that he didn't even mind the subject of their conversation—was enjoying the moment even. Enjoying her face that was kinda just floating, and her round little tits, and the fact that she'd been such a nice fuck.

"So, this is why you're living in one of LJ's trailers, then?"

He grinned. "How'd you know this was LJ's trailer?"

"Everybody knows." She paused for another toke, exhaled, made a little whistling sound between her lips when she did it. Then she said, "well, people who live around here do." Passing the joint back, she said, "were you part of that big bust up at The Villages a couple years back?" Exhaling a cloud of smoke, he said, "you heard about that?"

"Sure—who didn't? It was all over the news when it happened; cops made a big deal out of the bust—biggest car-theft ring in Florida history—worth millions, right?"

"I guess so," he said. "I mean, we did have a pretty big crew going—until one of our boosters turned out to be undercover."

"They said you guys would spend all night stealing cars, and that it was a sophisticated set up, because you used a car carrier."

"That was me, I was the transport driver."

"Really?"

"That was my job," Sebo said. "It's what I did all night long, man—remove the plates, load the cars, guard the truck—drive."

"So, you didn't actually steal any cars then."

"Technically no."

"What kind of cars got jacked?"

"Anything high-end that was new."

"The Villages is pretty posh." She took the joint back from him and finished it off... Sebo held his eyes on her as the last of the smoke left her lips. He breathed it in as she sat there in a nest of rumpled sheets—toked up, and naked, and looking amazing. Then her slender body gently twisted as she reached for the flowered plate. Stubbing out the roach, she said, "Sounds like a pretty smart setup if you ask me. I mean, old people like to buy nice new cars."

"Yeah, they do." Sebo moved his hand closer, gently stroking her thigh with the tips of his fingers, then he said, "The crew would always case ahead of time and work up a list—makes, and models, the car's plate numbers—stuff like that."

"Of course, during the day the cars could be anywhere around that place," said Sebo. "The Villages is just, like, huge—not the kind of place you wanna get lost in driving a stolen car. Our connections would get us the addresses that went with the cars we wanted. We'd map it all out, and I'd figure out the best place to spot the carrier. Then come about two in the morning, we'd all get to work. Once the crew got going I had to work fast, and those old folks…" Sebo let out a little chuckle. "They like everyone in the neighborhood to know they just got a new car, they like parking it right out in front for the neighbors to see—some of the rides we lifted still had the dealer sticker on the window."

"What'd you do with 'em?"

"Once the carrier got filled up, which only took, like, an hour, we'd wrap for the night, and that's when I'd drive the truck to Miami. Once I got down there, I'd unload, and that was the end of my job. The cars all got put into containers, then onto a ship heading south."

"Like Brazil?"

"Something like that." He gazed at her naked body some more, then he said, "None of this shit bothers you at all, does it?"

"No," she said. "Not really, I mean, everybody makes mistakes—you did your time, right?"

"It's just that..." He smiled at her, and still stroking her thigh, he said, "you're really great you know that?" He saw her smile—liked it. "Most people get nervous around me," he said. He rubbed at his scruffy chin with his left hand. "It's why I grow the beard, you know? Kinda hides it a little." He let his hand drop back to the sheets. "But it's more than that. I guess I affect people in the wrong way—makes some guys always wanna start shit for some stupid reason."

"You don't make me nervous." She pushed the plate aside, and then flopped back down beside him. "I could go another round—how about you?"

Eight

No guns…

T he grin on Alfi's face said it all. Sebo picked up a freshly filled coffee mug and took a sip. "Thanks man," he said. Alfi was cradling his own steaming mug in his hands when he said, "Do I get to meet her?"

"Sure you do…" Shelly answered.

Both men turned to look as Shelly strolled in from the bedroom wearing only Sebo's tee-shirt that fit her like a baggy dress. Alfi set his mug down, quickly grabbed a fresh one out from the cupboard, and had it filled and in her hands before Sebo could say another word. She thanked him. "So, you're Alfi, huh?"

"This is Shelly," said Sebo, but Alfi was still just staring at the girl—felt like nearly a full minute slipped past him before he finally said, "Piacere signorina…" Alfi gently squeezed the girl's outstretched hand, and said, "I've seen you at the Quick-Stop, am I right?"

"Yeah, that's right."

Shelly gulped down some of Alfi's coffee, then she said, "Thanks guys, but I really gotta go; my shift starts in an hour."

Alfi was peeking out from the doorway of the trailer when Sebo leaned in through the window of her little Ford hatchback to kiss her goodbye. "Amore…" Alfi sighed, "Bella amore…" Sebo stood near the street and watched until her car rounded the corner, and no sooner had the red Fiesta disappeared from sight, then from the opposite direction, the flashy front grill of LJ's Impala came into view.

Sebo had his thumbs hooked into the front pockets of his jeans, just admiring the approaching classic as he always did—1960, two-door coupe hardtop, his favorite model year, on account of the way they flattened out the tail fins from the 59's batwing, which had been overdone in his opinion. It was also the first year Chevy added the model's signature, six round tail-lights. Sebo liked the color too—horizon blue, factory choice. LJ's ride had the 348 V8, automatic power-glide transmission, a white accent stripe—all the chrome, and a customized, rolled Naugahyde interior in arctic white—nothing short of his own personal dream car.

Sebo stayed put and waited until the Impala rolled to a stop in front of him, watching as LJ shut her down and then stepped outside to face him; jingling his ball of keys in one hand. LJ didn't say anything at first, looking all cold and serious, until the guy finally flashed a wide grin, and LJ said, "You look like you just got laid, my man."

Sebo, with half a smile, gave a brief nod and LJ said, "Hell of a lot better than a tallboy, wouldn't you say?" LJ didn't wait for an answer from Sebo, instead, he made a graceful pivot and then strolled to the rear of his car. Sebo followed, looking on as his boss unlocked the car's trunk. LJ stuffed his ball of keys into his front pocket, lifted the trunk lid, and said, "I got a little job for you, my man."

Sebo leaned in closer and peered inside. "What's that for?" He asked.

Pointing at the uniform zipped inside plastic and lying neatly across the carpeted interior, LJ said, "It's for you, man." Reaching into the car's cavernous trunk, LJ said, "I hope I got the size right; I just asked for the biggest damn thing they had." LJ lifted the bag out by its hanger, and unzipping its clear plastic cover, he said, "This is official—none of that fake shit, this came straight from Brinks armored transportation."

Sebo stood with his arms folded in front of him as he stared back at LJ, thinking it through but knowing whatever it was LJ had planned for him, he'd have absolutely no say in the matter, Sebo said, "What's the job?" LJ flashed a big grin. "That's why I love you, man—you know that?" Handing over the uniform, he said, "It'll be a piece of cake—all you gotta do is drive." Sebo slung the uniform over one shoulder. "That's it?" He said. "Just drive?"

"That's it."

"No guns?"

"No way, man." LJ was shaking his head, but thinking of the compact nine inside the Impala's glove box. "I know how you feel about that shit", LJ said, "no guns."

"You know I'm restricted by my probation, right?"

LJ gave a quick wink Sebo's way. "No worries, my man, I got it covered—it'll all happen inside county lines—the drop is just over the bridge in Palmetto."

"What's the location?"

"The usual," LJ said, "out at the chicken farm—you still re- member where that place is, right?"

Sebo nodded. "Yeah, I know the place."

LJ closed the trunk of his car, pulled out his keys and locked it again, then he said, "I'll be picking you up tonight."

"What time?"

Jingling his keys some more, LJ smiled again before he answered, "Let's say twelve-thirty."

* * *

A quarter after midnight, and Alfi was in the kitchen, dressed in slim jeans and a black polo, and pouring steaming coffee into a thermos when he caught sight of Sebo's imposing new look. "You should've been a cop," Alfi said.

Sebo, tugging at the uniform's tight collar, answered, "it's scratchy, man—I hate polyester." Alfi took a step closer and then slowly moved in a circle around Sebo; looking him up and down with a scrutinizing gaze. "The fit is good," he said. Sebo, still working at straightening his tie, said, "You think so?" Alfi nodded his approval. "It's also good that you shaved the barba; I hardly recognize you." Then Sebo sees a new look from Alfi— confident, assured... "Come with me," Alfi said, "I will show you my shop."

With Sebo standing right behind him, Alfi unlocked the door to his trailer. "I keep a clean shop," Alfi said. "No prints— okay? Don't touch anything unless I tell you to."

This particular trailer being Alfi's own exclusive domain. Another of LJ's purchases, a deal completed just ahead of Alfi's paroled release, but unlike the old lady's trailer that Sebo and Alfi called home, this one hadn't been preserved; instead, it'd been gutted, its windows blocked from the inside, and its floor joists reinforced to better facilitate its repurposing.

It was tucked into the farthest reaches of the park, shrouded in overgrowth and shadowed by live oaks, their branches draped in thick Spanish moss that hung like curtains, and left the place virtually invisible from the street. Alfi waited until he'd fully closed the door behind them before he flipped on the lights.

"Holy fucking shit…"

Alfi stood back by the door with nearly a full grin as he took in Sebo's reaction. "You like it?" He said. Sebo breathed in the room's faintly odd, chemical odor, gazed across the pristine floor of Alfi's perfectly organized shop, and more specifically, at the two long, narrow, and neatly shrink-wrapped pallets of freshly printed cash. "Jesus, Alfi," Sebo said. "You're a one-man U.S. treasury."

Alfi smiled again. "Thank you, let me show you around."

Alfi went first to the biggest machine in the room, a gray metal behemoth nearly as tall as he was—half mechanics and half computer. Alfi said, "This is the heart of my shop. She is a top-of-the-line commercial intaglio press from China—she is my lover."

"That's some kinda machine," Sebo said. "How'd you get your hands on it?"

"Alibaba," Alfi replied.

Next Sebo eyed the large boxes of oversized paper stacked nearby—one of them open. Leaning in a bit closer, he said, "This paper looks like the real thing. How the hell do you find stuff like this?"

"It is the real thing." Alfi said. "It's just not as large—instead of 32 notes per sheet, I only get 12, but I still get the job done. This paper was milled in Belgium—special order of course—not cheap." Next, Alfi pointed at a collection of liter-sized tubs of quick-drying printer's ink in various colors. "Believe it or not, getting this right was one of the toughest parts of the job," he said. "Mixing the colors correctly is one thing, but there are secrets hidden inside the ink that take time to reproduce accurately—it's not just about how the note looks—it must perform. This ink came from Germany, and just one of these buckets costs five hundred euros."

"No shit?" Sebo said.

"It's true," Alfi replied. "But the ink and the paper are only a starting point in the process. Even duplicating the security features—this is a matter of technique and efficiency. The real challenge is in achieving the perfect finish; the way each note touches the light, and the way it feels in your hands—this is something I take particular pride in."

Sebo, paying attention to every word, noticed a rising intensity in the Italian's eyes when Alfi said, "If a note isn't perfect it hits the shredder and gets burned. I am telling you the truth when I say, I am better than the Iranians, or the North Koreans, or the Romanian Mob—my notes even beat a Peruvian super bill—this job is my life," Alfi said. "It's all that I do."

Sebo shifted from his left to his right and then studied more carefully the matched pair of fully loaded pallets which had been constructed in such a way as to fit through the trailer's narrow door. Each held hundreds upon hundreds of neatly banded stacks of cash, and each one of them, as Alfi went on to explain, being fully ABA compliant—strapped perfectly with a violet-colored band that held one hundred, twenty-dollar bills, which meant each strap held an equivalent value of two thousand dollars. The fact that it was all funny money was washed from his mind and replaced by a kind of euphoria. "So how much is here?" Sebo said.

"Five million dollars' worth." Alfi announced, and stepping closer to one of his shrink-wrapped pallets, "Each holds 1,250 straps; 2.5 million each."

Folding his arms, and rubbing at his chin with the heel of his left thumb, Sebo fielded a logistical question, "So how much does each of these things weigh?"

"The cash weight alone for each pallet is 125 kilos." Alfi answered, "or, 275.578 pounds, plus packaging? He tilted his head a little. "You are looking at 293.4 pounds each." Straightening again, staring back at Sebo, Alfi said, "Any problem with that?"

"No, man," Sebo responded. "No problem at all."

* * *

LJ was on time. But Sebo had expected nothing less—the guy was always punctual. LJ wasn't driving the Impala either. Instead, he was behind the wheel of a plain-Jane, closed-sided, panel-van; stripped out save for the two front seats, no interior lights, but everything else on it mechanically perfect—also expected. LJ stepped out from the van and then rolled open the sliding cargo door. "We're on a schedule, gentlemen," he said. "Let's get this shit loaded."

Sebo only had to remain folded up and wedged in beside the two pallets for a sum total of five minutes, but it was still a damned uncomfortable ride. From the trailer park the van needed to travel slightly less than half a mile in order to reach its destination; a warehouse off of Old Highway 301. Sebo figured it was a good thing too, and not only because he was cramping up inside the tight space, but because the van was riding low.

After taking a legal left off the highway, signal flashing, the van traversed a dimly lit, deserted parking lot, before LJ drove around to the rear of a sheet-metal clad warehouse. Rolling to a stop, LJ cut the engine, and said, "Everybody out…"

He was already fumbling with his ball of keys when LJ climbed out of the van. Alfi was out too and sliding open the side door for Sebo. The rattle of chain, the clink of keys, then a low rumble as LJ pushed at a large rolling door. Sebo watched closely, even forgetting his itchy uniform for a time, as LJ disappeared into the blackness of the building's interior. Then Sebo caught the glow from a small flashlight that shined across the polished front grill of an armored truck. "Mama Mia…" Alfi said.

"How do you like your ride?" LJ said.

Sweat was beginning to moisten his back as Sebo climbed up inside the armored truck's cab and took a look around. "Is she topped off?" He asked.

"Full as a summer tick," LJ answered.

"You and Alfi gonna follow me in the van then?"

"That's the plan, my man." LJ checked his watch. "Meet's in two hours, so let's get loaded and get the fuck outta here."

Nine

You said, no guns…

Two AM: Alfi drew thick night air into his lungs as he stood in dewy grass, and looking on, as LJ worked at a stubborn padlock. The two men standing side by side under a flood of light that beamed out from the van's headlights, and from those of the armored truck that idled just behind it. Light that was awash with the energetic swirls of a million insects.

"Why do they call this a chicken farm?" Alfi said. "All I see are roosters."

"Those aren't just roosters," LJ answered without looking up. "What you're lookin' at are fighting cocks." Alfi stood by as LJ rattled at the padlock some more until it finally gave way. Stuffing his keys back inside his pocket, LJ removed the chain, and with only a light push, the livestock gate swung open…

Alfi drove the van through first, pulling off to one side just after the gate. LJ stood beside the rough road and waved Sebo through the opening, the armored truck's taillights leaving behind a dusty red glow lifted from the road's rutted dirt. While Alfi waited for LJ, he looked out once more at the long stretches of low-roofed sheds that lined both sides of the road.

They had open sides and were packed in solid with cages raised up above the ground—hundreds of them. Inside each cage a single rooster stood and stared back at him. Beyond the chicken sheds, Alfi could see the edges of a thick jungle; subtropical, muted, brooding in the darkness, and no doubt, Alfi guessed—filled with snakes.

With LJ back at the wheel, the van trailed behind the lumbering armored truck. "I thought it was illegal to fight animals in this country," Alfi said. "It's illegal to fight 'em," answered LJ. "That's for damned sure, but there's nothing illegal about breeding 'em."

"Is there money in it?" Alfi asked.

LJ laughed, then he answered. "Fuck yeah. The guy that owns this farm? He used to breed race horses—did it for years—top bloodline thoroughbreds. I happen to know he rakes in a hell of a lot more from breeding these goddamned birds. He ships 'em down south to the Dominican Republic—all over Latin America, and shit like that. Dude just went and bought a beach house out on Longboat Key for Christ's sake. So yeah," LJ continued, "if you can stand the smell? There's a lot of fucking money in it."

The road made a bend to the left, and from behind the armored truck, Alfi spotted a glow from a sodium vapor light attached to a large barn just up ahead. "Remember to keep your mouth shut around these Cubans," LJ said. "When the tribe first got into the casino business? They naturally leveraged the mob, but that didn't last long—it's all Cuban muscle these days, and if you ask me? These sons of bitches are way the fuck worse than the old-guard Italian mob ever was. These cats all trace back to the Batista revolution—you piss them off? They won't say a word, they'll just send their Iceman after you."

"Iceman?" Alfi said. "You mean, like a hitman?"

"You catch on pretty quick."

"I am from Napoli," Alfi said. "You ever hear of the Camorra?"

"Nope…"

"The Camorra are the oldest mafia in Italy, much older than the Sicilian mafia, or even the 'Ndrangheta in Calabria, and they are the most ruthless. I can tell you they are much worse than these Cubans you're talking about."

"Dead is dead," LJ said. "Doesn't matter where the bullet comes from. One thing I do know for sure? If these Cubans decide to send their guy to take us down? We'll never see it coming. Nobody knows what the Iceman looks like—the guy's like smoke."

Alfi looked out through the windshield of the van as it bounced along the dirt road. Just in front of him was an armored truck carrying five million dollars in cash that he'd printed using plates that he'd engraved by hand, and the sight filled him with pride—not fear.

The taillights flared on the armored truck. LJ slowed the van to a stop and then shut down the engine. "This is it, Alfi," he said. "Show time." With the glow of the armored truck's taillights shining red across his face, LJ eyed the Italian more closely, and said, "If your shit doesn't pass the test? All three of us are fucked."

From the outside, the corrugated metal barn appeared deserted, but as the doors were opened in front of him, Sebo could see that the inside was filled with strong light and no less than a dozen men. Sebo eased the armored truck in through the building's wide doors as directed, and that queasy feeling was back in spades—*guns...*

Sebo shut down the engine, lifted both hands above the wheel, and kept them there. Just outside, and directly in front of him, three men stood shoulder to shoulder near the truck's front bumper—all three dressed in the exact same uniform that he was wearing. The difference being that these guys were armed—each with a Five-seveN, and all three handguns were pointed at him.

"Fucking guns..." Sebo mumbled under his breath.

Out of the van, LJ, and Alfi too, kept their hands in plain sight, and held out wide as each man was searched. Then Alfi caught sight of Sebo climbing down from the armored truck's cab. Alfi was trying hard not to show his excitement when the Cubans opened up the rear doors of the armored truck. He briefly glanced in LJ's direction—read only the man's cool, blank expression as Cuban mobsters unloaded his twin pallets of handmade cash. Sebo was watching too, briefly making eye contact with Alfi as he stood off to one side, and a full head taller than any of the armed men who were guarding him.

Alfi's attention was then drawn to a long folding table that sat off to his left—a table with only one chair. Occupying the chair was an older man of rotund stature. He was dressed in a short-sleeved, button-down, a pair of dress trousers, and was busily adjusting a magnifying lamp.

As Alfi felt the full weight of the scene unfolding in front of him, his fingers trembled ever so slightly. Then he saw someone pull out a knife and slice through the shrink-wrap. A single strap of his hand-made bank notes was then handed off to the rotund man seated in the chair. The moment the man tore off the violet colored paper band—Alfi realized he wasn't breathing.

Alfi, motionless, and invisible—his presence totally ignored, as the rotund man in the chair spread the twenty-dollar bills out on the table. The man then put on his reading glasses and looked closely at the smooth fan of fake twenties—thumbing through all of them carefully, turning each of them over, before he proceeded to examine one with the magnifying lamp.

Complete silence followed for the next several minutes as the man meticulously examined four more randomly selected straps of Alfi's twenties. But just as Alfi thought the man might be satisfied with his work, Alfi saw him signal to the thugs hanging around nearby, and from seemingly out of nowhere, an electronic banknote counting machine appeared on the table next to the rotund man.

At the sight of the money counter, LJ whispered, "Oh just fuck me right now and get it over-with…" LJ, glancing briefly at Alfi's breathless expression, then Sebo's stone-cold face, before he looked back again at the table—just as the rotund man unzipped a bank bag and pulled out what appeared to be a legitimate stack of cash. The man then slipped several of Alfi's twenties in with the real thing, fed the entire stack into the counter and then started up the machine.

LJ held his breath as the machine whirred and quickly shuffled through the stack of banknotes—fully expecting the counter's ultraviolet eye, or magnetic detectors, to choke on Alfi's cash as it scanned for counterfeits. It took only a matter of seconds for the machine to complete its task. The feeding tray at the top was now empty—every bill having been counted as clean.

Ten

Come to think of it...

"My mom and dad's first date was at the Trail Drive-In," Elaine said, "but back in those days, if you were black? They would tell you to park in the back."

"Pepto-Bismol pink—you could see it from a mile away driving on 41; who could forget that place?" Bill said. "Had a screen twice as big as an IMAX. I remember the day it burnt down, holy cow, what a fire that was." Bill stared down at his stack of paperwork, and quickly shuffled through a few more pages before looking back at Elaine, he said, "how about the Bradenton Roller Rink? You remember that place, right? It was on the corner of Cortez Road and 26th—your mom and dad ever go there? I met my wife there." Bill continued. "We went to different high schools; I was at Manatee, she went to Southeast High—my parents didn't approve at first."

Elaine glanced up at Bill from her desk, and from her own stack of paperwork. "You mean that place that had the big terrazzo floor? And the organ player?"

"That's the one." Bill pointed at her. "Remember old Mr. Warner? Guy must have played that organ for thirty years—my wife cracked her elbow on that terrazzo floor."

Elaine chuckled, said, "You ever notice any black folks in that place? Like, ever?"

"Come to think of it…"

"Well that's all I need to say about that then…"

"You're doing a good job of ruining my childhood, Elaine."

"Just adding some clarity—ain't truth a bitch?" The words hardly leaving her mouth before Elaine looked up to see Freddy coming through the office door. Rather than say anything she merely observed as Freddy's portly profile passed her by only to plant himself in front of Bill's desk instead. "Hey Bill, I ran into your guy the other day."

Mazurek, his reading glasses low on his nose, looked up from his paperwork, and said, "Hello to you too, Freddy." Then Bill said, "Now which guy would that be?"

"The big one—you know, the one they call Sebo."

"Didn't give you any trouble, I hope."

"Didn't give him a chance to."

Bill, glancing up again, said, "What's that supposed to mean?"

"As soon as I saw the fucker, I cuffed him," Freddy said.

"What'd you do that for?" Bill was about to repeat his question when Elaine did it for him, then she listened to Freddy's story some more before she said, "Hang on—you mean that counterfeiter? The Italian guy?"

"Yeah, that's the one," Freddy said. "Alfi Lanzano—skinny little shit. Come to find out he's sharing a trailer with Bill's guy

Sebo. They're both living over at the Pelican Court—you know, that dump off East 44th Street." Elaine, with her eyes on Bill this time, said, "And that would be one of Little Junior's trailers—were you aware of this?" Bill, now with his glasses off, and pinching at the bridge of his nose, said, "Uh huh… I was aware."

"Smells rotten as all hell to me," Elaine said.

"LJ's clean, Elaine, remember?" Bill was fully focused on her now. "The man doesn't have so much as a parking ticket. He's a member of the county initiative that helps local businesses hire ex-cons." Bill held her gaze as he continued. "Then there's the fact that neither Sebo, nor Alfi, have any prior association." Bill stared at Elaine from his desk, said, "Look, I've only been over there the one time so far, but the place smelled fine to me—it was like visiting your grandma's house."

* * *

It was late morning by the time Sebo finally climbed out of his sound sleep. He pulled on his jeans and then made his way into the old lady's kitchen. That's when he saw Alfi standing at the stove. "Last night was fucked up," Sebo said. "I never saw so much cash in my life."

"It wasn't real money," Alfi said. "Just an accurate reproduction."

Sebo, with a shrug, said, "What's the difference? It's all just fancy pieces of paper."

"*Very* fancy, yes…" Alfi's voice trailing off while his eyes never strayed from the true focus of his attention. Sebo bent down and then stared at a tiny upside-down coffeepot cooking atop a spiraled electric hob. "You're an artist, man," he said, "you're a fucking genius." Alfi didn't respond at first, he just stood and stared at the little aluminum coffeepot. Then he said, "I thought it would be better once I had finished the job."

"What do ya mean?" Sebo said, and, still watching Alfi's activity closely, he added, "Once you're inside this shit? Especially with a guy like LJ? You're just in it, man, and you're never gonna feel good about it."

"I thought there would be more satisfaction."

"Not getting caught—that always works for me," said Sebo, and holding his eyes on the tiny coffeepot, he asked, "I don't get it. How can this thing make real coffee? I mean, no offense, man, but it looks like a kid's toy."

"That's because you've never had real coffee before," Alfi said.

Sebo straightened, and then he reached for one of Alfi's little espresso cups that were sitting near the stove. Pinching the demitasse between thumb and finger, he lifted it close to his face and stared at it, chuckled... "I don't know anything about this kind of stuff," he said. "My idea of good coffee comes in something big enough to fit my fist inside."

Alfi, shaking his head, said, "Just wait. Watch and learn, okay?"

Sebo took a step back, did as Alfi asked, then he said, "So how long did it take you to make five million dollars?" Alfi stood with his arms folded, and his eyes still fixed on the tiny coffeepot. "Around five months," he said. "Working ten hours a night, every night—seven days a week."

"For the kind of top-quality product that you produced? LJ's gotta be getting at least thirty cents on the dollar—what's your cut?" Sebo caught a hint of a smile as it flashed briefly across Alfi's face. Then the Italian stared up at him and said, "What's yours?"

Sebo nodded. "Yeah, good point."

A slight hissing sound from the coffeepot sent Alfi into action. "For Italians," Alfi said, "our passion for coffee is difficult to explain… it's better to taste." Sebo observed as Alfi carefully lifted the double-ended pot from the stove by its tiny black handle. "The timing must be perfect," Alfi said as he flipped the coffee pot right-side up and then set it down off the heat.

"What do we do now?"

Alfi, with more of a smile this time, said, "We wait."

Sebo bent down close again. "Why is it shaped like that?"

"This is something special you find only in Napoli," Alfi said. "My sister sent this one to me; it's called the *Napoletana*. I grew up with this way of making coffee. From the time I was three, my mother always made it like this."

"You started drinking coffee when you were three years old?"

Alfi shrugged. "Of course—all kids drink coffee, don't they? I liked mixing it with the milk in my cereal each morning before school." Alfi waited a bit longer until the strong espresso had filtered down completely from the coffeepot's upper half and into the serving pot at the bottom. He checked if it was finished by lifting the pot. "Ah, she is ready." He first loosened and then removed the upper filtering section, then secured the lid onto the serving pot that formed the base of the delicate apparatus.

Alfi filled two of his espresso cups. "A bit of white sugar…" Alfi said as he stirred each one gently, then he handed a demitasse to Sebo. "Don't drink it too quickly. Enjoy…" Sebo took a sip, then another, before he finished it off.

"That's really good coffee, man."

Alfi smiled. He was reaching for his own cup but his hand was stopped by the sound of a heavy fist pounding against the trailer's front door—the sound froze Alfi mid-motion. Sebo set his cup down, saw Alfi's fear. "You're cool, man." Sebo said. "You're cool, all right?" Sebo left Alfi standing in the kitchen, went to the door, and opened it.

The guy standing outside the front door recognized Sebo on first sight. The two men stood nearly eye to eye, and toe to toe, for only a moment before the guy said, "Why the fuck would LJ keep a loser like you around—I just don't get it." Then the guy said, "Where's Alfi?" Sebo stared back at the former professional wrestler for one, perhaps two seconds before his left fist clinched tight and Sebo punched him right in the face.

A classic, straight punch that landed with hammer-like ferocity; Sebo felt a satisfying sting rack the knuckles of his left hand when his fist made contact—even greater satisfaction when the guy folded in two in front of him and then dropped. The wrestler going down hard across the three molded concrete steps—slid down on his back before finally landing on his ass in the carport. Sebo wanted to laugh but he held it back; he felt almost sorry for the guy. The man had once been a powerful athlete, but these days, Sebo knew he was just aging, cheap muscle. A man who didn't know when to pack it in, and who even still insisted on going by his old ring name—*Hatchet-Man*.

Sebo shook the sting from his left hand as he stood in the doorway and waited for the guy to recover. As much as he wanted to pound on the guy some more for threatening Alfi and his girlfriend, Sebo knew it wouldn't be right to beat on a guy when he was already down. But also, on account of the way *Hatchet-Man* had let himself go since Sebo'd last seen him.

Then his partner finally showed himself, and at the sight of the second old wrester, Sebo chuckled again, quickly reasoning that this guy was either too smart or too lazy to make a move. After a closer look, Sebo went with *lazy*... The guy was just as soft and out of shape as his buddy had been. Sebo had figured right too, because the second wrestler *didn't* make a move. Instead, he went to help Hatchet-Man get his feet back underneath him. "You're a dead man, Corrado!" The second old wrestler shouted. "You hear me? A dead man!"

Sebo chuckled some more at the guy's hollow insult. "What is it they used to call you?" Sebo said, "*Sling-Shot?*"

"Sling-*Blade*, asshole."

"Sling Blade Asshole," Sebo said. "That's a good one—I like it."

Eleven

I'll see to it you get what you need…

"That'll be thirty-four dollars even, ma'am." Shelly was handing the woman back her six bucks in change when a glint of sunlight flashing off polished chrome caught her eye. She looked out from behind the register just as a show-quality, 1960 Impala rolled to a stop in front of the gas pumps. Shelly watched LJ step out from his car and then stroll toward the door. The moment LJ entered the Quick-Stop he made eye contact. Flashing a big smile her way, he said, "Sure is a nice day today."

"Looks like it's gonna be another hot one," Shelly replied.

"The weather's not the only thing around here that's hot," LJ said as he approached the counter, and then added, "give me a fill up on pump four please, Ma'am—no plastic, I'm paying with cash."

"You got it." She activated the pump, and LJ was still staring at her. "My man Sebo was sure in a cheerful mood the other day…"

"Is that so?" Shelly answered. LJ was still focused on her face, and still staring right at her. "I've got your pump turned on," she said. "Top off as much as you need." LJ leaned in against the counter and kept his eyes on hers. "I appreciate that," he said. "It's one of the reasons I like coming in here." LJ's wide grin reappeared, then he said, "The friendly service."

Not knowing what else to do, or what she should say, Shelly just stood behind the register and smiled back at him. Then LJ let out a chuckle, and said, "You got nothing to worry about, girl. I just wanted to let you know that making my man Sebo happy, makes me happy—you hear what I'm say'n?"

She nodded...

"Good," LJ said. "That's real good." LJ spun back on his heel and strolled outside. Shelly watched her control panel as the gallons clicked off while LJ stood out by the pump and filled his Impala with gas. After he topped off, he came back inside.

"That'll be $62.00 even," Shelly said. "Would you like to add a quick-pick to your total today?"

LJ pulled out his wallet, and then handed her four twenties. "No thanks," he said. Then he looked back at her. "Let me ask you something—how much do you get if you sell someone a winner?"

"It depends on the jackpot," she said, "but the vendor can win as much as $100,000."

"No, no," LJ said, "I don't mean it like that, I mean, how much would you get? I mean, you personally."

She stared back at him. "Umm, I think the most I could get would be a thousand dollars." Shelly handed him back his eighteen in change, and LJ smiled at her again. "I don't want a ticket or nothing, but what's the jackpot up to this week anyway?"

"For Mega Millions? Or Power Ball?" Shelly said.

"Mega Millions."

"The jackpot rolled over again last week," Shelly said. "For tonight's drawing it's up over two hundred million—I've been selling a lot of tickets for that one—you sure you don't want to play?"

With a wink, LJ said, "No thanks. I only asked because I just wanted to hear you talk, that's all." Then he smiled, and said, "I liked what I heard too, so if you ever need anything—anything at all? You just give me a ring." LJ slipped a card out from his wallet and then slid it across the counter toward her. "You hold on to that card, girl, okay?"

She took the card—nodded...

"Anything at all," LJ said, "you just call me, and I'll see to it you get what you need."

* * *

Sebo opened his front door, and this time, he liked what he saw. Shelly's expression sparkled as she held up a pair of extra-large take-out pizzas. Grinning at the sight, Sebo said, "Hey Babe, right on time." She handed over the two huge pies, just as Sebo stooped down to give her a brief kiss before she followed him inside. "Cold beer?" Sebo asked. He set the two pizzas down on the dining table, heard her say—"You bet."

"Ah pizza..." Alfi tipped back the lid of one of the boxes and took a whiff of the rising heat—crinkled his nose. "What's wrong?" Shelly said. "Don't you like pizza?"

"He loves pizza," said Sebo. "It's all he talks about—this is the problem." Sebo swung open the fridge, grabbed three beers, spun back around, and said, "He just doesn't like American pizza."

Shelly giggled. "American pizza?" she said. "Pizza's Italian."

"Not this pizza," Alfi said, pointing at the two pies. "Look at this?" Shelly opened her beer before she stepped over and peered down. "What's wrong with it?" She asked. "It's so covered in crazy stuff that you can't even tell what kind of pizza it's supposed to be." Alfi watched Shelly pick up a plate, and then a slice. "One day, if you both come to Napoli," he said, "I will show you what real pizza is—then you will understand."

"I don't know anything about Naples other than what you've been telling me," Sebo said. "But this right here?" He reached down into the box. "This is just the way I like it…" Sebo lifted a thick slice with both hands, folded it in two, and took a big bite. "Mmm… thanks Babe," he garbled. Then Sebo caught Alfi wrapping his plate in foil. "Whatcha doing, man?"

"I have to work."

Sebo dropped the half-eaten slice back inside the box, "What are you talking about, man? You should take a break. Why don't you hang with us?" Shaking his head, Alfi said, "It doesn't work that way for me." Then he smiled. "It's better this way—gives you two more time alone."

* * *

Sebo had his eyes closed for what seemed like only a brief interlude before he felt her little hand again—her small, soft fingers playing with his cock. Without moving, he said, "Don't you ever get tired?" He heard her giggle, so he rolled over to see her freckled face.

"Is there any pizza left?"

Her hand slipped away before she twisted back and looked down at the floor. Then she flopped onto her belly in order to reach the box. Sebo was eyeing her little bottom again, and thinking about the postcard she'd showed him—Yep… a perfect match…

Then he saw her hand reappear, but this time it was holding a hardened scrap of pizza crust. "No thanks," Sebo chuckled. He heard the crust hit the box and she twisted back to face him. Then Shelly quickly sat up with her legs crossed in front of her. "What time is it?" she asked.

"Have no idea," Sebo answered with a shrug. Shelly scrambled from the bed and went for her purse. "What's going on?" He asked.

"The drawing!" she chirped.

"What?"

He saw her pull her phone from her bag and look at it. "Shit." Sitting up himself now, Sebo said, "What are you talking about?" He saw her shoulders slump a bit.

"We missed it."

"Missed what?"

"The Mega Millions drawing." Then she said, "You still have your ticket, right?"

Sebo pointed toward the old lady's dresser. "Yeah, sure, it's over there somewhere."

Shelly went for the dresser, her hands pushing around the small clutter of cash and receipts, until she came up with Sebo's lottery ticket. She spun back to face him with the ticket held high, and he saw her grin. "Let's check your numbers!"

With her phone in one hand and the ticket in the other, she climbed back into bed, wriggling until she was back beside him again. Shelly placed the ticket in the center of his chest, and it tickled a bit as it lay there perched atop his crop of hair. He didn't move, he just watched her thumbs dance around as she clicked away. Then she reached for his ticket, plucking it, and a few hairs, from his chest—"Ow!"

She giggled. "Sorry!"

Shelly held Sebo's ticket up next to the bright screen of her phone... waited.

"Did we get any numbers right?" Sebo said. The profile of her quiet face was painted in the phone's pale glow. She continued to stare at the screen until Sebo finally said, "Hey, Babe? Did we get any right?"

Then he heard her small voice whisper a single word... "Yeah..."

Twelve

Got a pen?

Her hands were trembling. Sebo was still just watching her. He waited a few more seconds, then he said, "What's up, Babe?"

"Shhh!"

He lifted his hands in surrender. "I'm cool, Babe," he said. Then he heard her start to cry, so he shifted to get a better look at her. "What's going on? Why are you crying?"

Shelly hadn't even realized yet that she was crying. Sebo's voice came at her like a distant echo. She was staring hard at the numbers printed on Sebo's ticket—*searching for her mistake...*

Shelly held up her phone and stared again at the drawing's results that were posted on the Florida Lotto website—then back again at the ticket. She held the ticket closer to her phone, and her face, and this time she really worked to be mindful, and to focus. She rechecked the date of the drawing, and rechecked the numbers, until the whole thing went fuzzy, and her eyes began to sting and go blurry, and she could no longer recognize anything.

"Let me see it."

With the tears now flowing freely down her cheeks, Shelly handed her phone, and the ticket, over to Sebo. He pushed himself more upright and took a look for himself. He laughed. "Hey, check it out?" Sebo said. "I won something—no shit?" He nudged her. "So what did I win, Babe?" Rubbing the heels of her hands across her wet face, she sniffed, and said, "You won the Mega Millions."

Sebo was quiet for a moment as her words settled inside his head. "You mean, like, the whole thing?" She shook her head. "Not the whole jackpot," she said. "For sure there's gonna be other winners, but you've definitely won a bunch of money." He laughed again. "Really?" Sebo held the slim paper ticket up in front of his face. "So how much do you think I won?"

Shelly thought for a moment then she said, "well, there's sixteen states that participate in the drawing. It takes a while for the central office to get back all of the results and announce the winners." Shelly glanced over and saw the back of his ticket for the first time. "You have to sign the back." Sebo flipped the ticket around, examined it, and she said, "Yeah, like, sign it right this minute—it's super important."

"You got a pen?"

Shelly went to grab her purse then returned with a ballpoint in her outstretched hand, and Sebo really looked at her face this time—she wasn't happy. "Hey?" He said. "This is all cool, right?"

"Here." She handed him the pen. "I'll feel better after you sign the back." He took the pen from her, but just held on to it while he focused on her face. "You okay, Babe?"

She smiled a little. "Yeah, sure—now will you sign it already?"

Without another word, Sebo twisted around toward the old lady's nightstand. He leaned over, and with his left hand, signed the ticket. Twisting back, he let out a sigh, and said, "So you gonna tell me why you're upset?" He saw the tears again... "Babe?"

Shelly sniffed and then rubbed at her runny nose. "It's just..." She choked up again before she finally found her voice. "We can't see each other anymore."

"What?" Sebo barked. "What are you talking about?" He saw fear on her face for the first time. "Hey, I'm sorry..." He leaned back against the headboard—folded his arms across his chest. "Look, uh..." he said, "it's okay, just tell me what you mean?" She was already out of bed by now and pulling on her jeans. Sebo just sat there and watched her get dressed.

She gathered the last of her things, took in a long breath, and then said, "I sell the tickets at the store—that's the problem. If the lottery commission finds out we're seeing each other, we could get into trouble—they might even forfeit your prize money over it."

Sebo smiled at her. "If that's all it is, then fuck this thing." He crumpled the ticket up in his hand and tossed it to the floor. Shelly watched him do it and it shocked her to the point that she couldn't speak, or even move—she could only stare down at the little ball of crumpled paper lying atop the midnight blue, wall-to-wall.

"I'm serious, just leave it there," said Sebo.

"No way!" She said, "you can't do that—you don't even know how much it's worth!"

"I don't care," he said, "leave it." Then Sebo smiled at her, he held his arms out toward her, and motioning with his hands, he said, "can you please come back to bed now?

She giggled…

Thirteen

Do better than try…

B ill Mazurek swung his Bronco off of 9th Street East, and
then onto 35th Avenue. What lay in front of him now was
a double-row of low-rent duplexes crowding both sides of a
dead-end street. Beyond that was a thicket of scrub-oak, a ten-
foot drainage ditch, and beyond that, the west parking lot of the
campus of Southeast High—his wife's alma mater. It was still
morning, but already edging up toward ninety. In the distance,
humid air hanging above the roasting asphalt shimmered under
the scorching sun.

Inside his vintage Bronco, Bill had the windows rolled up
and the AC blowing cold. An iced, fountain-soda sat in a cup-
holder. He slowed to peer out at the mailbox numbers moving
past his window, while, Spanish language lesson number 24,
played on the tape-deck. "Lo siento," Bill repeated, "todavía no
está en casa."

Then he spotted a group of kids just ahead, playing with a
water hose, five or six at least—grade-school age, and taking
turns spraying each other down at the end of one of the concrete driveways. Then Bill saw one of them look his way; the kid
pointing in his direction, and it made the other kids all stop to

look too. Bill could see them shouting now as they all quickly scattered. The kid holding the hose left it running across the driveway as he too, turned-tail, and sprinted for home.

Bill chuckled at the sight. The kids all knew his Bronco—knew he was a probation officer too. Now they were all running home to tell their moms that there was a badge coming down the street—happened every time he visited the neighborhood. Even though Bill currently had only two parolees that lived here, and today he was checking up on just one of them.

After a brief knock, and a short wait, the front door to the duplex opened. "Hey Pablo, how are things going?" Bill said. A man with close-cropped hair and a scruffy beard, and whose muscled outline filled the doorway to capacity, smiled at Bill. "¿Cómo van las lecciones de español?" He said.

"Muy bien," Bill answered, "gracias por preguntar." With an approving nod, Pablo said, "Not bad, chief—you're really getting the accent down." Then Bill noticed the large bandage on Pablo's left forearm. "You get another one lasered?" Glancing down at the bandage, Pablo nodded again. "Son of bitch came off a lot harder than it went on, that's for damned sure."

"It'll be worth it, I guarantee," Bill said, "which leads me to my next question." At that moment he saw the former gang member and drug dealer wince.

"You already heard about that, huh?" Pablo said.

"You have to keep a job going—you know that, right?" Pablo nodded, and Bill said, "Which means you have to be useful, and valuable enough to someone's business that they are willing to pay you for your time—right?" Bill saw another nod of agreement. "So I'm certain you've realized by now that telling off your boss is not what a hard-working business owner needs, or wants, to hear from their employees—am I right?"

"Yeah, Chief," Pablo said. "I'm really sorry about that—I'll try to do better next time, okay?"

"You have to do better than try," Bill said. "What I have to see from you is success—are you hearing me?"

Folding his arms in front of him, Pablo said, "Yeah... I hear you."

"Look," Bill said, "I spoke with Jerome, and he said to tell you he's willing to give you a second chance, but you'll have to go down to the tire store and personally apologize to the man, face to face." Pablo flashed a tight-lipped grimace, but nodded his agreement, he said, "I'll do it. I'll go over there today, and thanks, I appreciate it."

"Tienes un buen día," Bill said, "y te veré la próxima semana."

"Sure thing, Chief," said Pablo. "I'll do that—Gracias."

* * *

After hearing the light rap against his door, Sebo spun back toward the bathroom, and motioned for Shelly to stay out of sight. He quickly pulled on a pair of jeans, grabbed a fresh tee-shirt, and then left his bedroom. On his way to the door, Sebo peeked in on Alfi—the guy was still sound asleep. Sebo then continued on to the front door and opened it.

"Mr. Mazurek," he said. "Hello sir."

"Call me Bill, Sebo, and I'm serious—forget the *sir* bit, okay?"

Back in the bedroom, Shelly was still rubbing a towel over her shower-wet hair. She tipped her head back and allowed her damp blond hair to fall loosely against her tee-shirt. Then she paused to overhear the voices of the two men as she slipped on a pair of panties. She was still listening to their conversation when she spun back to hang up the towel. By the tone of the visitor, Shelly could tell it was most likely a drop-by from Sebo's probation officer—their voices passing clearly through the trailer's thin walls.

"So, whose car is this?" Bill said as he briefly looked over the red Ford Fiesta sitting under the carport.

"Just a friend."

"Male or female?" Bill asked.

"Female…" Sebo flashed a brief grin, and Bill said, "All right then—moving on. How's the maintenance job going?"

"I like it, it's a good job—I'm gonna stick with it."

Shelly zipped up her jeans and then glanced again at the crumpled lotto ticket she'd rescued from where Sebo had tossed it the night before. With the two men's conversation still going strong outside, Shelly picked away at the crinkled paper with her small fingers until she was able to spread the ticket out flat, and still intact, on top of the dresser.

"LJ tells me the place has never looked better," Bill said.

Shelly carefully examined the ticket as Sebo's baritone voice filtered back though the walls. "That's really good to hear," he said.

Shelly pulled out her phone and checked again to see if the lottery commission had announced how many winners there were—still no news. Shelly knew what it most likely meant too—the odds that only a single winning ticket had been purchased were going up.

"My wife bought me a riding mower for Christmas a couple years back," Bill said. "I've been thanking her for it ever since."

Shelly stared at the rumpled lotto ticket a bit longer before she let out a frustrated sigh, and then slipped it into her wallet.

Fourteen

We run a pool…

S helly smiled briefly at her boss before she said, "I'm really sorry if this puts you in a bind, Mr. Mettle."

The Quick-Stop's manager let out a sigh, and said, "I'd like to talk you out of it if I could—I knew I was in trouble when I saw you coming in on your day off."

"I really do need this transfer," Shelly said. She watched the man's face drop a bit.

"Personal issues? Family problems?"

She nodded. "Yes. I don't wanna get into details, but a transfer would really help me out a lot."

"You're a good worker, Shelly," the man said. "I hate to lose you, but I'll go ahead and make the request on your be-half." Then he added, "I know there's an opening over at the Palma Sola store—it'll be a bit of a drive for you, but you'd be a shoe-in; I'm friends with the manager over there."

With her transfer secured, Shelly climbed back into her red Ford Fiesta, and with a nervous flutter in her stomach, she turned over the car's little four-banger and proceeded to drive to the nearest post office.

The line for the service counter was already a long one when she arrived. Shelly first selected an envelope for USPS Priority Express. Then she stood off to one side and filled out the paperwork—using Sebo's full name, his current address, and the old lady's land-line phone number. Next, Shelly filled out the shipping address after scrolling through menus on the Florida Lottery's website with her phone. As she was completing the forms, she once again stopped to check if the lottery commission had announced any winners—still nothing. With the ticket prepared for shipment, Shelly joined the line and waited.

"Next."

The postal clerk took Shelly's sealed envelope from her. The woman first checked the information on the form, and, smiling at Shelly, said, "Florida Lottery Claims Processing, Tallahassee? Is that right?" Shelly nodded. "Yeah, it's nothing big though, and the only reason I'm mailing it in is because I have to catch a flight."

Still smiling—still curious, and a bit envious too—the woman said, "How much did you win?"

With a shrug, Shelly said, "I'm sure it's not that much, and to be honest? I don't even know—they haven't announced the winners from last night's drawing yet."

"Oh, they sure have!" The woman answered excitedly. "You didn't see it yet?"

Shocked, the girl shook her head before she responded with a breathless, "No." Then Shelly said, "Are you sure? Because, I was just looking at the website a little while ago."

"After the big ones, I look all the time," the woman replied. "We run a pool."

Shelly watched as the clerk weighed her envelope, and as she did, the woman muttered quietly, "There was only one winner last night." After she inputted the envelope's tracking code into her computer, the woman made direct eye contact with Shelly, and said—"What do you think about that?"

Shelly felt her next breath catch inside her throat—her face turning ghostly in the process. Eying the girl's reaction, the postal clerk said, "That'll be twenty-three dollars and seventy-five cents." Shelly's hand trembled as she gave the woman thirty dollars. The postal clerk handed Shelly back her change, her receipt, and the tracking number for her package. Then the woman winked at her, and said, "I hope it works out for you, dear—good luck."

Fifteen

Smarter than she lets on...

S helly caught sight of the black Tahoe through the glass of
the post office doors. She hesitated, her hand dropping
away from the door's handle, and with it, all thought of Sebo's
ticket, and the prize money, was obliterated. As soon as Shelly
saw him exit the SUV she turned away from the door. Spinning
on her heel, she left the building's front entrance. From there,
Shelly went back inside, and back onto the main floor of the
post office, where she quickly looked left, then right—searching
the room for another way out.

"Shelly."

The man's voice was firm, and sharp, and as soon as she
heard him speak her name she froze in place.

"Shelly, turn around."

His face had the eyes of a hungry lion—she wanted to run.
But as powerful as her urge to flee was, she hesitated—knowing
full well that he was carrying a gun, and a badge, and also knowing that he owned her.

Folding her arms in tight against her body, Shelly lowered
her head and looked down at the floor—felt his firm grip on her

83

elbow. "We're walking back outside," he said. With his hand clamped tight to her right arm, and his fingers digging hard into her flesh, she was forcefully marched out of the building. They crossed the parking lot together, and when they reached his black Tahoe, he pushed her up against it, opened the rear door with his free hand, and said, "Get in."

Shoved into the backseat, Shelly looked up only briefly at the woman seated beside her. She could tell right away that this woman was different from the one she'd seen before. The woman said nothing; she only stared back as the driver's side door opened, and FBI Special Agent Martinez climbed inside.

Agent Martinez settled himself in behind the wheel with the Tahoe's engine running softly at idle and the AC steadily pumping out cold air. Shelly could feel the chill against her skin. The interior smelled of disinfectant, and the black leather rear seat felt cool and smooth, but the female agent still wasn't saying a word—she just continued to stare at Shelly.

Martinez twisted back from the driver's seat. "What's going on?"

Shelly wasn't looking at him when she said, "I don't know what you mean."

"Why are you here?" Martinez demanded.

"It's a post office," Shelly said, and still looking down at the floor. "I needed to mail a letter."

"You think you're being smart or something?" Martinez barked. Shelly cringed, and still with her eyes on the floor, she rolled her lips into a tight frown. "You wanna play games?" Martinez snarled. "Because I can think of a whole lot of shit I can throw your way—you sure you wanna play games with me?"

Shutting her eyes against the brute force of his voice, she drew her arms in even more tightly around her chest.

A few seconds of silence went by before Shelly heard Agent Martinez let out a sigh, then he said, "Why did you ask your manager for a transfer?" Shelly lifted her chin with her eyes wide open. He took in her shock and smiled. "I know everything, Shelly," said Agent Martinez. "Haven't you figured that out by now?" He chuckled and shook his head. "I know every fucking thing there is to know about you."

Pointing a finger at her now, he said, "You went in on your day off this morning and asked your manager for a transfer. I also know that he agreed to let you shift to another store— Palma Sola—wasn't that it?" Martinez, now grinning, rubbed at the bristled scruff that covered his chin. "I also know that you've been fucking Sebo Corrado."

He watched her reaction… *savored it*… "No accounting for your taste in men," he added. "But given the fact that your last boyfriend's currently rotting in maximum security? I guess I'm not that surprised." Agent Martinez shot a quick glance at the female agent in the back seat beside Shelly. He nodded, and right on cue, she said, "You had direct contact with LJ yesterday, is that right?"

Shelly looked up at the woman. "Yes," she said.

"Shelly," the woman said, her voice softer this time, "you do understand how important this investigation is, right?"

"Yes…"

"And how important *you are* to this investigation—right?" The woman watched as Shelly nodded in response. "So why would you ask for a transfer?" The woman said. "You were ex- actly where we needed you to be—you can't just decide to up and leave." The female FBI agent gauged Shelly's reaction, then she said, "You sure you're hearing me? Because you don't have the ability to make a decision like that—you're working for us, Shelly—we made an agreement, and not one single aspect of what you've done today makes any kind of sense to us—you have to tell us what's going on."

"I was scared, okay?"

"You made a deal with us, Shelly," Martinez interrupted. "You want out of the deal? Well, all right then—fine with me. You just give the word, Agent Carson here will make the arrest, and you can spend the next couple of decades in a cage..."

A few minutes later, Special Agent Martinez watched from behind the wheel as the girl passed in front of his vehicle, moving at a half-run back across the post office parking lot to her car, and Martinez said, "You were too soft on her."

Back in the front passenger seat now, and buckling her seatbelt, Agent Carson answered, "You're gonna lose that girl if you don't back the fuck off."

"You don't know that little twat like I do—she's smarter than she lets on—her ex is in lockup on a RICO because she flipped on him."

"You're the one who asked me for a favor, remember?" Adjusting her air vent, she said, "You give me all of ten minutes worth of a briefing on the case, and you still got the result you wanted, okay?" Then Agent Carson added, "So don't give me any shit about how it got done, because it did get done." She took in a long breath, waited a few seconds, and then watched as Agent Martinez reached for the shifter of the still-idling Tahoe. "How did you know she was sleeping with this guy Sebo?" She finally asked. "You told me you haven't been able to get ears inside the trailer yet."

"It was a hunch."

She chuckled. "Well, your hunch paid off, so what now?"

"Now we have to get ears inside that trailer." Martinez pulled out of the post office parking lot, rolled to the intersection of 24th Street East and 57th Avenue, where he hung a left and accelerated in the direction of Old Highway 301.

"What about getting the girl to plant it then?" Agent Carson said. "I mean, if she's sleeping with the guy?"

"After the stunt she pulled today?" Martinez said. "She's not reliable enough, and if LJ hadn't taken an interest in her? I'd already be finished with her and she'd be in cuffs right now. Our number one focus is LJ, and getting this girl tapped into his operation—into his overseas connections higher up. Now that she's had contact with LJ? I want her focused on him, and only him."

"What about your phone tap?" Carson said. "You said you have the trailer's land line—what've you turned up there?"

"So far we got nada."

"Cell phones?"

"Nope," Martinez said. "Neither one of them owns one."

"How about putting a tracker on Sebo's car then, like you did the girl's?"

"Sebo doesn't have a car."

"The Italian then, what about him?"

"Nope—no car."

Carson thought for a moment, then she said, "Both those guys are on paper, right?"

"Yep."

"So why not just bring them both in? I mean, they'd have no choice but to cooperate with us."

"LJ's too smart for that—he'd know."

"Cameras?"

"He's got eyes all over that shit-hole trailer park of his."

Martinez glanced her way, said, "For now at least, I need both of those guys in the program and working for LJ—not fertilizing some east-county citrus grove."

"What about leveraging the probation officer?"

Slowing for a traffic light, Martinez said, "I thought of that, but then I looked up the two peace officers assigned to these guys."

"And?" Carson questioned.

Martinez said, "One's a straight-up, local-yokel, and close to retirement." Carson, listening, then asked. "And the other guy?" Martinez let out a brief chuckle. "Does the name 'Barney Fife' mean anything to you?"

"Barney who?" Carson asked.

"Barney Fife," Martinez answered. "The goofy dumb deputy on the Andy Griffith show—you never heard of him?"

Carson shook her head. "No, I never heard of no guy named, 'Barney Fife.'" Then Carson said, "Tell me you do, at least, have a tracker on LJ's car then."

"Yes, we do."

"And?" Carson questioned again, and this time she looked directly at Martinez—saw his disgusted reaction. "He's clean, isn't he?"

"Yep."

"So, what's next?" She said. "I mean, if you still want me to work this case with you, that is."

"You're not planning on getting pregnant any time soon, are you?" Martinez asked.

"Hell no," she said, and Martinez smiled. "Good, then the answer is yes—I definitely want you working this case with me." Slowing for a turn, Martinez said, "I guess what we'll have to do next is talk to the peace officer."

"Which one?" Carson said, "The local-yokel? Or the Barney Fife?"

"I haven't decided yet."

Sixteen

You knew it was a fake…

"I liked the deal we had before," Meteo said. LJ shrugged off the comment like it didn't mean anything to him—which it didn't. LJ took another bite of his fried grouper sandwich before shifting slightly on the concrete bench, a bit further down in order to catch more shade, but not so much that he'd lose his eye-line with the beachfront showers, and the wet bikinis. Meteo was enjoying the soft aroma of coconut suntan oil filtering through the air, and the accompanying scenery, as much as LJ was, but more from a business perspective; thinking about how much the girls playing around in the showers would bring him on the open market—if he ever got the chance, that is…

While Meteo continued to watch, taking in the scene, the sun, and a pleasant view of the Gulf of Mexico, LJ was still chewing, and staring into his sandwich, then he said, "I remember when these things were made with real grouper."

"You need to see Las Rocas, my friend," said Meteo, and while glancing down at his own plastic basket: the paper lining, the fries that swam in their own grease, and the fake slab of fried grouper that had been squashed inside a hamburger bun—he pushed it aside, deferring to his beer instead.

"Las Rocas, huh?" LJ said. "Can you get real fucking grouper down there?"

"I have my own boat," said Meteo. "We catch them fresh."

LJ smiled fully this time. He dropped the half-eaten sandwich back into the basket. "Sounds a hell of a lot better than this shit."

"It's tilapia," Meteo said. "It's a cheap, ugly, freshwater fish native to Africa—we used to farm them in Estado de Zulia, but there's no money in it anymore." He pointed. "What you've just been eating came out of some crap-filled pond in Cambodia."

"Oh man... that's it." LJ reached for his beer, gulped some down, and then he said, "You've just ruined this place for me— I've been coming here for years; why'd you have to go and tell me that?" Wiping his mouth with a paper napkin, LJ said, "How is it you know so much about fish anyway?"

With a shrug, Meteo answered, "I know enough to recognize when I've been served a fake. I know it every time, and around here the restaurants all like to pass off cheap shit as the real thing, but the tourists don't know the difference. I can tell just by looking, but the taste says everything; freshwater fish tastes like a muddy river—the good stuff tastes like the sea." Pointing again at LJ's lunch, Meteo said, "You knew it was a fake—I didn't tell you anything."

"Let's talk about the deal then."

"Yes," Meteo said, "let's talk. I'd like to get more cars."

LJ shook his head. "Sorry, but that window has closed for good." Then he let out a little chuckle. "I knew you were gonna ask about those goddamned cars—why did I know that?" LJ started snapping his fingers to an imagined rhythm, and then he

91

said, "Yeah… that's right—because every time I see you that's all you ever ask me."

"The cars move."

Nodding his agreement, LJ said, "I hear you bro, but what I have for you moves the world, man, and I don't mean on wheels—I'm talking about old-fashioned, cold hard cash."

Meteo, his mind still on the cars, said, "Past two years I've had to work out of Biloxi." Meteo groaned out his next breath, as tourists strolled by their outdoor table, and by an over-crowded display of inflatable beach toys, and beneath a cluster of cabbage palms in need of trimming. "The supply is good but they can't get me the same level of product—Biloxi only draws in the cheap crowd, Kia's and Hyundai's—shit like that. I don't like the way those guys do business either, always trying to rip me off."

"All the more reason to cut that shit loose," LJ said. He pulled out his wallet. LJ knew he finally had Meteo's attention when he dropped the bills on the table in front of him—Meteo reached for one of the twenties right away.

LJ took in Meteo's reaction, but he didn't stare. He just sat quietly and allowed Meteo to spend a few minutes alone with Alfi's artwork. Meteo mostly just held the counterfeit notes between his fingers at first, but then he really examined them closely. A couple minutes later, LJ finally read the expression he'd been waiting for. "You like what you see?" LJ said.

"Chévere…" Meteo whispered.

"Nice?" said LJ. "That's it?"

Shaking his head, Meteo said, "You need to work on your Spanish, mi Pana—chévere means much better than nice." LJ, still showing half a smile, waved them off when Meteo tried to pass back the five fake twenties. Then LJ said, "You'll be needing samples, so it's best if you hang on to those." Slipping Alfi's twenties into his own wallet, Meteo said, "I've never seen work like this—not ever."

Flashing a grin this time, LJ said, "You and me both."

"It's more than that." Meteo's voice slipped back to a whisper. "I'm fucking serious—these notes are even better than what the CIA produces to fund their payoffs—it's better than anything I've ever seen."

"This mean you're ready to ditch those Mississippi morons and work with me again?"

"The world still runs on oil and U.S. dollars," Meteo said. "Ever since the Americans put us Venezuelans under embargo, we're drowning in oil, and starving for dollars. After seeing what you got? Why should I keep pawning Korean cars for pennies? My answer is yes, mi Pana—I'm in."

Seventeen

I guess you noticed…

S ebo reached inside the old lady's Frigidaire and grabbed a beer. Taking a nice long pull from the ice-cold bottle, he pivoted in bare feet on the gold and orange linoleum; artificial tiles that bore their designer's upscale, Roman-square motif. Then he took a step further to stand on the matching high-pile shag that still looked and felt perfect.

Sebo's mind was on the sofa, and then a shower after he'd finished his beer. Dirt and bits of shredded vegetation still scratched at the back of his neck. But he was of the mind to sit down on the brown chenille couch anyway. A glimpse of bright red paint passing in front of the window stopped him. It was the hood of her Ford Fiesta, still in motion as she maneuvered in to park beneath the carport.

He was still holding the half-finished beer in his left hand when he opened the trailer's front door with his right and saw her getting out her car. The look on her face made him want to say something straight out, but he held it back.

The first thing he wanted to ask her about being the fact that she'd taken his lottery ticket—he'd noticed it missing right after she left that morning. The booze, and the pot, and the pretty damned good sex, not having totally blurred his memory of actually winning something. Even if he wasn't quite sure how much money he'd actually won—that part was a bit fuzzy.

Sebo was on the verge of opening his mouth when he got a better look at her face and decided to wait. He finished off the beer instead. She came up the three concrete steps and then passed him by without a word on her way inside. He just closed the door behind her. Sebo took a step over and set the empty bottle on the piano, watched her sit down on the couch in a little folded up position. On first impression, he thought she looked like she'd just outrun somebody, or perhaps, just cheated them. He took a step back, sat down on the piano bench, and waited for her to say something.

"Yeah, so…" she started to say, but then she mumbled something else that he didn't quite understand. She was fidgeting with her hands, rubbing them together like they itched, rocking forward and then back again with a steady swaying motion like she needed to pee or something. She looked pale. Her eyes were red, but he'd already decided he wasn't going to say anything until she explained herself first. So, he just sat and waited for her to fess up. Then she said, "Um, yeah—so, I guess you noticed, huh?"

Nodding his response, Sebo just held his eyes on her. She was still fidgeting, still rocking back and forth, until she finally said, "I did take it, okay? But it's safe, I mean—seriously, it's safe. Okay? I mailed your ticket into the lottery claims office."

"You mailed it in?" Sebo said. She thought his voice sounded surprisingly calm. "Why would you do that? I told you to leave it—you remember me telling you that, right?" She nodded, and he said, "I was serious when I told you to leave it on the floor. Why would you go and mail it in without asking me? You didn't even let me know about it before you did it—what kinda shit is that?" Her eyes went to the far wall and stayed there. Then Sebo spoke again and this time she felt the full weight of his voice. "You need to tell me everything—I mean everything."

"I thought it was the best thing I could do for you." Her eyes briefly met his before they settled on the floor. "I did it for you—okay?"

Sebo, working hard to hold back his anger, said, "The only way you ever do something for me? Is if I ask you to." She started to get up from the couch, and he said, "You go for that door and you'll be real sorry."

She went for the door...

From the piano bench it only took him a single stride to get ahead of her. The second his hand clamped down onto her arm she felt paralyzed. Her heartbeat now pounding hard up inside her ears as Sebo dragged her away from the door. By this time he already had his other arm around her waist. She fell limp and he could tell already that she wasn't going to try and fight him off.

Shelly glimpsed the texture of gold shag framed inside her golden hair as it swung in front of her face, and she knew she had no options at this point; anything she did would only make it worse, because she knew full well what was coming next—a beating. She braced for the first blow—they always liked to hit her in the face first for some reason.

She could tell her feet were no longer touching the floor as Sebo moved back to the piano bench. She was surprised he hadn't hit her yet, but by now it was all a blur anyway. She had no idea what was happening until she felt him yank her jeans down. Four hard smacks to her bare ass followed; the pain searing her skin like acid, and the pure shock of it all; what he was really doing to her. It had happened too fast to fully process. Then it stopped.

Sebo took in a breath. "You had enough?"

"No…"

The word that had somehow escaped her lips seemed like it came from someone else who was in the room, but she'd said it all the same. Loud, and clear, and for once at least, a purely honest reason—because it was the truth. No hesitation from him; Sebo gave her four more, hard and fast. With each succeeding jolt of pain Shelly felt her body violently quake, and inside each excruciating moment, as his strikes hit home, what she saw were all of the monsters haunting her head—bad choices being exploded into bits, as they were gunned down one by one; obliterated by his huge hand against her naked flesh: LJ—smack! Agent Martinez—smack! Her ex who ran the check fraud ring—smack! The previous arrests she'd lied about—smack!

For a single brief pure moment Shelly felt her mind go completely clear while the agony he'd inflicted rifled through her. Tears streamed down her face but she wanted to ask for more. Not only because of what she'd already done to him—for what was still coming…

Sebo, breathing hard, could hear that she was crying. Drawing his stinging hand back, the red bloom of her soft flesh blossoming in front of him, he said, "How about now?" She stayed quiet this time, so he shoved her off his lap and she landed on the floor.

Shelly, scrambling to get back on her feet, struggled to catch her breath as she wriggled fast into her jeans again while her body shook uncontrollably. Then she heard him tell her to go home.

After picking up her purse, she reached for the door—still quiet, and he said, "You thought I was going to hit you in the face, didn't you?" She paused at the door, didn't look at him, but he could see her small chin answer yes from beneath her messed-up hair. "I don't do that kinda shit," said Sebo. "Truth is, I've never hit a woman before just now." She looked up—made eye contact.

"It's not just about that fucking ticket, you know that, right?"

She could only stare back at him while the all-too-briefly bolted doors inside her mind flew open, and the river of filth the spanking had cleansed her of flooded right back in. Sebo, still holding tight to her stare, said, "When you're ready to tell me everything, you know where to find me."

Eighteen

Damn the torpedoes…

"Shake Pit," Bill said, "now that place is the real deal."

"I don't eat that shit," Elaine said, and Bill answered, "Too bad, you're missing out on a classic. They still mix the shakes to order, just like when we were kids—place has hardly changed in sixty years."

Elaine, still looking at him, and still with half of her organic chickpea and quinoa salad sitting on her desk, said, "What were you doing way out on the west side of Manatee Avenue anyway?"

"Had to drive out to Riverview Boulevard," Bill said. "The stockbroker."

"Oh yeah, I forgot about that guy—how much time does he have left anyway?" Fumbling with a ballpoint that had suddenly gone dry, Bill said, "Six weeks." She watched him struggling to get the pen to work, chuckled, then she said, "That's good news."

"He sure is happy about it."

"I don't mean him," Elaine said. "I mean, that's good news for your cholesterol."

Bill tossed the dead pen into the trashcan with a clang and reached for a fresh one. "What's wrong with having a double-cheeseburger, and a strawberry shake, now and again? Simple pleasures, Elaine—that's what they say life's about. Don't short an old man out of a smile."

Elaine, her gaze fixed on his face, said, "Now you're admitting to something."

A few minutes later, Bill looked up from his paperwork to find Freddy standing in front of his desk. "You got something to tell me?" Bill said. Freddy, with of both his hands shoved down into his pockets, and with a nervous grin plastered across his face, said, "Something big is going down." Leaning back in his chair, the fresh pen still in his right hand, Bill said, "And what would that be?"

"I'm not allowed to say—it's top secret."

"So why say anything at all then?" Bill was still leaning back in his chair, still twirling the new ballpoint between his fingers. "What are you trying to tell me, Freddy?" Leaning in close to Bill, and with his knuckles nervously rolling inside the pockets of his chinos, Freddy said, "Look, uh… I'm serious, okay? I'm not allowed to talk about it, but you need to be extra careful around Sebo."

"I'm always careful around Sebo," Bill said. "What's going on?"

Jerking his jittery right hand free, Freddy then patted the compact nine-millimeter-semiautomatic clipped to his belt, and said, "you need to be even more careful."

"I've never carried, Freddy, and I don't have any plans to either."

"Well, you should—that's all I can say."

Bill, shaking his head, watched Freddy move with a noticeable swagger as he exited the office, and Elaine said, "What the fuck was he just going on about?"

With a shrug, Bill bent back over his paperwork. "I have absolutely no idea."

* * *

"A thousand dollars?" Shelly said. "Really?"

"Well," her boss said, "it is company policy to reward the team-member who sold the winning ticket." The thought of a thousand bucks landing in her meager checking account suddenly outshined the rest of the shit she was going through, and as a result, she giggled...

"I'd like to add that I am also very happy you've decided to stay with us, Shelly."

Smiling back at her boss, she said, "Thanks, Mr. Mettle..."

* * *

Sebo rubbed at his eyes before rolling over to look at the analog clock radio on the night stand: 9:04 AM. His headache was still going strong, along with a queasy knot in his gut—a holdover from the day before. A feeling that always showed up whenever he realized he'd just been screwed—or was about to be...

The crushing headache inside his skull had been there all night long—her face flashed through the pain again... *Shit*... Nearly awake, and with his awareness of impending doom growing stronger, Sebo considered the option of cracking open a tall beer—maybe a few of them, and then lighting up the spliff she'd left him from the other day, but the sound of a lightweight's fist against the trailer's front door shoved it all aside.

Sebo let out a groan. "Alfi!" He shouted. The fist against the door rattled through the trailer again, so Sebo shouted even louder this time—"Get the fucking door, man!"

On the move, but still zipping up his jeans, Alfi was already reaching for the front door when it opened in front of him and his red-faced probation officer said, "What the fuck, Alfi? You don't even lock your front door?"

Alfi, with a shrug, and taking a step back, said, "I guess I forgot."

From his bed, and still lying prone, Sebo could clearly hear the conversation taking place outside, but the only part he cared about was the fact that it didn't involve him. Rolling back over, he made another attempt to tune everything out.

"You forgot?" Freddy answered as he invited himself inside, and briefly scratching at the back of his head, he said, "Let's see—what is it LJ has you doing around here anyway?" Freddy snapped his fingers a couple of times, and then he pointed back at Alfi. "Oh yeah, now I remember—*night watchman*... Do I have that right?"

Nodding, Alfi answered, "Yes."

"And you go and leave your own front door unlocked?" Freddy chuckled. "Good thing you're only allowed to carry a flashlight—LJ sure picked a couple of winners." Pointing again, but this time at Alfi's bare chest, Freddy said, "Go put a shirt on—I'll wait right here."

The moment Alfi disappeared from view, Freddy spun around on the thick shag and headed straight for the kitchen. He briefly glanced around before zeroing in on the drip-coffee maker sitting in a corner of the Formica countertop. Moving the boxy old machine out from the wall, Freddy spotted an outlet just behind it. Digging quickly into his right-hand pocket, he retrieved what would otherwise have appeared to anyone else as nothing more than a standard outlet adapter. Fitting the FBI issued listening device into place, Freddy quickly shifted the machine back to its original position.

The peace officer then rushed back to the spot where Alfi had left him standing, waiting only a few seconds more before Alfi reappeared from his bedroom wearing a faded concert tee. "Damn the Torpedoes." Freddy said. "You like Tom Petty?"

Glancing down at the front of his vintage Goodwill find, a circular red and black design featuring a youthful Petty cradling a 12-string Rickenbacker, Alfi said, "Of course, but who doesn't?" Freddy, his right hand resting on a canted hip, and with the tips of his fingers lightly touching his holstered, 9mm pistol, said, "Yeah, well, I have better places to be."

Back inside his Crown-Vic, Freddy eased out from beneath the carport of the old lady's trailer, followed the asphalt loop back out to the front entrance, and paused for traffic. He swung left, and then caught the light two blocks down, passing a cheap strip mall, the East Bradenton Baptist church, a cemetery, and a bingo parlor. Another left-hand turn, and now he was heading back in the direction of the trailer park. Freddy slowed when he spotted the black Tahoe parked along a residential side street.

"What the hell is he doing?" Special Agent Martinez eyed his rear-view mirror as the grill of Freddy's car rolled up to the Tahoe's rear bumper. "Goddamn it…" Martinez barked. The veteran field agent continued to grumble as he watched Freddy open up his driver's side door and then step out from his car.

Twisting back to take a look for herself, Agent Carson said, "You want me to go wave him off?"

"No," Martinez ordered. "Sit tight." Shifting into drive, Martinez shoved his foot down on the gas and pulled away. As he did, Carson was still keeping an eye on Freddy through her side mirror. "Look at his face!" Carson chuckled before smacking her hands together and bursting into full-blown laughter. Then she eyed Martinez's cold expression—quit laughing. She waited a few more seconds before she said, "You want me to call him?"

Accelerating until he rounded the next corner, Martinez then braked to a hard stop, and reaching for his phone, he said, "It's okay, I got this…"

Freddy was still standing in the street and waiting beside his car when his phone's ringtone sounded off from his pocket. with his phone held to his ear, and a knot in his gut, he first took a chewing out from Agent Martinez, then Freddy said, "But, sir—I thought you'd wanna hear how it all went down?" Once more the graveled voice of Agent Martinez bellowed back into his ear, "We had a plan, Officer. You had specific instructions. You were to make a slow pass, make eye contact if you were successful—that was it."

"Yes sir, but—"

Martinez cut him off, and, shouting into his phone this time, said, "Do you want to be the guy who blows it? Is that the kind of man you are? The one who fucks up?"

"No sir."

"Good, then follow my fucking orders—that is your one and only job, Officer."

"Yes sir."

Martinez, on the move again, passed his phone over to Carson. "Confirm the op for me, will you? And get details—I can't talk to this guy anymore."

Nineteen

You never heard of Barney Fife?

"I told you never to call me on this number," LJ said. He was eastbound on the Palma Sola causeway, and on his way back into town after a weekend spent on Anna Maria Island. LJ cruised along nice and easy in his Impala; this after his lunch with Meteo the day before, followed by a wild overnight with Cynthia at her beachfront condo—his current number one. A night LJ was still recovering from in fact, as he listened to Hatchet-Man's request to "stop by the office."

"Yeah, sure," LJ said. "Be there in twenty."

* * *

"Look, Boss, I apologize, I must've hit the wrong entry." The lumbering, has-been wrestler was facing away from LJ, and talking from over one shoulder, while moving at an unusually swift pace through a narrow hallway. Waving his phone above his head for LJ to see, Hatchet-Man said, "These fucking glass screens are tricky as all hell—what the fuck's wrong with buttons anyway?"

Forced to listen through his aching head as he followed close behind, LJ grumbled, "I don't have time for this shit."

"You said to keep an eye on the feeds coming in from the trailer—am I right?"

"Correct," LJ responded, "I did say to keep an eye on the goddamned feeds, coming from the goddamned trailer."

Hatchet-Man was still rambling when he unlocked a door, and then entered the rear office of a buy-here-pay-here car lot on East 14th Street. One of four legitimate businesses LJ owned, and used, for various purposes. The other three being a dry-cleaning shop still run by his mother, a limousine service, and a pool hall. The wrestlers ran the car lot.

Hatchet-Man passed quickly through the office, while digging into his pocket for another key. Still a few steps ahead of LJ, the old wrestler had the final door unlocked just in time for his boss to stroll right through without having to slow down.

"You said to make those guys a priority," Hatchet-Man said, puffing out his words as LJ strolled by.

"I'm busy; just show me."

A sprawling bank of flat screen security monitors filled three walls of the windowless room. The screens were stacked four rows high; Hatchet Man pointed at one of them and said, "Take a look at that one there; halfway up and third over from the left. I saved the video feed; I'll run it for you."

LJ, with his arms folded and his oversized keyring jangling steadily off his right index finger, focused on the black and white surveillance camera's silent playback. "Hold the fuck up," he said. Still with the ball of keys in his right hand, LJ pointed at the frozen image of Freddy moving the old lady's Mr. Coffee. "What the fuck is that shit?"

"You better see the whole thing," Hatchet-Man said, so LJ watched the rest of the playback—chuckled.

"Fucking Feds went and recruited themselves their very own Barney Fife."

"Barney who?" Hatchet-Man questioned.

LJ glared at him. "A white dude your age?" LJ said. "You telling me you never heard of Barney Fife?" LJ read Hatchet-Man's blank expression, said, "Don Knotts was the actor's name—played the stupid cop on the Andy Griffith Show? The man was a comic genius." LJ, still looking and still getting a blank in return, said, "I loved that show. I used to watch the re-runs after school when I was a kid."

"There's more," Hatchet-Man said.

"Make it quick," LJ said while glancing at his Rolex.

Hatchet-Man took a step to his right, and with two of his fat fingers, he pecked at a keyboard. "This one's pretty kinky," he warned. At first LJ only stood silently, and somewhat agitated, as the video feed played back in front of him—the one from the camera hidden inside the bookcase beside the old lady's upright piano. The camera with a clear view of the action that took place at the piano bench the day before.

"Whoa!" LJ shouted. "That shit's fucking raw, man." Folding his arms again, and shaking his head in disgust, LJ said, "That shit right there is not my man Sebo's style—that, is just a fact."

Hatchet-Man chuckled as he watched the video along with LJ, then he said, "I liked it better when they just fucked each other."

Glaring at Hatchet-Man again, LJ said, "Can't you give the man some privacy?"

"You said to keep an eye on everything they did—am I right? Besides, the chick's pretty hot."

Back in his Impala and heading across town, LJ had the radio playing and the AC blowing cold, tapping his fingers against the wheel, keeping time with a Motown golden oldie, and thinking about his next move—feeling pretty good about his newly discovered advantage. The song ended and the DJ's voice came back on air:

…Eddie Holland Jr., truly one of the greats in front of the mic, or in the studio; songwriter, producer—what a talent. That last track was recorded in 1963, "From The outside Looking In", up next, I'll be spinning more pure gold with Martha and the Vandellas, Mary Wells, Shirley Wahls, and the Marvelettes, all this after the news, so be sure to stick around for more great golden sounds from 96.6 on your FM radio dial…

LJ slowed for a yellow light, and now the news was coming over the Impala's customized, high-fidelity sound system, LJ no longer listening because the hands-free was buzzing in his ear—he answered the call. "Hey babe… it sure was… Mmm… I miss you too—tonight? No, tonight won't work for me. How about next Saturday? Oh yeah… see you then." Tapping at the hands-free again, LJ picked up the tail end of the news broadcast as he waited for the light to change:

…A Florida resident is the one and only winner of this week's Mega Millions jackpot totaling 224 million dollars. Officials spent several hours tabulating the data from all sixteen states in Wednesday night's drawing. After receiving the winning ticket by mail, the Florida Lottery Commission has officially named Sebastian Corrado, of Bradenton, as the lucky winner…

Twenty

Just my luck…

LJ sat silent in his car until a driver's blaring horn finally rattled him loose from his state of stunned disbelief. Accelerating through the intersection, LJ took the next available side street, and then made a quick K-turn before peeling off in the opposite direction toward his trailer park.

* * *

A few miles away, Trudy's door opened and Bill smiled back at her. "How are you today?" He asked.

"Good, Bill, thanks—I'm doing all right."

Bill smiled at the baby in her arms, and said, "And how is little Derek?"

"Growing like crazy—still teething," she said, "but he's finally getting better." Bill was listening—observing every possible detail about the person in front of him as he always did, and processing what it told him. Then he caught a sudden shift in her expression, as if she'd suddenly remembered something important, then Trudy said, "Hey, uh, did you hear the news?"

"What news would that be?"

Shifting the squirming baby from one hip to the next, Trudy said, "The news about Sebo—you didn't hear, yet?"

Shaking his head, Bill said, "Wanna fill me in?"

"He won the lottery—can you believe that shit? A guy like him?"

Shaking his head again, Bill said, "Are you sure about that?"

"Oh yeah—it's been all over the news already—fucker won the Mega Millions jackpot: 224-million-fucking-dollars. The whole fucking thing."

* * *

In a diner on the west side of town, FBI Special Agent Carson, staring at her phone, said, "Oh wait... here's another one." Carson then glanced up from the screen and across the table at Special Agent Martinez. He let out a soft groan before he said, "Spare me, will ya? This shit's making me ill."

Shifting in his seat, he set his coffee mug down in time for their waitress to pour him a refill. Meanwhile, Carson had returned to her phone. Martinez took a sip from his freshly filled mug; could hear her chuckling, and even though he found it grating, he liked her enough to leave it be. He was just watching her stare at her small screen, and then without looking up, she said, "No, no, you got to see this tweet—there's a cartoon attached." She smiled up at Martinez. "Here, have a look."

She stretched her arm across the table and Agent Martinez peered at the screen, and at an animated gif image of a smiling convict in prison stripes being showered in a mountain of cash. "I can't believe this shit—what the fuck is wrong with this world anyway? How can a shit-wipe felon be allowed to win the fucking lottery?"

She took her phone back. "No law against it." Carson said, and Martinez answered, "Well there outta be." Martinez was still grumbling under his breath when he saw her look up from her phone again—really smiling at him big this time. "What?" He said. "What's going on?"

"You're not seeing the bright side," Carson replied. "There's a bigger picture here—don't you get it? This is a plus for us—*AND* for this case." He picked up on her line of thought and allowed himself a small grin. Not only for the potential upside on the case, but because she was smart. "I guess 224 million buys us a hell of a lot of leverage—Sebo never rolled on LJ in the past, but he sure as hell will now." Martinez paused a moment, then added, "The girl could end up being a problem."

"I agree." Answered Carson. "What do you want to do about it? Pick her up?"

"More like shake her up." Answered Martinez. "I want to make sure she knows who she really belongs to—keep her from doing something stupid."

Nodding her agreement, Carson said, "Yeah, sure, I follow, but forget about the girl for a minute, because there's a lot more to this. You're still missing the bigger picture—*our* bigger picture." Martinez shrugged, and she said, "No law says he can't win the money—but under the law, we can sure as hell take it from him with a conviction—all of it."

Martinez, grinning even wider now, and liking his new partner even more, said, "Oh the sweet, sweet joy of asset forfeiture."

* * *

From his corner office on the third floor of the Sun Coast Bank building in downtown Sarasota, attorney Joseph Crest's fingers furiously clattered against his keyboard as he searched for hard data. "You got him yet?" He called out from his desk.

"I'm working on it!" his legal assistant shouted back from the next room.

"Not good enough, Barb, not good enough." Crest then added, "It's been more than two hours since the official announcement—we're already in the weeds here." No sooner had the words left his mouth then Barb's attractive figure in a tight dress appeared in his doorway— "I got something!"

"Good—let me see it."

She scurried across the room and handed him a printout, which she quickly followed up with a caveat: "You're not going to like it." Crest scanned down the single page of information about his prospective new client. "Florida Department of Corrections?" He looked back up at Barb. "Seriously?"

"I'm afraid so," she said. "Turns out his last known address for the past two years was a state-sponsored, gated community in Hillsborough County."

Crest chuckled as he continued to read the printout. "Just my luck, huh? The one time I get a clear shot at a lottery whale, and he's a felon." Tossing the sheet onto his desk, Crest said, "This guy's even on paper, for Christ's sake."

"I didn't catch what he was he in for," Barb said.

Lifting the page back up from his desk, Crest looked at it again—"Says here the guy's a car thief."

"Oh, is that all?" she said. "Well at least it wasn't drugs or sex crimes." Then she looked more closely at her boss's face. "No... Please... You're not actually thinking of taking this guy on, are you?" Crest smiled at her. "There's no law against this guy winning the lottery—he deserves the same representation as anyone else, and I can guarantee we'd be the only ones crazy enough to take him on as a client." Still shaking her head, but knowing his mind was already made up, Barb said, "What about the fact that we have no idea where this guy is."

"A minor detail," said Crest. "Call that skip-tracer pal of yours—tell him to find out, and as soon as he does, I'm going to go pay Mr. Corrado a visit."

* * *

From inside the agency's headquarters on H Street, in Washington DC, United States Secret Service Special Agent Margit Spencer handed her written report over to her supervisor. He first paged through the document, but then looked more closely at the pair of pristine cellophane sleeves that Spencer had carefully attached to the front.

"So, there's just these two so far?"

"I expect we'll be seeing a lot more," she answered. "The scary part is, neither of these bills were picked up by machine counters—in both cases they happened to be culled out on a hunch by two separate bank employees—it was purely by chance." Spencer then leaned in closer, and pointing, she added, "Note the individual serial numbers—those two bills were sent to us independently from two separate banks, located in two different states, and a thousand miles apart from each other."

Setting the report aside, he said, "Give me the compressed version for now."

Clearing her throat, Spencer said, "We're obviously dealing with first-class work. No computer printers or photo scanning technique—no offset printing methods either. What you see in front of you was produced using a traditional intaglio press, and from multiple sets of engraved plates. The ink came from Germany, and the paper came from Belgium."

Reaching for the report again, he turned back one of the cellophane sleeves and eyed the reverse side of the counterfeit twenty. "Possibly foreign government production then?" He said. "The Iranians? The Turks?" He looked up. "What's your gut feeling so far?"

"My honest opinion?" She said. "I think the perp's domestic."

"How so?"

"It's the plates—lab analysis has determined that they weren't cut by machine, but engraved totally by hand, and most likely by a single individual."

"So you think we're dealing with a home-grown Rembrandt?"

"Not necessarily home grown," answered Spencer. "I've been scouring case files as far back as the last decade, and I believe I have a solid lead."

He smiled at her. "By all means, Agent Spencer—tell me more."

Folding her arms in front of her, she said, "There was a case in Florida a few years back—very high-quality work. Turned out the counterfeiter did his own engraving, and all by hand—he used his plates to print up forty thousand in $20-dollar silver certificates from the 1960s."

"That just jogged my memory…" Returning to the report, he began flipping through the pages, and said, "You include a rap sheet?"

"Page six."

Spencer's supervisor turned to the last page, eyed the black and white of Alfi's mug shot. "Alfonzo Lanzano—right, the Italian, I remember him." Looking up from the report he said, "So I take it Lanzano's not in jail anymore?"

"Out on probation and currently living in Manatee County."

Grinning at Spencer, he said, "Book a flight—I'm sending you to Florida."

Twenty-One

Two quick taps from the horn of a vintage Impala...

After another hour of failed sleep, Sebo realized his headache wasn't giving up an inch of ground in his battle to get some rest. After finally dismissing the thought of spending it stoned, he decided instead that he'd make an effort to maybe, possibly, just have a normal day. Swinging his feet to the floor, Sebo stood, stretched, and then pulled a clean tee-shirt over his head. After dragging on his jeans, he left his bedroom to find the front door standing wide open and the trailer's AC struggling to cool the outside world. Sebo was about to close the door but thought better of it; he decided to peer outside instead.

The first thing Sebo saw was a car he didn't recognize parked beneath the carport. Looking around some more, he caught sight of Alfi. The Italian was standing with a slight, slender girl who had long dark hair. Sebo continued to observe as Alfi held her close in his arms, the couple as one—*passionate...*

Staring for a few more seconds, Sebo found the sight of them together to be something pure, and even beautiful. He wanted to say something, but instead he quietly took a step back. Turning away from the door, he left it as it was—standing wide open with the trailer's AC bleeding cold air; he didn't care.

In the kitchen, he found Alfi had left his small *Napoletana* coffee pot sitting on the stove. Immediately, unconsciously, and out of habit by this point in their brief friendship, Sebo reached out with his fingertips to touch the side of the demure and elegant implement—*still hot...* Without hesitation he proceeded to pour two shots of the smooth, strong coffee down his throat.

He'd just set the empty demitasse down on the Formica when Sebo heard the car's engine turn over outside. The sound compressed beneath the carport and flooded into the trailer through the opened door, but Sebo didn't move—he just stood at the sink and waited for Alfi to come back inside.

Closing the door behind him, Alfi spotted Sebo standing in the kitchen. "I can't stay to explain," Alfi said. "I have to go do something."

"Was that her?" Sebo asked. "Angela? The girl from before?"

Nodding briefly, Alfi answered, "Yes..."

"If you need any help—if you need anything, man, just ask."

"Thank you, but..." Alfi paused a moment, then forced a thin smile. "I won't be gone long," he said. "I just need to go outside and think."

Twenty minutes later and Sebo had finished off the rest of Alfi's coffee. He was considering asking Alfi to cook up some more of his special pasta, when Sebo heard two quick taps from the horn of a vintage Impala.

Opening the front door, Sebo looked out as LJ's car rolled to a stop beneath the carport. Sebo just leaned against the door frame and waited as LJ stepped out from his car with his big ball of keys, and an even bigger grin on his face. "My man!" LJ shouted.

Sebo chuckled but didn't move from his position—still leaning against the doorframe with his arms folded. LJ stood with his hands on his hips and stared up at Sebo from beside his car. "Look at you," LJ said, "cool as a mother-fuckin' icebox."

"What's going on?" Sebo asked.

"What's going on?" LJ said. "I heard the news—that's what's going on. I heard the fucking news!"

"What news is that?"

LJ froze for a moment. He studied Sebo's face again, and said, "Your news, man—you're the big lotto winner!"

"Oh that…" Sebo straightened, stretched his sore back and then rubbed at his temples. "Shit's been giving me a headache, man."

LJ chuckled. "You fucking amaze me. If I'd just won 224 million dollars? I would not be complaining about a headache—that's for damned sure."

Gazing back at LJ, his expression flat—a total blank—Sebo said, "Wait… what was that?"

At that precise moment, the two men heard a stranger's voice call out to them from just beyond LJ's Impala. "Hello? Excuse me—are you Sebastian Corrado?" LJ spun around to see a stubby-looking dude in a suit and a tie striding toward him in a straight line from the street. The unfamiliar man had nearly reached the rear bumper of his Impala, when LJ said, "Who the fuck are you?"

Holding out his business card, the man said, "Joe Crest, attorney at law—at your service."

Sebo was down in the carport by now and standing next to LJ. "No thanks," he said. "I don't need a lawyer." Crest looked up at his towering, potential new client—chuckled a bit—and then he said, "Oh you certainly do, Mr. Corrado—a man in your position? I guarantee that what you need more than anything in this world, and at this very moment in fact, is a good lawyer."

"Did you not just hear what the man told you?" LJ said. "Now get the fuck back in your car and go away—I won't tell you again."

"Are you threatening me, sir?" Crest said.

Crest, his eyes on LJ, watched as the man's attention shifted away from him and instead, focused on the street. Crest then saw LJ immediately back off, lift his hands as if in surrender, and staring back at Crest, he said, "No… Not at all, sir—I apologize."

Following LJ's line of sight, Crest spun around to see what was behind him. What he saw was a vintage, two-tone Bronco—white over blue—just coming to a stop along the edge of the driveway. Crest spun back toward Sebo and LJ. "Who's that?" He asked. "Somebody you guys know?"

"My probation officer," answered Sebo. The surprise turn of events brought out another chuckle from Crest, and then he said, "A cop when you need one—I guess this is my lucky day."

"He's not a cop," Sebo corrected, "he's a peace officer."

Sebo stood by and watched as Bill got out of his car, while LJ, breathing out a long frustrated sigh, leaned back against his. LJ, with his arms folded and with his keyring hanging off one finger. Then Sebo leaned back too, and right next to LJ with his thumbs hooked in the front pockets of his jeans and waited.

Bill didn't say anything at first. He just held his eyes on Sebo as he walked right past Crest—pegged the man in the suit right off the bat as a lawyer; an opportunistic money-chaser. Bill kept walking until he found himself face to face with LJ and Sebo. After pausing to have a look around, Bill said, "Am I interrupting something?"

"They were just leaving," said Sebo, and Bill, still observing every detail of the odd situation, not liking the vibe he was getting either, or the odd stench for that matter, said, "You guys smell that?"

"Smell what?" LJ said.

Bill first swiveled left, and then right, before he looked back at LJ and Sebo. "Smells like smoke."

Twenty-Two

Straight to voicemail…

As she approached her gate at Reagan National, the TSA uniform on duty blocked her path and ordered her to take a step back. "This gate is closed," he barked. "You'll have to re-schedule your flight." Without a word, Speial Agent Margit Spencer held her badge up in front of the man's face, and without another word from him, he stepped aside and allowed her to pass.

On board her flight, in an aisle seat, agent Spencer checked her phone one last time, and the text she'd been waiting for finally flashed onto her screen—*Received your report, we'll be waiting when you arrive in Tampa, see you in a couple of hours…*

* * *

Glancing back at Shelly through the rear-view, FBI Special Agent Martinez said, "Heard your boyfriend hit it big in the Mega Millions drawing."

"He's not my boyfriend," Shelly answered.

Agent Carson, sitting next to her in the back seat of the black Tahoe, said, "What a shame, but I guess that makes it eas-ier for you to keep working with us then, huh? We won't keep you long Shelly, we just wanted to be sure we're all on the same page, and to let you know that we'll be watching you even more closely from here on out."

Martinez then shifted in his seat so he could look the girl directly in the eye. "You're not missing out on anything, but you already knew that, right? Stick with the program, Shelly, and your luck could turn out to be a hell of a lot better than Sebo's."

* * *

Staring at the bank of security monitors spread out in front of him, Sling-Blade said, "Hey, you better come take a look at this."

Hatchet-Man was ten feet away and sitting at his desk. He gave his partner only a single glance before his attention returned once more to the stacks of counterfeit twenties he'd been counting. "Not now," he said. "Can't you see I'm busy?"

"This is serious," said Sling-Blade. "You need to come have a look at this right now."

Standing shoulder to shoulder inside LJ's surveillance room, Hatchet-Man, and his partner Sling-Blade, stared in stunned disbelief at the live video feed streaming in from Alfi's print shop. "What the fuck is he doing?" Hatchet-Man said. Sling-Blade pointed at the black and white image on the monitor, and said, "He's trashing the place, that's what he's doing—why the fuck do you think I called you over here to see it?"

The pair of has-been wrestlers continued to stare at the screen for another minute or two, transfixed by Alfi's activity.

Inside his print shop, Alfi methodically moved around the long, narrow room; dumping buckets of expensive German inks, pitching containers of industrial solvents, and tossing other exotic materials, before proceeding to empty dozens of boxes filled with oversized sheets of custom-milled, Belgian paper. The liquids and paper spilling and splashing onto the floor and mixing together before Alfi next turned his attention to the freshly shrink-wrapped bundles of his hand-made counterfeit cash—slashing at them in a fury with a trimming knife.

"You better call the boss," Sling-Blade said.

Hatchet-Man already had his phone out, jabbing at the glass screen with his fat fingers. "Fuck!" He growled. "I can never get this stupid thing to work right."

"You want me to do it?"

"No, I got it, okay?" Hatchet-Man jabbed at the screen some more before he finally lifted the phone up to his ear and said, "It's ringing…"

LJ was standing beside his Impala and wondering how best to get rid of the low-rent ambulance chaser; a total stranger who'd so rudely interrupted him at a critical moment. Then LJ heard his hands-free beeping inside his ear, and yet another interruption was not what he was willing to tolerate, so LJ simply reached up, tapped at the device, and sent the call straight to voicemail.

"Fuck!" Hatchet-Man shouted at his phone. "He won't take my call!"

Sling-Blade was still staring at the surveillance feed. "Shit—try him again."

Hatchet-Man did, and, once again, he was left shouting at his phone after his second call went straight to LJ's voicemail. He looked back up at the live surveillance feed, and Hatchet-Man said, "Where'd Alfi get a gas can?"

Joe Crest, following Bill's lead, sniffed again at the air's rapidly rising acrid order. "You're right," he said, "smells like some kind of chemical fire."

LJ, turning to Sebo, said, "I'll go check it out—I'm sure you three have plenty to talk about."

"Let me give you a hand," Sebo said, before LJ waved him off—"It's okay, I got this."

Taking up a lanky jog, LJ took a shortcut in between two of his empty trailers. He crossed another's small, neatly mowed front lawn, and then followed the edge of the paved, loop road toward the rear of the trailer park. LJ could already see thick lumps of black smoke billowing up from behind the trees, along with the moss-covered oaks and underbrush—which were rapidly catching fire. By the time LJ reached the print shop, however, he was no longer looking at the flames, but instead, at a lone, slender figure standing just clear of the growing inferno.

Bill walked back to the edge of the driveway with Joe Crest right behind him, each of the two men looking in the direction of the billowing smoke cloud until both of them spotted the flames climbing up above the treetops. "Jesus," Bill said, and reaching for his phone, "We better get a fire crew out here fast, or this whole place is gonna go up."

LJ marched in a straight line toward Alfi. The slim Italian, with his back to LJ, was standing with his hands on his hips as he watched the flames grow—mesmerized by his hand-made inferno. Alfi, just taking in the pure joy of it, and relishing his momentary sensation of near weightlessness—a euphoria that came with the print shop's destruction—he never saw the first punch coming...

Knocked to the ground, and fully exposed to LJ's wrath, Alfi suddenly found himself caught up in a violent storm of flailing kicks and vicious punches. With every blow, the full force of the pain that LJ was inflicting rifled through Alfi's body. He was trapped inside a blur of agony and incoherence, the Italian attempted without success to shield himself from LJ's rage, while the man's fists pounded into him like jackhammers.

After a 911 call for help, Bill turned back toward the old lady's trailer, and toward LJ's Impala. "Where's Sebo?"

LJ took full advantage of his furious anger, his superior position, and the surge of adrenaline that came with it. Alfi screamed as LJ continued to punch him, first in the head, then the kidneys, then back to his face again. In the moments in between, Alfi pleaded for him to stop, but the man wasn't about to stop—he was just getting started. LJ had just taken a quick step back to gain a better position, preparing to deliver the real pain, when a heavy hand landed on his shoulder.

Sebo spun LJ around to face him, drawing back with his south paw while lifting LJ up from the ground with his right. LJ, scrambling to free himself, before he slipped his right hand behind him, and then came back out gripping a compact nine. At first sight of the P-380 in LJ's hand, Sebo let go.

"What the fuck is wrong with you?" LJ screamed as he held the pistol up in Sebo's face. "What the hell? You belong *to me* you big, dumb fuck—*you're my man!*" LJ laughed at Sebo, then he said, "Haven't you figured that out yet? You're *my* man—*I own you!*" LJ took another step back and put more ground between himself and Sebo. Then he said, "Pick up Alfi—we're getting out of here."

"The fire crews should be showing up any time now," Bill said.

"They better get here quick," Crest added, before he lifted one hand, and pointing, he said, "Hey, hey—what's that guy doing? What's happening?" Crest looked back at Bill with a pleading face, and said, "What's going on?"

"LJ's holding a gun on my parolee," Bill answered, "that's what's going on." Bill briefly made eye contact with LJ as he marched toward them—still about twenty yards away, but with a rock-solid grip on the pistol—Bill knew the man meant business.

Sebo was heading in their direction too; walking just in front of LJ, but Bill was already focused on Alfi. The poor guy appeared to be unconscious, and badly bleeding; looking like a sack of potatoes in Sebo's arms. Sebo then made eye contact with Bill, and immediately Bill read the scoreboard. Letting out a sigh, Bill held his empty hands out in plain view.

"What the hell? You're a cop, right?" Crest shouted.

"I'm not a cop," Bill answered, "I'm a peace officer."

"Don't you have a gun?" Crest said, and Bill just shook his head. "What the hell?" Crest demanded—"You have to do something!"

"I *am* doing something," Bill said. "And I strongly suggest you do the same before somebody gets shot."

Twenty-Three

Watch this...

"And $9.63 is your change—you have a nice day, sir."
Closing the register, Shelly glanced out through the
Quick Stop's front glass, and toward the pumps, just as the
flashy Impala glided in for a smooth stop. The sight of Sebo
getting out from the Impala's front passenger seat caused her to
choke on her next breath. Shelly spun away from the register
and headed for the store's rear passageway and her manager's
office. "Mr. Mettle?" Shelly called out. "Can you take over the
register for a couple minutes?"

She peeked around the corner to find her boss's desk
empty. *Damnit... He's in the can again...* Spinning back toward
the register, Shelly found herself face to face with Sebo, and unable to speak, she could only stare up at his hulking presence.

"Did you hear the sirens?" Sebo said.

Still unable to breathe, or say a single word to him, she nodded...*Yes...* "Pretty big fire broke out at the trailer park," Sebo
said. "I need a fill up on pump two, please ma'am." Shelly
moved back behind the register, while Sebo dug into his pocket.

He tossed three fresh twenties on the counter. "That should cover it."

He watched her take the cash and then open the register. When she looked back, he was leaning in close and staring right at her face, holding tight to her gaze, and said, "Those friends of yours—the one's you didn't wanna tell me about? They're cops, right?" He paused, studied her reaction, and spotted what he was looking for…

"You better call 'em," said Sebo. "Call right now and tell them you saw me with LJ—you tell them now's the time."

Still staring at Shelly's silent face, Sebo said, "You listening to me? Because this is me, asking you, to do something for me—call the cops." Then he briefly smiled at her. "I'm sorry about the way things went between us—I never did care about that ticket, Shelly, the only thing that mattered was being with you."

Outside, Sebo pumped gas into LJ's car. LJ, leaning out of the window, eyed Sebo, then he said, "What the hell? Were you making time with your girlfriend in there?" Sebo looked right at LJ and grinned. LJ laughed, said, "Oh I like you, man—you know that, right? I always have liked you."

* * *

"The chicken farm, huh?" Sling-Blade said, and Hatchet-Man, after slipping his phone back into his pocket, let out a chuckle, and then he said, "That's right, so we better get moving—he wants another hole dug."

"How big a hole?" Sling-Blade asked—hopeful.

"Big." Hatchet-Man answered. "Real big."

* * *

Sebo walked back around to the passenger side, popped open the door, and then slipped down into the white Naugahyde seat beside LJ. "I hope that's all you were doing—just makin' time," LJ said.

Sebo nodded. "You and me made a deal."

"That's right, my man, that is right." LJ shifted the Impala into gear. He edged out from the fuel island and then into late morning traffic. Sebo was just sitting quietly and watching LJ's every move; tracking his fingers on the wheel as it spun back smooth out of the turn, the hard look on his face, and the 9mm semi-auto—just visible above his waistline.

The car's AC blew cold as she floated down the road; smooth and quiet like they were on a cloud. Smokey Robinson drifted out from the radio. From 44th, LJ swung left onto Old Highway 301, after catching the green. Now LJ was driving north, and Sebo knew they were heading for the bridge over the Manatee, and Palmetto, but then LJ slowed.

Sebo was still sitting silent, and LJ said, "I Just need to stop here for a minute—shouldn't take long." Steering the Impala into a discount strip mall, LJ pulled into the first open spot near the rear of the lot, but kept the engine running. Then Sebo saw LJ lean forward past the wheel and strain to reach something under his seat.

When his hands came back out into view, LJ was holding a black metal cylinder. It was about a foot long, close in dimension and near enough in appearance to a cop's flashlight, but Sebo thought it looked more like a pipe-bomb. Eyeing Sebo's expression, LJ said, "I read you—this thing freaked me out too until I found out what it really was." Holding the device up in front of Sebo, LJ let out a chuckle, and said, "Turned out to be just a little harmless gift from the FBI."

"No shit?" Sebo said.

LJ nodded. "This is some antique kinda shit too—you'd think a man of my acuity would deserve a more high-tech approach. Budget cuts I guess. I found this hunk of junk mounted to the undercarriage about five months ago—been carrying it around ever since."

Then LJ flashed a grin at Sebo, and said, "Watch this..."

Opening his driver's side door, LJ unfolded himself into a standing position before strolling over to one of the parked cars nearby. Without hesitation, he knelt down and then clamped the FBI's GPS tracking device to the car's underside; the device's powerful magnets making a clanking sound as it attached itself to the frame of a Toyota Prius. Back inside his Impala, and behind the wheel, LJ said, "That felt good."

Twenty-Four

Saw it on YouTube...

Jesus H. Christ it's hot in here... Joe Crest was feeling the full weight of his gray gabardine as he lay folded up on his left side, and in the center of the trunk of LJ's classic ride. The car was on the move again, shifting, swaying, and bouncing along. The disconnected motion was starting to make Crest feel ill. His neck was aching and his back hurt. Then there was the skinny Italian guy who'd been stuffed in behind him—not moving... *quiet...*

Crest moaned at his own discomfort—at his incomprehensible circumstances. Like the fact that he was shoved up so close to the peace officer lying in front of him, that he could smell the guy's aftershave. *Aramis... God help me...*

Dark as night inside. Tight on space, and short on air—his phone in the black guy's pocket. His wrists clamped together with a heavy plastic cable-tie, a second one around his ankles. Crest could feel the peace officer moving and jerking around. He wanted to tell the guy to cut it out, but the duct tape across his mouth had made him a mute.

A couple of minutes later, Crest realized the peace officer must be facing him because he no longer smelled *Aramis*, but the man's labored breaths. Then he felt the guy's fingers touching his face.

Groping in the dark, Bill felt for Crest's mouth, and then peeled back the tape. "What the hell?" Crest barked before Bill's hand mashed down hard over his mouth. "They'll hear us," Bill whispered. He took his hand away, and Crest said again, but in a whisper this time, "What the hell?"

Bill didn't bother to answer the guy, or even pay attention for that matter. He was too busy digging his phone out from his pocket. The light from the screen illuminated the trunk's interior in a dim blue haze. A soft hum rising up from the tires told Bill the car was picking up speed. In the pale light, Crest finally got a look at Bill's face. "How'd you break free?" He whispered. "They teach you that at the academy?"

Bill wasn't looking at Crest, he was still staring at his phone. "Nope," he whispered back. "Saw it on YouTube once, figured I should give it a try." Tapping at his speed dial list, Bill lifted his phone to his ear, and Crest said, "How'd you keep the big guy from taking your phone?"

"I didn't," Bill answered. "He passed it over on purpose."

* * *

Shelly stood outside while leaning against a block wall at the back of the Quick-Stop on her smoke break. She was next to the dumpster, with a Marlboro 100 balanced in one shaking hand, and her phone in the other. "Yes, it was LJ's Impala... yes... it was about twenty minutes ago."

FBI Special Agent Martinez listened over the hands free, and with the speaker activated, so agent Carson could listen in on it too. "Sebo told you to call us?" Martinez repeated.

"Yes."

"How would he know you were working with us?" Carson said.

"He didn't."

"I should believe that?" Martinez snapped back. "Did you just go and blow this case? Is that what just happened?"

"What happened is what I just told you!" Shelly shouted into her phone. "You know everything I know—okay? You wanted information, right? Well that's what I just gave you, and if you want LJ? You better go after him."

Twenty-Five

Not for that skinny little girl...

"Where the hell are you?" Elaine said. She bit at her lower lip as she listened to Bill. "Wait a minute," she snapped. "Wait just a goddamned minute—did I just hear right?"

Bill shielded his phone from the road noise as he lay on his back next to Joe Crest. "Yeah," he said, "you heard right—I'm locked in the trunk of LJ's Impala, right now—right this very minute."

"Get the fuck out!" Elaine shouted into her phone.

"I wish I could," Bill answered. "But I'm stuck in here with two other guys, and we're moving." As Elaine continued to listen to Bill, she spotted Freddy coming in. Snapping her fingers to get his attention, she said, "Call the Sheriff's Department."

"What's going on?" Freddy asked, and Elaine, working hard to keep her cool, said, "Bill's in an armed hostage situation—do you hear me? Call the Sheriff's Department, right now, and tell them one of our officers is being held captive."

"By who?" Freddy said, and Elaine, screaming at the man, "Do what I just told you to do!" Taking a breath, Elaine then

135

added, "It's Little Junior; he's got Bill locked in the trunk of his Impala."

With his phone out and dialing the Manatee County Sheriff's Office, Freddy said, "Right, I'm on it—I got this."

Rolling her eyes at Freddy, Elaine said, "Just tell them what's happening. Give them a description of LJ's car. You got *that*? Because that's all I want you to do."

Turning back to her own phone, and Bill's situation, Elaine said, "Are you injured?" She listened to Bill describe what happened to Alfi, and the fire, and how LJ had beaten Alfi badly over torching one of his trailers.

"He did what?" Elaine said. "Why would Lanzano do that? And why would LJ beat him up over it?"

"I have no idea," Bill said. "But right now, I have bigger problems to deal with."

"Look, I have to know where you are."

"We're heading North on Old 301."

"Are you sure?"

"Sure I'm sure," Bill said. "I've been driving around this county for over thirty years—I could do it with my eyes closed."

* * *

Digging into his pocket, rummaging for his hands-free earpiece, LJ said, "No fucking way…"

"I don't know what else to tell you, man—it's true."

"You crumpled up the ticket? You crumpled up a *winning* Mega Millions ticket?"

"Yeah…" Sebo said, smiling a little, "I did."

"That's the most fucked-up shit I've ever heard," LJ said. "That's the most fucked-up shit I've ever heard in my entire life—*and for that skinny little girl?* No fucking way, man, I'm sorry, but there's just no fucking way." Still fumbling with the ear-piece—one hand on the wheel—LJ glanced across at Sebo. "You're crazy, you know that, right?"

"Whatever you say, man. I'm just telling you what hap-pened." Sebo looked back out at the road ahead just as a chunk of twisted scrap metal came into view; about two feet long—jagged and lying nearly dead center in LJ's lane. "Watch out for that." Sebo warned, and LJ, still trying to fit his hands-free back inside his ear, said, "Watch what?"

Twenty-Six

Sí, claro…

In the parking lot of a rundown strip-mall, Special Agent Martinez knelt down low onto scorching-hot, oil-stained asphalt, and with his hands and knees fully committed, he strained his neck to peer beneath the rear bumper of a parked, Toyota Prius. By the time he was able to pry the GPS tracking device loose, Martinez's button-down clung to his body like damp tissue. Huffing out labored breaths, and expletives, he climbed back to his feet.

The chunk of dated tech felt like a brick in his hands. Martinez walked back to the opened rear hatch of his department-issued SUV, and that's when Agent Carson heard the heavy *clunk*, as the hunk of metal-encased electronics, high-powered magnets, and lithium batteries hit the floor of the cargo area. Carson twisted back toward Martinez, and said, "You did say the guy was smart."

Without a word to Carson, Martinez closed the Tahoe's rear hatch. Back inside, and behind the wheel again, Martinez first adjusted his air vent for maximum coverage. "It's a fucking oven out there," he grumbled, as he used his free hand to mop sweat from his brow with a fast-food napkin. Martinez then reached across Carson's lap, and popped the glovebox. With his right hand, he rooted around inside for a couple of seconds before coming out with a handheld GPS receiver—Carson flashed a grin...

Staring at the receiver's LCD screen, Martinez said, "Let's see how smart LJ really is..."

Carson chuckled. "So the old one was just a decoy then, huh?"

"You could say that," Martinez answered. He waited for his second signal to appear. "A working decoy," he added, "but yeah."

* * *

Jerome stood at the edge of his service bays and watched as LJ's 1960 Impala limped across the center turning lane of Old Highway 301. "I'll be damned..." he said.

The car's left front tire was in shreds, the crippled classic on a direct line leading straight for his tire store. Jerome kept his eyes on the shiny two-door coupe, even smiling a bit, as she bobbled and bumbled her way into his parking lot, and then to a stop in front of his service bays. "Hey Pablo!" Jerome called out. "Look alive—we got ourselves' a customer."

Pablo looked up from a mid-job, oil change on a 1983 Celica Supra, and spotted the familiar Impala. "On my way," he called back to his boss.

"I don't believe this shit," LJ said, after laying eyes on the man striding out toward his car. Rolling down his window with one hand, LJ used the other to hide his pistol.

"It's just Pablo, man," Sebo said.

"Hey, LJ..." The ex-gang member said as he bent down to rest his muscled arms across the Impala's driver-side door. He looked in through the opened window. "What happened?" He asked. "You hit something?"

"What the fuck do you think?" LJ said. Then he flashed a big grin at Pablo. "Look, seriously, man, how fast can you fix me up? I'm on a schedule, and my spare's flat—I'll be needing a new tire."

"No worries," Pablo said. "I'll have you back rolling again in no time."

* * *

Bill took his hand away from Joe Crest's mouth. "Will you stop doing that?" Crest whispered.

"Will you keep quiet when I tell you to?" Bill answered. Looking back at his phone again, Bill thumbed through his long list of contacts.

"You calling the cops again?"

"Not yet. I need to be sure where we are first, but I think I already know."

"How can you tell?" whispered Crest, and Bill, still scrolling through his contacts, quietly answered, "Because there's only one place around here to get a blowout fixed." Bill tapped at the number he'd been looking for, lifted the phone to his ear, and Crest said, "Why are we still sitting in here? I say we start kicking a screaming—get some attention, right?"

"Wrong," Bill said. "LJ's armed—remember that part? You wanna be the one who gets shot? Because I sure as hell don't."

* * *

Flashing another smile at Pablo, LJ said, "That's exactly what I needed to hear—make it happen."

"Sure thing," Pablo said. "Let me go get the floor jack—I can change it out right here—you don't even need to leave the car." Pablo left the Impala and went back inside the shop for the jack. On the way he felt his phone buzzing in his pocket. Digging into his coveralls, Pablo glanced at the screen and answered the call.

"Hey Chief, what's up?"

Hearing Pablo's voice, Bill said, "Necesitamos hablar solo en español, ¿está de acuerdo?"

"Sí, claro…" Pablo said. His parolee then listened closely when Bill asked him if LJ's Impala was sitting in front of Jerome's tire shop. "Sí, sí. Pablo said, "él tiene un neumático desinflado."

Next, Bill told him where he was at that very moment, and that Sebo had helped him by allowing him to keep his phone—adding the all-important detail that LJ was armed. "Look, Pablo," Bill said, "just change the tire—don't do anything else, help's on the way—are you hearing me?"

"Sí," Pablo said, "te escucho."

Twenty-Seven

Who's driving?

"Just tell me where you are. . ." Elaine said, listening, nodding, and snapping her fingers at Freddy again. "Tire King, on Old Highway 301? What the hell? Yeah, I got it." Slipping her phone back into her handbag, Elaine pointed at Freddy. "You got that, right? Call the department back and let them know where Bill is." His phone up to his ear already, Freddy gave her a thumb's up. "Good," Elaine said. "You're driving—let's go."

Turning over the engine of his Crown Victoria, Freddy said, "I always knew LJ was no good."

"Don't give me that," Elaine snapped back. "You didn't know shit." She was digging into her handbag, and said, "But don't sweat it—you hear me?" Then Elaine reached out and put her hand on Freddy's arm. "None of us knew for sure—all right? Not even me." Freddy watched as Elaine's attention returned to her bag. Lifting out a compact, .38 revolver, she smoothly opened the cylinder.

"Is that a Colt Cobra?" Freddy said. "I prefer the nine."

Inspecting her fully loaded firearm—six, plus-P hollow points—Elaine said, "I prefer to stop the son of a bitch."

* * *

FBI Special Agent Martinez punched in the latitude and longitude from his second GPS tracker into the Tahoe's onboard navigation.

"Tire King?" Agent Carson questioned. "What the hell?"

The SUV in gear and on the move, Martinez said, "The car's parked, that's all that matters—call it in."

"What do you want me to ask for?"

"Everything," Martinez answered.

* * *

"Welcome to Tampa, Agent Spencer." Secret Service Special Agent Margit Spencer reached out and briefly grasped the hand of Special Agent Miller.

"Thank you," she said. "What's the word from our agents in Bradenton?"

"You're not going to like it."

Buckling her seatbelt, agent Spencer looked out through the SUV's windshield as Miller pulled away from the curb and exited TIA's arrival pickup. Passing traffic on his way to the highway, Agent Miller said, "You were right—they found Lanzano's counterfeit operation hidden in the back of an old trailer park."

"Sounds more like good news to me," she said.

"I guess it is…" Miller added, "but the bad news is that somebody's already torched the place—it was burnt to the ground." Glancing her way, he said, "My agents tell me it was one hell of a print shop—hell of a fire too. Fire crews were still on the scene when they arrived, but there's almost nothing left."

"*Almost* means there's still evidence," she said. "What about Lanzano?"

"They're still looking."

* * *

Pablo's pneumatic torque wrench pulsed out loudly: *Zing! Zing! Zing!* The sounds pumping in through the Impala's opened windows. Sebo sat in the front passenger seat—sweating. LJ was still behind the wheel—*three men in the trunk...*

LJ's thumbs were busily texting away, while Sebo just sat beside him expressionless, with his eyes facing ahead and a fixed jaw, but on the inside, his gut was churning so hard he thought he might lose what he last ate. His probation officer still had possession of a phone, and now Sebo was regretting the decision to pass it over, backsliding on his momentary conviction to *do the right thing...*

"You need to relax," LJ said, without looking up from his texting. "Everything's being handled."

Sebo took in a long breath but kept his eyes looking ahead, as Pablo's rapid-fire torque wrench spun the last of the lugs into place; Pablo working fast as instructed, but also waiting—anticipating that a couple of dozen heavily armed deputies would descend on the tire shop at any moment.

With the fresh tire in place, Pablo gathered up the wrench's air hose and climbed back to his feet. He was lowering the Impala off the floor-jack when he heard LJ say, "What do I owe you?"

"Three hundred and twenty plus tax," Pablo responded, before adding, "Cash or credit?"

"Cash," LJ said. His wallet was already out, and he was peeling off twenties. "Here's four-hundred." Pablo rolled the floor-jack clear of the car before returning for the bills in LJ's out-stretched hand. "Let me go get your change and receipt," he said.

But LJ shook his head. "Just hold onto them for me—I'll drop by and pick it up later."

* * *

"That's the car," Elaine said, pointing.

"I see it," said Freddy. "Who doesn't know that Impala?"

Looking around some more, Elaine added, "Where's our backup?"

Freddy eased off the gas as his Crown Vic approached the tire store. "Looks like LJ's leaving," Freddy said. He slowed further—changed lanes, and Elaine was already on her phone again.

"We're moving again," Bill said. "It's hot as all hell in here—where's the cavalry?"

"Still putting on their party clothes, I guess," Elaine answered. "Look, don't worry about that, they'll be here. The important thing is, we have eyes on LJ's car—we're following you."

"Who's driving?"

"Freddy's driving—what the hell does it matter?"

"It matters," Bill said. "LJ knows that Crown Victoria of his."

Twenty-Eight

Just trying…

"Look, I apologize," LJ said. "I'm sorry about what happened back there—I know how you feel about guns."

"I just wanna get through this," Sebo said. "What's our next move?"

"*Our* next move?" LJ chuckled. "I do like the sound of that." LJ, still heading north, cruised at an easy pace for another three blocks before turning off of Old Highway 301, the Impala rolling smooth on four good tires again. The AC blowing cold, and LJ's favorite radio station playing a Motown classic by the Velvelettes—"A Bird in the Hand (Is Worth Two in the Bush)." For a moment everything felt like it was back to normal, and Sebo very nearly allowed himself to enjoy it.

The car slowed for another turn, LJ's fingers gliding smooth over the wheel, and Sebo was the first to spot Meteo's rig; a one-ton crew cab, towing an enclosed car trailer. The rig was parked up along the edge of a residential side street.

"You gotta be shitting me," Sebo said, and LJ responded, "I told you to relax—didn't I? Just be cool, my man—we *are* getting through this—you don't have a thing to worry about."

* * *

Rolling past the empty parking lot of Tire King, Agent Carson said, "I don't see the car."

Martinez briefly scanned the tire store's deserted front lot before glancing back at his tracker again. "LJ's less than a mile away. We're out of time—I'm not waiting for backup."

* * *

"Are you far enough back?" Elaine said. "I don't like this—I don't like this one bit." She looked out through the windshield of Freddy's idling Crown Vic; she and Freddy sitting side by side in the front seat and watching from only a block away.

The two peace officers looked on as LJ's Impala slowed to a stop behind an enclosed car carrier. Not a commercial carrier, Freddy noted, but a one-off type for racing hobbyists, and this one pulled by a heavy-duty diesel pickup. Then Elaine pointed out that the trailer's rear ramp had already been lowered, and it had an interior compartment just the right size to accommodate a classic Impala. "I still say we're too damned close," Elaine said. "We need to back off."

Freddy glanced around again at the low profile, cinderblock houses lining both sides of a working-class neighborhood. Then he pointed at a box truck parked in a driveway just ahead of them. "Look how we're lined up with that other truck over there—we're fine; from his angle he can't see us."

"We are not fine," Elaine snapped back. "We are anything but '*fine*'" Pointing at LJ's Impala, the car already in the process of being moved inside the trailer, she said, "That man right there in front of us is armed, and he's got Bill—we have to have backup." Elaine, flustered enough to spit, shouted, "What we need is some mother-fuckin' assistance!"

147

* * *

Special Agent Margit Spencer looked out at the gently shimmering waters of greater Tampa Bay from an altitude of 430 feet. Her moving vantage point being near the peak of the four-mile-long, southbound span of the Sunshine Skyway Bridge. The city of St. Petersburg was behind her, while off to the right, Agent Miller had pointed out the sliver of white sand that defined Egmont Key, then the north end of Anna Maria, and the Gulf of Mexico beyond.

A steady tempo of beaming sunlight intermittently flashed across the hood of Agent Miller's Secret Service-issued Suburban, while the shadows cast by the Skyway's cable-stays winked by. The pair were driving south at a good speed and in moderate traffic on the I-275 causeway, with Agent Miller behind the wheel, and currently crossing from Pinellas to Manatee County, en route to Bradenton.

Agent Spencer's hopeful anticipation of a significant arrest was balanced against the anxiety of possible failure—a likelihood she refused to focus on for long. Instead, she put her mind off the anxiety part by taking in the spectacular view from the bridge. Her phone cut the moment short. "What do you have for me?" She said.

"We spoke to a witness," an agent on the ground in Bradenton reported. "The guy's over eighty, but credible. What we're looking for is a 1960, blue Chevy Impala in mint condition."

Copying down the details, she said, "Anything else?"

"According to our witness, Mr. Lanzano's locked inside the trunk of that car."

"What?" Spencer gasped. "Say again?"

"Our suspect's locked inside the trunk of a 1960 Impala—you hear me that time? Oh, and he's not alone either—there's two more hostages in there with him."

"Acknowledged," Agent Spencer answered. "What else?"

"It was Lanzano who set fire to the print shop—we've been picking up chatter over the local police frequency—they're onto the Impala too. They're trying to get their SWAT unit up and going."

"Just trying?" Spencer said, before the agent in Bradenton responded, "Yeah, well, they still haven't left the station—their MRAP armored vehicle broke down."

Twenty-Nine

Apparently not…

"I better cut this short, Elaine," Bill said. "I hear voices outside the car."

"We're staying close by, we won't leave—do you hear me?"

"I hear ya. Thanks."

Elaine ended the call just as Freddy was looking up at his rear-view. "What are you looking at?" Elaine asked before she twisted back in the Crown Vic's front seat to have a look for herself. The view out through the car's rear glass, however, was now blocked by the imposing grill of a black Chevy Tahoe. "Who the hell are they?" She demanded.

"It's the FBI," Freddy answered.

"The FBI?" The unfiltered shrillness of Elaine's voice caused Freddy to wince. Then she took in a breath and said, "How do you know that's the FBI?"

"I've been working a case with them," Freddy answered. "They've been investigating LJ."

Freddy cringed as Elaine's wide eyes drilled into him. "At what time were you planning to tell me this?" She screamed.

"I couldn't!" Freddy pleaded. "It was top secret!"

FBI Special Agent Martinez sat behind the wheel of the Tahoe and let out a long sigh as he eyed the rear of Freddy's idling Crown Vic. "The guy did manage to tail LJ," Carson said.

"I don't care," Martinez answered. "We gotta get rid of him before he blows our bust." Carson, reaching for her door handle, said, "I'll go order him to leave." Martinez, sighing again, said, "Please do, and make it quick."

"I am not accepting your explanation," Elaine said, still shouting at Freddy. "Not one bit—Bill's life is at risk, do you hear me? Do you understand how serious this is?" Freddy was keeping quiet, but he *was* watching when Elaine's hand moved again to the pistol inside her purse. The thought of arresting LJ, and rescuing Bill, with the aid of the FBI, flashing through her mind, she said, "I say we go talk to the FBI then, and get them to help us."

Elaine's attention was focused on Freddy when his eyes moved past hers and his expression suddenly went blank. "What's going on?" Elaine said—shifting in her seat just as a woman's face stared back at her through the passenger-side window: slim, attractive, the woman wore a navy-blue pantsuit, had nice hair, and held a badge in her hand.

Moving her hand away from the pistol inside her purse and powering down her window, Elaine looked the woman in the eye, and said, "I gotta badge too—you want to see it?" Elaine held her badge up in front of the woman's face, and agent Carson said, "You two are impeding a federal investigation—we have jurisdiction. I am ordering you both to leave the premises at once."

Pointing in the direction of LJ's Impala, Elaine said, "Do you see that trailer over there? What we need is your assistance, and we need it right now." Still pointing in the direction of the car carrier, her finger moving forward and back with the rhythm of her speech, Elaine said, "One of our officers is being held hostage inside the trunk of that car." Staring back at Agent Carson; reading the woman's reaction, Elaine said, "You didn't know that, did you?"

"No," Carson said, "I didn't."

A frustrated huff left Carson's lips and then she said, "Look, we do have backup on the way, and we will resolve this situation. I will inform my superiors of the hostage situation immediately, but I'm sorry, you're in the way, and I can't allow you to stay here—you'll have to leave."

"We have backup coming too," Elaine said. "We're waiting for our county Sheriff's SWAT team to arrive, and they'll be showing up here any minute—we're not going anywhere." Then Elaine said, "If you don't like it? Then you'll just have to put us both under arrest."

"Step out from the car," Agent Carson ordered, while Freddy, still watching the trailer, observed the fact that the Impala had now been loaded inside, and the trailer's rear ramp was closed.

"Hey, you two," Freddy interrupted, "LJ's on the move."

* * *

LJ twisted back from the front passenger seat of Meteo's dual-cab Ford pickup. "Meet my man Sebo," he said, before he gestured back toward the truck's driver, and added, "Sebo, this is my good friend, and business partner, Meteo."

Looking up into the rear-view, Meteo said, "I've heard a lot of good things about you, Sebo—you're the stand-up guy—nice to finally meet you."

152

With a nod from Sebo, Meteo pulled away from the curb and steered his rig west. Two blocks further and he took a right before doubling back to rejoin again with Old Highway 301.

* * *

His head felt as if it had been kicked multiple times—which it had. Alfi opened his eyes to darkness, but he knew he wasn't alone—he could hear voices. He said, "What has happened?" He tried to move his hands and then his legs before he realized they'd been bound with cable-ties. "Where are we?"

"We're locked inside the trunk of LJ's Impala," Bill answered, before lifting his phone back to his ear. This time speaking to the Sheriff's department directly, he said, "What do you mean it broke down? How the hell does an MRAP break down?"

Bill listened some more to the deputy's explanation as to why the SWAT team had yet to be dispatched. "I don't care," he said. "Look, we're being held hostage, LJ's armed, and we have a man injured—you've got squad cars, right?"

Crest listened to the rest of Bill's exchange with a friend at the department. When Bill ended his call, Crest said, "Are they coming?"

"Apparently not," Bill answered.

"What?" Crest shouted, and by now Bill no longer cared how noisy the man was. "The FBI's claimed jurisdiction," he said. "The local Sheriff's department's been ordered to stand down."

"That's good news," Crest responded. "If the Feds have taken over, that means they're sending in their own team." The light from Bill's phone was moving around the trunk's interior, and Crest was still waiting for an answer. "What are you doing?"

"Looking for a way out."

"Can you do that?" Said Crest, and straining to see what Bill was up to, he added, "How about getting me out of these zips?"

"Me too, please," Alfi chimed in.

Bill bumped into Crest, elbows and knees, before hitting his head hard against metal. Reaching up after the sharp pain, Bill felt his forehead, and he could tell the wound was bleeding, but he kept working until he'd managed to bend himself around enough to reach the release rod attached to the old car's trunk lock. Bill slipped his phone into Crest's bound hands. "Try to hold the light so I can see, will ya?"

Fiddling with the lock assembly bolted to an inside panel, Bill slipped his hand up and felt for the release rod, and with his other hand, he then turned the assembly. The lid popped open. Fresh air washed over the three men inside the trunk and instantly blended with the dank, damp, overheated sludge they'd all been sucking in—but there was no light from the outside.

"Where are we?" Crest said.

Pushing the trunk lid fully open, Bill rose to his knees before climbing out. Stiff, sore, head pounding, sweating—angry... Bill breathed in deep, looked around, and said, "It's pretty much what I thought; we're inside a trailer, and we're moving."

Thirty

The man could die...

T he floor of the trailer shifted and rumbled beneath Bill's feet as he slowly worked his way forward. Grasping the Impala's passenger-side door handle, he took in a wishful breath before giving it a squeeze—felt a rush when it opened.

The car's interior lights blinked on and then shined across its immaculate white vinyl interior. The intense brightness forced Bill to briefly squint against the glare until his eyes adjusted, and he was able to clearly see inside. The first item to draw his attention being the over-stuffed keyring swinging from the car's ignition; the second was the glove box.

* * *

FBI Special Agent Carson straightened from the passenger-side window of Freddy's Crown Vic. She swiveled back toward her partner, Martinez aggressively waving at her before he shouted from his opened window to "Get back in the car!"

Elaine, grinning, watched as Carson left her window and ran back to the Tahoe. Freddy was smiling right along with her when the FBI vehicle chirped its rear wheels, roared past them, and sped off in pursuit of LJ.

Freddy shifted his car into gear and said, "Hold on to something."

Elaine managed to refasten her seatbelt before the sudden motion shoved her forward. The strap snapped tight and dug into her chest as the Crown Vic's 4.6 liter, V8 launched into reverse. She braced hard against the dash, while Freddy picked up speed until he skidded into a K-turn.

"You think LJ's going back toward 301?" Elaine said.

Shifting his car back into drive and mashing the gas pedal again, Freddy answered, "It's his only option—the rest of these blocks go nowhere."

"You think the FBI knows that?"

"By the time they figure it out we'll be way ahead of 'em."

* * *

Pablo grabbed two big pumps from a jug of Gojo beside the shop's sink. He hadn't laid eyes on Sebo since before the big Villages bust. Sebo, the guy who'd taken the fall for LJ, even though most everyone knew by now that LJ and his Venezuelan connection had been shorting the crew's cut from day one. Pablo felt his phone buzzing inside the front pocket of his coveralls. He let it go a couple more rounds so he could rinse the last of the heavy degreaser from his hands in a filthy sink. What he needed now was details, and backup; only one guy had the connections to make that happen.

That guy was calling him back at that very moment. Pablo knew even talking to Justin was off the reservation—he could be picked up and remanded just for that one single act, but there were no other options. Seeing Sebo with LJ had been the trigger, but the call from Bill made him pull it. Pablo wiped a damp hand across the front of his coveralls before answering his phone.

"Cabrón," he said. "A viente! What you got for me? De verdad?" He shook his head at the news he was getting, the cops not having shown up when LJ's car was a cripple because they couldn't find their asses if they used both hands. "Las mamadas…" Pablo said. "Thanks man, I appreciate it… yeah, I'm on my way."

Pablo spun back from the sink, already shedding his coveralls, and getting a rush off the idea of delivering some well-deserved payback. His boss was blocking his path. "Where the hell you think you're going?" Jerome said.

"You saw what happened?" He answered, maneuvering to get past his boss. "Bill Mazurek's in trouble—the man could die, all right? The cops ain't doing shit about it."

"You think you can do anything about it?"

"Yeah, I do."

Pablo had shed his coveralls by now and grabbed his jacket off the seat of his bike.

Jerome wasn't giving up that easy. "The hell you can—LJ's bad news, and that dude Sebo's a mother-fucker too—let the cops handle this." Jerome watched Pablo straddle his 95' Heritage Softail. "I'm serious, he said. "What the hell can you do but get yourself in trouble again?"

"No worries, jefe," Pablo said. "Nothing illegal about going for a ride."

* * *

Special Agent Margit Spencer shook each of the hands of her counterparts in Bradenton. Both men were experienced agents with sharp noses that Spencer was already grateful for, the advance team of two having completed their prelim after locating the print shop and tracking down a resident eyewitness. Now it was time for her to take the lead and bring this investigation to its logical conclusion—*an arrest.*

Spencer stood for a couple of minutes and stared at the blackened burn sight... *Not much left*... The remains were still too hot to examine. Remnant heat and an acrid, chemical order still hung in the air. All of this signaling to Spencer that this had once been one hell of an operation. Now it was little more than a sheet of aluminum slag and some twisted metal framing, but then there was the girl.

"Who is she?" Agent Spencer asked. She turned back to get only shrugs from her investigative team, so Spencer pulled her badge and flagged the girl over.

Handing the female officer her ID as requested, Shelly eyed the woman's smart-looking suit, and the other three suits that were with her, and the two black SUVs parked nearby. "So who are you guys?" Shelly asked. "More FBI?"

Spencer stopped examining the girl's license and briefly locked eyes with her. Turning back to her fellow Secret Service agents, she said, "Is the FBI involved in this case?"

Agent Miller first took in the puzzled reactions from his fellow agents, then he said, "Not that any of us were aware of."

"But you guys are after LJ, too, right?" Shelly said, and now Spencer's interest had piqued and she was fully focused on the girl. "Who's LJ?" She asked. Shelly was getting that feeling again, the one she always got whenever she stepped into a pile of shit—something that seemed to happen to her on a regular basis. She took in a breath, and said, "You're not FBI? You look like FBI." Lifting her badge again, Spencer identified herself as Secret Service before repeating her question, "Who's LJ?"

"Uh, Just a guy," Shelly said. The girl's nervousness was really starting to show, and the last thing Spencer wanted to get into that afternoon was a foot chase. She'd already decided she was holding onto this girl. Agent Spencer softened her tone, and then asked more gently, "We're just looking for information—what does LJ look like?"

And the girl, still looking pretty caged, but no longer like she was about to bolt, finally said, "Um, black guy? Sort of tall, like, forties-or-something? Short haircut, oh, uh—you know? Pretty good shape? Right? Always wears nice stuff—pretty easy to spot."

Still holding the girl's eye contact, and after the other three agents had moved in closer behind her, Spencer said, "Sounds like you know him pretty well—why would he be easy to spot?"

"Well, yeah? I mean, but it's not so much *him* as his car, like, LJ drives this flashy Impala—metallic blue? With a lotta chrome? You know the kind I mean?"

Thirty-One

That kind of cash alters your business model…

T he car's interior smelled like a closet in an old house. Opening the Impala's glove box, the first thing Bill saw was the nine-millimeter Luger, 115 grain, 100 round, value-pack sitting on top the car's manual. The ammo box felt light. The Chevrolet owner's guide was in perfect condition, just like the car. Pale blue and white paper, a line graphic of the car's front grill on the cover with *1960* in plain text.

Bill shoved it and the ammo box up and onto the dash and then quickly returned to rummage some more, picking up speed as he knocked aside a tube of hand sanitizer, surgical gloves folded up in a clear baggie, and a set of handcuffs with pink fur lining. It was only after he'd pawed through everything, and colored strips of exotic condoms had spilled out onto the car's carpet, that Bill came across the Leatherman.

* * *

"Two hundred and twenty-four million? No fucking shit!" Meteo let the number roll off his lips and out of his mouth a second time before he turned the incredible figure over again in his mind and whispered once more, "No fucking shit…" Sebo was sitting in the back seat, quiet, and listening to LJ run the conversation. Sebo wasn't thinking about the money. He only wanted one thing at that moment and that was out of the truck.

"That kind of cash alters your business model," LJ said, calm and cool, and feeling back in charge again. With his thumb and gesturing behind him, he said, "My man Sebo here? We're already making plans, you know what I'm sayin'? I'm including you in those plans, Meteo—you hearing me?"

"You want to be King of Venezuela, Pana?"

Meteo was talking to LJ, but still thinking for himself, he said, "Because that's what that kind of coin can buy you in my country."

* * *

"What's on the tracker?" Martinez said, calmer now after losing Barney Fife in his wannabe-whip, and his partner Ms. Jackie Brown. He would've enjoyed seeing Carson make an arrest; two black chicks with badges—the action would've been epic. One thing he truly hated was a missed opportunity, and god knows he could've used the entertainment.

Martinez swung the big SUV into a sharp right, then tapped the gas to hit the next corner and get ahead of LJ's rig. Martinez knew he wasn't equipped to make the arrest on his own—even though the thought was in his head because his backup wasn't moving fast enough.

Just two more turns before the highway, so Martinez dropped back. Now he was where he needed to be; just one street away and rolling just under the speed limit—running parallel to the car-carrier, but one block ahead. Martinez knew that if he'd just played this right, the next street up ahead would take him back to Old Highway 301, which would be the exact same street as the one LJ was currently on. Martinez was rolling almost at idle, waiting to see if he was right, and looking ahead at the cross street when he spotted the rig as it rolled right on through; one hundred yards away and directly in front of him.

"I still have a strong signal," Carson said. She looked up from the tracker's LCD just in time to catch a tail-end glimpse of the truck and trailer rig as it glided past her view. "Damn, you're good."

* * *

With the Leatherman, Bill first cut Joe Crest free. Bill helped the sweat-soaked attorney sit up, peel off his suit jacket, and then climb out from the trunk of the Impala, the guy bitching and moaning the whole time. "We're moving," Bill warned. "Make sure you hang onto something." Crest could feel it too. He could feel every jerking motion in fact as the floor of the trailer shifted and bumped beneath his dress shoes.

Crest breathed in deep and steadied himself just as Bill had advised, grabbing ahold of one of the car's most prominent features—a tail-fin. Next came Alfi, but Bill could see right off that the guy was in tough shape. Helping Alfi up and out, Bill grimaced at the young man's swollen face; it was badly bruised, he was bleeding from his mouth, and also from his right ear; it was obvious he needed to get to a hospital.

Together Bill and Crest were able to move Alfi into the back seat of the car, the blood from Alfi's wounds leaving behind a thick red smear across the gleaming white Naugahyde. Bill felt bad for the guy. Not only because Alfi had taken such a harsh beating, but because Bill knew Alfi was most likely on his way back into lockup, and that part always left him depressed.

Another couple of minutes and Bill was behind the wheel of LJ's classic ride. He grasped the overstuffed keyring, while Crest looked on from the passenger seat. Crest pointed the heavy keyring and said, "You know that's really bad for the ignition switch, right?" Bill wasn't really listening to Crest as he turned the key and the starter motor engaged—loud from inside the closed space. The car's V8 cranked over easy enough before it settled into a smooth idle, and the sound of it made Bill smile. "What's your plan?" Crest said.

Reaching for the shifter, his feet on the floor-pedals, Bill said, "I'm gonna take a friend's advice."

"What kind of advice?" Crest asked, and Bill said, "She told me 'get the fuck out', so that's what we're gonna do."

Thirty-Two

I only remember the shit I'm supposed to...

B right afternoon sun baked a weed-infested parking lot of a boarded-up Dollar General. From his viewpoint behind the wheel, Freddy could see ripples of heat rising off the Crown Vic's hood as he sat parked, and partially hidden, by a pair of construction dumpsters, but his view of Old Route 301 was good enough.

They'd been there less than ten minutes. Freddy had the engine off, the windows down, and, just like him, Elaine could already feel the sweat forming as she sat on the front seat's vinyl and looked out through Freddy's binoculars. Both officers focused on North-bound traffic streaming at them steady from the nearest intersection, which happened to be 53rd Avenue East, Freddy having doubled back to rejoin with the highway from the opposite direction. This after the FBI had split—a turn of events he was feeling pretty happy about. Mostly because he'd done his part, and in return the FBI had been arrogant jerks.

"Wait just a goddamned second."

Elaine's voice sounded off like a song, so Freddy swiveled in her direction. Elaine was sitting up, leaning toward the dash, and looking out, sharpening the focus on the binos. Freddy watched her face to catch any further reaction. After a couple of seconds, he said, "You got 'em yet? You see the car carrier?"

"Uh huh…" Elaine hummed back.

Freddy, not wanting to waste any time, fired up the Crown Vic's big block V8. The vehicle was a retired, FHP interceptor unit he'd picked up at auction for next to nothing, repainted in midnight blue metallic, rebuilt and retuned as a hobby, and thus returned to her former glory. Shifting into drive, one foot on the brake, the other on the gas, Freddy eyed the high-profile rig closing in from under an eighth of a mile. The truck and trailer rig were boxed in by surrounding traffic, but visible all the same. "I see it too," said Freddy. "Buckle up. We're moving out."

* * *

"Am I under arrest?" Shelly asked.

With a subtle shake of her head, Agent Spencer replied, "*No*, but we do need your help." Still holding eye contact with the girl—her three fellow agents still standing ready to make a grab if need be—but the interesting bit, from Spencer's perspective, was the fact that she was now reading less fear from the girl.

What was left on the girl's face was a kind of fatalistic resolve, which told Spencer she had been arrested before, and probably more than once. Adding up the pieces, ready to take a chance based on what her gut was telling her, Spencer decided her best opportunity to make her play was right at that very moment. "Look," she said. "I don't know what kind of deal you may have made with the FBI, but I can personally guarantee that the Secret Service will offer you a better one—does that work for you?"

Shelly only had to think on it for a second or two before she nodded her agreement. "Good," Agent Spencer said, before gesturing back toward Miller's black Suburban. "Let's go—you'll be riding with me."

* * *

The truck and trailer rig crossed the intersection of Old 301 and 51st Avenue East, heading north. Meteo was behind the wheel and keeping to the left-hand lane. He stayed with the main road after the split with 15th Street, passing Curly Joe's salvage yard, the Bowles Creek Asphalt Plant, and the Haitian Ministry Theophile Church. The church was opposite an expanded median that separated 15th Street from 301, the median consisting of nothing more than waste ground filled with broken concrete and grown over with weeds.

"There's the turn," LJ said, pointing. "You see it? Just up there on the left—across from the old hubcap shop." Already slowing his heavy-duty Ford, Mateo said, "Yeah, sure—your crappy warehouse, right?"

"It's been years, man," LJ answered. "You remember everything."

"You know me, Pana—I only remember the shit I'm supposed to."

Sebo's oversized frame still filling the backseat and still paying attention, but also staying quiet, observing the familiar surroundings as Meteo swung a left and then proceeded across the warehouse's empty parking lot. The rig then drove on, passing by a heavy line of trees that ran down the left-hand border of the property's south side. Next, they entered a narrow alleyway, before finally rolling to a stop in front of the building's huge sliding door. Sebo knew exactly where they were, even though the last time had been at one o'clock in the morning, and he'd been wearing a scratchy polyester security guard's uniform.

His gut churning hard again, just like it had been that night, no, *worse...*

Sebo watched LJ pop his door and step out from the truck. LJ rolled his shoulders back while his body stiffened as if he were readying himself to take the stage in front of a large crowd. He then marched in a straight line for a padlock hanging from a thick chain. Sebo was thinking of making his move. But before LJ reached the locked warehouse door he stopped dead in his tracks. "Where's my fucking keys, man?" LJ spun back toward the truck's opened passenger door and searched inside, and Meteo said, "You probably left them in the car."

Taking a step back, LJ adjusted himself before pointing at Sebo. "Go get my keys, man—make it quick."

Sebo nodded and opened his door. He was out of the truck in only a second or two, and striding toward the back of the rig with purpose, so he could open up the rear doors and lower the ramp but all the while, what Sebo was actually doing was scouting for a way out. Once he'd reached the back of the trailer, Sebo worked the latches, and sized up the alley.

Scaling the eight-foot high chain link that lined the alleyway would be tough enough, especially given the fact that climbing anything was something he strongly avoided. Sebo's one gift had always been an unfailing ability to pound the shit out of his opponents until he could simply walk away from the problem at hand. Running never being much of a strength either; he considered even the short distance he would need to cover to reach the fence to be a nonstarter.

By now, LJ was getting impatient. "Sebo!" He shouted. "Get my mother-fucking keys!" Reaching for his pistol, LJ walked back to where Sebo was standing—had the compact nine out and in his hand when he got there. Meteo was watching from the side view, with the truck's engine still running. By now Sebo had the trailer's rear doors open, swinging them both wide. He then went for the release on the loading ramp, and that's when he picked up the smell of gasoline exhaust; Sebo knew it wasn't coming from the pickup.

"What the hell, man?" LJ said as he popped his head around the corner and just as Sebo was releasing the ramp; the spring-loaded mechanism unwound, and the ramp started coming down slow and smooth. The shiny rear bumper of the Impala and her fighter jet fins came into view.

It was at that moment that Sebo realized the car's engine *was* actually running. LJ too, and in LJ's brief state of confusion he locked eyes with Sebo's equally puzzled gaze.

From the opposite viewpoint, however, the one from inside the pitch-black darkness of the trailer, and from behind the wheel of the idling Impala, the only thing Bill could make out was the intense glare from the daylight that had just opened up behind him.

Thirty-Three

Somebody's making a break for it…

"Better get down." These were the only words that Bill spoke aloud to Joe Crest before his right foot mashed down hard on the gas. Twisting back with his left hand gripping the wheel and his right arm wrapped over the back of the seat, Bill felt the old car strain under the stress before she finally launched into full reverse.

Bill squinted at what was behind him on his way out of the trailer; caught only a brief glimpse of Sebo's big outline jumping clear. Then a much brighter flash of light as the outside sun raced in at him head-on and filled the car's white interior. The sound of LJ's pistol going off never registered.

Joe Crest's screaming didn't register either.

The old Impala's 348 V8 had wound up quick enough, but the rear tires had only spun at first before finally finding grip against the diamond aluminum floor of the trailer. Bill's vision closed down after that, narrowing into a pinpoint blur when what he was actually doing reached full consciousness. By then his throat had closed in so tight that he was no longer breathing. The whole series of events moving fast as light and piece by

169

piece at the same time—all of it packaged into a single instant that felt like forever.

Then the fact that LJ was shooting at the car finally caught up to Bill: the pistol pumping out rounds in rapid succession just before an explosion of glass pelleted against Bill's neck and back. First from the passenger-side window, and next, when the windshield blew into the car's interior; both rapid-fire impacts scattering fragments like snow. Bill briefly closed his eyes; he felt the car's front bumper bounce off the pavement at the bottom of the ramp and bits of glass piercing his skin, but he kept his foot down.

Feeling the car pick up speed, straining to see, Bill fought to keep the Impala in a straight line until he was ready to try for a turnaround. The car sped in reverse across the parking lot, and still with his foot to the floor, Bill managed to put about fifty yards between himself and LJ's gun—now was the time. Bill went for the brakes. As he did, he cocked the wheel hard to the right, and three thousand, seven hundred pounds of vintage Detroit steel lurched to the left even harder.

Bill's body chucked sideways with the swerve—one hand on to the wheel, and the other on the shifter. He kept his foot on the brakes until the front end completed a full, 180-degree-skid; the highway came into his view—he popped her into drive.

* * *

From the parking lot of an auto salvage yard, Agent Carson was the first to catch the glint of chrome as she looked out through a broken line of trees and the chain link fence that separated her and agent Martinez from the warehouse and LJ's rig. With his reasonably decent view, and from a distance of perhaps fifty yards, agent Martinez, still fuming over the fact that their backup had yet to appear, was regretting his decision to claim federal jurisdiction and bench the local cops.

He'd focused his binoculars and his attention only on what he could see clearly from his angle. This included the truck's driver—an unknown suspect Martinez had never seen before—and most of the truck and trailer's left side. Sebo not currently on Martinez's radar because Sebo was on the right side of the trailer and therefore hidden from the agent's view. Everything that happened after that particular moment though, happened quickly.

The sudden motion that had first grabbed Carson's attention took a couple of seconds to fully register. When it did she was able to get out only one word, and that word was "*Wait*". It took a couple more seconds for Martinez to catch up to her. He'd been sitting in the front seat of the Tahoe, just like she was, and had pretty much the same view she did; semi-obscured, driver's side of the rig, with nearly a full view of the trailer. Still, it was Carson who was the first to realize what was going on.

Martinez was able to briefly lift a finger, point, and then croak out the words, "What's happening?"

Carson, still a couple of beats ahead, was now in a state of full discernment. "Somebody's making a break for it," she said.

* * *

"What do you mean, you've been ordered to stand down? Who tells you to—*stand down?*" Elaine listened to the voice on the other end of the phone; a guy she'd served with back when she'd carried another badge and worn a Sheriff's department uniform. This being before the shooting—the one that nearly killed her. A drug bust gone bad, a year spent in recovery, and nobody blamed her when she decided to make a change.

Elaine listened to a few more seconds of the deputy's droning explanation of federal, versus state authority, and something about Homeland Security, before she finally cut him off. "Let me get this straight," she said. "This *is* the Manatee County Sheriff's Department I am speaking with—am I correct? Uh huh... and we are—you and me—currently speaking from within the borders of Manatee County, are we not? Uh huh... that *is* correct, so *why* in the *hell* have you not sent your SWAT unit out here? We have an active hostage situation going on— one of our officers is amongst the hostages—do you fully understand the gravity of this situation? Look here, I don't care what the Feds said—I don't care that your vehicle broke down—you people have a job to do!"

Freddy was listening to Elaine's side of the conversation as he drove his Crown Vic, keeping his speed up as much as the flow of traffic would allow, but mostly what he was doing was scanning the cars in front of him, oncoming traffic too, along with the side streets—searching for LJ's truck and trailer. He let a few more seconds go by, listening until she'd finished reaming out the Sheriff's department, and then, hesitantly, he said, "I, uh... I lost sight of LJ's trailer."

Elaine tossed her phone back into her purse. She let out a huff and then took in a long breath before she realized what Freddy had just said. "What?" she yelled. "Did you just tell me you lost them?"

His hands tightened around the wheel while Freddy cringed at Elaine's shrieking voice. "I just lost sight of 'em is all, okay? They have to be close by."

Elaine looked ahead through northbound traffic before twisting in her seat to see what was in back of them. "Double back. They must've made a turn somewhere—make another pass."

* * *

Two black Suburbans rolled in tandem, both of them Secret Service-issued vehicles; both traveling dark, and at the posted speed. They were southbound on Old Highway 301. This after being forced to circle back a second time. Shelly was riding along in the back seat; watching and listening to the two agents' exchanges, but mostly she was thinking about how this whole thing might play out in her favor. Smiling a little, but not enough to get noticed as the Secret Service agents drove around in circles.

Shelly overheard agent Spencer let out a huff of frustration. Then Spencer glanced across at agent Miller and said, "Are you sure you know where it is?"

They were looking for a particular location, but Shelly had no idea where it was. A piece of information that Miller had managed to pick up from the FBI's radio exchanges—something about a rundown warehouse. "Close to abandoned," were the words the FBI used, and based on that alone, Miller figured it had to be close by and likely just off the highway.

"I'm pretty sure I saw something a short ways back—just give me a minute," Agent Miller said. After a nod to signal her agreement, agent Spencer turned her head. She looked straight out across the hood of their vehicle in time to catch a flash of sunlit chrome. The flash had come from a blue blur of motion cutting a path almost directly in front them, and from the right—moving fast. "There!" she shouted. "Over there!"

Thirty-Four

I could sure go for a Checker Burger...

In a remote corner of the three-hundred-acre *chicken farm*, which was slightly south of Rubonia. At one time mostly swamp, but long drained off before the EPA stepped their foot down on such things. The farm's owner still kept a handful of thoroughbreds on the property as a vanity, cattle for the tax discount, but he bred fighting cocks for the payout. The area was still largely agricultural, mostly populated by old yokels who grew sod for the developer's tract housing, and still voted Democrat out of habit. This particular farm was located north of the Manatee River by about six miles. Still west of the old Tamiami Trail; Highway 41, but east of the newer, faster, I-75.

It was here that Hatchet-Man stood at the edge of a palmetto thicket crowded in by slash pines and in grass that had been cropped short by a herd of Brangus. The old wrestler had one hand resting on his hip, which he held cocked to one side, while the rumble from a bright yellow backhoe's diesel idled steadily. The machine's boom slowly cycled again in front of him. Hatchet-Man let out a huff as he watched the scarred steel bucket swing past him, his eyes following the hydraulic boom as it leisurely reached out and then extended downward into the hole once more. Taking a step closer to peer over the edge, he watched the bucket's teeth cut another thick swath through damp earth and a tangle of stringy roots.

Shaking his head in disgust, Hatchet-Man folded his arms and let out a groan as the bucket slowly curled back, scooping up another load of sandy earth streaked with black and gray loam. The hole's diameter had been steadily expanding for the past few hours to the point that it now resembled a small swimming pool. One that was nearly large enough to accommodate a vintage, 1960 Impala.

Pointing again at the hole, Hatchet-Man yelled up at Sling-Blade, "It's still too shallow!"

From the cab of the backhoe, his partner shouted back, "What da ya mean? I got eight feet!"

"The hell you got eight feet."

"You want to run this piece of crap?"

Nodding his intention and striding toward the cab, Hatchet-Man said, "Yeah, I do—get the fuck down from there—we don't got all day. LJ's gonna be here any minute."

* * *

The roar of the Impala's V8 engine, even at full throttle, couldn't drown out the sound of Joe Crest's screaming. Bill's right foot was still pressed hard to the floor as the car's slushy steering caused it to rabbit-swerve right and then left. Bill had both hands on the wheel—still not breathing as the stream of cars traveling the highway just ahead of him rushed into sharp focus. Bill only managed to get the Impala straightened out after the two-door coupe had already bolted across the highway—Bill *had* planned to turn.

Traffic braked wildly to avoid the old classic, but Bill was moving too fast to notice. The Impala cut across the southbound lane, next came the turn lane, then the northbound; all of it streaking by him in about two seconds. Bill's foot was now firmly on the brake pedal but he was getting no response.

From Special Agent Miller's line of sight he guessed the Impala was doing close to sixty. The Secret Service veteran hit his brakes to avoid a collision as traffic shut down in front of him. Freddy and Elaine in the Crown Vic caught the action unfolding too, but from the opposite direction. FBI Special Agents Martinez and Carson had only just reached the highway when halting traffic blocked their path. Martinez was only able to catch a glimpse of LJ's car first cut across the highway from his left, but the veteran FBI agent caught a much better view when the Impala clipped the display in front of the hubcap shop. The car then careened into the broad median of waste ground that separated Old 301 from 15th Street.

Bill's foot desperately pumped at the floor pedal as a collection of dislodged hubcaps flew up in front of him. The silvery discs bounced over the car's hood before flying inside through the opening where the windshield had been. It wasn't until Bill yanked LJ's ball of keys from the ignition that the car finally coasted to a stop, and just a few feet shy of Sunday's sermon placard in front of the Haitian Ministry's Theophile Church, which read: *Slow down and take in the word of God...*

LJ lowered his pistol and sized up the remaining action for a few more seconds before turning back to Sebo. "If you weren't worth 200 million," LJ said, "I'm pretty sure I'd have shot you already."

Sebo was listening but still looking in Bill's direction as LJ's precious classic cut across the crowded highway. The sounds of screeching brakes and blaring horns that rose up in response was followed closely by a cloud of dust and debris kicked up a quarter of a mile away. Sebo was grinning slightly at the nerve of the old guy. Then behind him, Sebo heard LJ complain, "Jesus! I still don't have my mother-fucking keys, man." LJ shifted back to face the pickup in time to see Meteo hold up a pair of bolt cutters. "Hey Pana," he said, "I got your key right here."

A choking cloud of dust had flooded in through the Impala's shattered glass just as Bill remembered to breathe again. Joe Crest was still screaming the same words he'd been rapidly repeating ever since Bill had decided to take Elaine's advice, stomp his foot down on the gas, and 'get the fuck out.' On hearing what seemed like the hundredth *Holy Shit!* from Crest, Bill took in another long breath, reached out and patted the guy's shoulder. "We're okay," Bill said. "You can shut up now." It was just about that time that Bill heard the sirens.

Sebo shoved his shoulder into the rusted rolling door to the warehouse, moving it aside just enough for Meteo to pull through with the pickup and the now-empty trailer. Inside, the warehouse was cavernous and mostly empty, with enough floor space to accommodate three rigs the size of the one Meteo had just parked. Gone was the Brinks armored truck, and in its place sat an aluminum bass boat. The far wall contained a sizable collection of brand new appliances still in their boxes, mostly stoves but also refrigerators. LJ's van was parked beside the refrigerators.

Pointing again at Meteo, and then at the van, LJ said, "You got a key for this too?" Two minutes later Meteo was behind the wheel of the van and the van's engine was running. They made a relaxed departure, Meteo hardly driving above idle, LJ in the passenger seat and Sebo in the back. Meteo, casual and cool as he eased the van out. He rolled though the alley and then to the far edge of the parking lot. Meteo even paused for a break in traffic.

Sebo leaned forward from the rear seat to eye the carnage unfolding in the median directly in front of them. "That's a lotta cops, man," Sebo said.

LJ smiled, and answered, "Look at that, uniforms every-where, the Feds, hell, they even sent the SWAT team—I'm im-pressed."

From behind the wheel of the Impala, Bill lifted up both hands as Manatee County's finest surrounded the car with guns drawn. Bill smiled up at the officers. "Nice to see you guys."

On recognizing Bill, the SWAT's commander ordered his team to lower their weapons. The senior officer then lifted his helmet and said, "Mazurek, what the hell?"

From the warehouse parking lot, Meteo, his turn signal flashing, eased out onto Old 301 and continued north. LJ still had a grin on his face. He first reached for the AC, flipping it on full blast before his hand moved next to the radio. The last cho-rus of Marvin Gaye's *I Heard It Through the Grapevine* came over the speakers. LJ relaxed back into his seat just as the van crossed the 9th Street intersection and continued traveling north on 301.

From the westbound side of 9th Street, a group of six bik-ers, all of them riding Harleys, joined the flow of traffic.

"Where to, Pana?" Meteo said.

"I don't know about you guys," LJ responded, "but I could sure go for a Checker Burger."

Meteo chuckled. "Whatever you say. Where to after that?"

"The chicken farm," LJ said.

Thirty-Five

Nice guys don't commit federal crimes…

B ill Mazurek was outside of the car by now and leaning against the driver's side door—feeling pretty damned lucky and still buzzing over the outcome. Bill's smile left his face when officers dragged Alfi, battered and bloodied, from the back seat of the Impala. "That man is injured," Bill called out.

"He's my suspect," FBI Special Agent Martinez answered. Then Martinez paused to look more closely at Bill, and pointing his finger at Bill's bleeding right shoulder, he said, "Hey, buddy, looks like you're the one who got tagged—you better get that looked at."

Bill twisted to have a look and spotted the small slice a nine-millimeter bullet had left behind. When he looked back four uniforms had already laid Alfi out face down in the dirt. They searched him and cuffed him before rolling him over and onto his back. Sand clung to Alfi's bloody face and formed a ring pasted to his mouth. Bill could hear Alfi moaning from the pain, and the sight of it all hit him like a punch to the gut.

Bill kept his eyes on the slim Italian, he was watching a cadre of local officers, and FBI, lift Alfi to his feet, when the figure of a smartly dressed young woman came into view. She wore a trim suit, had a badge hanging from her neck, and was shouldering her way in through the wall of local and federal cops. On first sight, Bill figured she must be another Fed.

Secret Service Special Agent Margit Spencer stepped in to block the path of FBI Special Agent Martinez, Agent Carson, and their fellow agents who now flanked Alfi. Lifting her badge in front of Martinez's face, she said, "Under the authority of the United States Secret Service, I claim jurisdiction over your prisoner."

Martinez balked at the order, sneered, "I got him first—take a number." Spencer didn't budge and Martinez said, "You mind?" He flashed his badge: "FBI."

Spencer, not moving, slipped a sheet of paper out from her jacket pocket. She opened it and held it up in front of Martinez's face. "I have a signed federal warrant for this man's arrest. He's wanted for counterfeiting."

Martinez growled as he pushed her hand aside and said, "You can have him when I'm done with him."

Agent Spencer stood her ground. "Show me see the date on your warrant, and if it predates mine? I will step aside."

Agent Martinez grimaced, his thick shoulders dropping a little—Spencer almost smiled. "You don't have a signed warrant for this man, do you?"

"No ma'am, we don't," Agent Carson answered.

* * *

Inside the Crown Vic heading north on Old 301, Elaine said, "Are you *sure* you saw LJ inside that van?"

"I'm telling you I saw him," Freddy answered. "There's no way I'm wrong about this—it was LJ."

"You're certain?"

"Yes—yes! How many times do you need to hear me say it?"

"I don't like this," Elaine said. "I don't like this one bit." She folded her arms, exhaled. "We should be back there helping Bill." She looked over at Freddy behind the wheel. "If you are truly *that sure* then we should be calling for assistance; the police should be handling this."

"You're right," Freddy said. "Make the call." Freddy looked out again at the van he was tailing. A white Chevy, late 90's vintage, three cars ahead. Elaine glanced down at her phone. She hesitated at the thought of pulling resources away from an active crime scene, and based solely on Freddy's lone, fleeting glimpse. "What if you're wrong?" She said.

"I am not wrong," Freddy answered. "I know what I saw." He pointed at the van again. "LJ is in the passenger seat of that van—hey, look there." Freddy pointed again. "They're making a turn."

Elaine caught sight of the van's flashing right turn signal. "Looks like they're pulling into Checker's." She let out a sigh. "I seriously doubt that LJ would be stopping for a burger right now—don't you?"

Slowing his Crown Vic, Freddy said, "I say we keep up the tail; confirm that it's LJ."

"Or not," Elaine answered.

* * *

Shelly stood off to one side, and near the front bumper of a black Suburban. She had her arms folded against her body, and

181

a Secret Service agent standing next to her. His hand dug into her shoulder, but not as hard as Martinez's grip. He heard her gasp when his fellow agents dragged Alfi past her—cuffed and stumbling. "You know that man?" The agent said.

Nodding, Shelly answered, "Yeah, his name's Alfonzo, but everybody just calls him Alfi—he's a nice guy."

"He's a felon and a counterfeiter," the agent responded. "Nice guys don't commit federal crimes."

"Everybody makes mistakes," Shelly said. "I'll bet it was LJ who made him do it."

Turning to make direct eye contact with the girl, the agent said, "That's the second time you've mentioned this guy LJ. What's your connection?"

"I don't know what you mean?"

The agent took a step closer and stared down at her hard. "Let me tell you something—you talk around a lot, and you're not so smart about it either. It's what gets you into trouble, so I'm gonna be clear—you want to stay out of jail this time?"

She nodded, kept quiet. The agent held her gaze, tightened his grip on her shoulder. "I want to know everything you know about LJ: his business, his associates, his employees, other vehicles he owns—all of it. You got five minutes to impress me before I cuff you just like we did Mr. Lanzano over there, and you can start with LJ's connection to Mr. Lanzano."

* * *

FBI Special Agent Martinez now stood in the opened doorway to LJ's warehouse with his hands on his hips and a flat expression on his face. About twenty feet in front of him, six of his fellow agents were actively combing through the empty pickup and the empty trailer still hooked to it.

Martinez, observant, and processing details as they came to light: like the fact that the chain hanging from the warehouse door had been freshly cut. The abandoned truck, which was in perfect running order, had even been left fully topped off with fuel—including the spare tank. Then there was the smaller stuff. Like the multiple oil stains that littered the concrete floor of the warehouse; only one of them was fresh, and it wasn't beneath the truck.

Martinez twisted back toward the opened, rolling door to study the edge of the concrete apron and the sandy lot just beyond it. He'd knelt down for a closer look at tire marks when Agent Carson approached. "Nothing from the trailer," she said. "The truck's clean too, no tickets or warrants, and no prints either—it's registered to a construction company in Miami."

Carson wasn't getting any reaction, so she observed Martinez for a few more seconds before she added, "You're thinking he had another vehicle waiting."

Martinez grimaced, answered, "He had to have, but it wasn't part of the plan—they were forced to improvise." Martinez straightened and swiveled back toward Carson, and she said, "He's got at least a twenty-minute jump on us. The road out front goes either north or south; law enforcement arrived from the south—my gut says LJ turned north."

Martinez nodded. "I agree. Let's go."

"Hold on there, Colombo," Carson said, and lifting her hands for added effect. "Wait a second—we're just guessing here; we have no idea what kind of vehicle LJ's in? The guy could be anywhere."

His face went blank for a few seconds before Martinez said, "Where's our Barney Fife?" He got an odd look back from Carson so he said, "Freddy."

She caught up and Martinez said, "All day the guy's been a leech—he and Jackie Brown have been turning up everywhere we've been, right? I never saw that Crown Vic of his on scene, did you?"

With her eyebrows raised, Carson answered, "I did not."

Martinez had a grin on his face by now. "You still have the guy's number, right? Call him."

Carson pulled out her phone, but hesitated. "You sure you want to pull these agents off an active crime scene, and send them out on a goose chase? Because I don't think that's a good idea at all—we haven't even been able to question Lanzano yet." She was staring at Martinez's face and didn't like what she saw.

"Just call Freddy—if my hunch is right, we'll follow up on our own."

Thirty-Six

You gotta real badass streak…

F reddy shadowed the van until he'd confirmed they'd taken the turn. Elaine kept the vehicle in sight while Freddy dropped back to enter the parking lot of an auto parts store next door. He took a middle spot that faced the drive-thru. A pickup parked on Elaine's side, an SUV on his; Freddy kept the car running. He guessed that from his vantage point the van was maybe sixty yards away. Between them were a few more parked cars, a couple of Melaleucas, and a decent enough line of sight to the burger joint.

Leaning forward over the dash, with the binos out again and focused on the van, Elaine said, "They're taking the drive-thru." She eyed the van as it rolled to a stop at the speaker. "I can't I.D. the passenger; his back's to me."

"Keep looking," said Freddy, just as his ringtone went off—something like sirens to a sixties vibe, and it caused Elaine to turn her head as the theme music for *One Adam-Twelve* played inside the Crown Vic. She chuckled. "What the hell is that all about anyway?"

"My phone," Freddy said, fumbling to read the incoming.

"I mean that stupid-assed music—what the hell?"

Staring at the screen now, Freddy said, "It's just my ring-tone—"

"You got a serious cop hard-on, you know that?" Now she was looking right at him. "How come you never became a real cop?"

Lifting the phone to his ear, Freddy held a hand up in front of her face. "Watch the van, okay? I gotta take this."

Elaine cleared her throat and lifted the binos again, but she was listening to Freddy's phone conversation. From his reaction, Elaine figured the caller must be FBI.

Through the binoculars, she could see the van's passenger still had his back turned toward her. She knew it could be anybody, but out of her left ear she could hear Freddy trying to convince agent Martinez that the white Chevy van they were tailing was LJ's. From what she was picking up so far Martinez didn't seem to be buying it, his hesitation based on the fact that Freddy was his only witness. She couldn't blame him. She had her doubts too—nobody stops at a drive-thru during a getaway. Elaine kept her eyes on the van's passenger as the vehicle inched forward inside the drive-thru lane.

Freddy was still pleading his case when the figure in the van's passenger seat briefly twisted toward Elaine's focused view and looked out through the van's window. Dropping the binos in her lap, she reached across and snatched the phone from Freddy's hand. "*We've* just made a positive I.D. on Little Junior," she said to Martinez

Inside Martinez's black Tahoe, Agent Carson listened in on the exchange as Martinez repeated, "Are you certain?"

"I've known this man for years," Elaine said. "I know it's him—we went to high school together."

* * *

"That's two double Buford's, two Kool-Aid Slushies, and an extra-large seasoned fry—that'll be twenty-three-eighty-two." Meteo gave the drive-thru attendant a pair of fresh twenties before handing the bag with the food over to LJ. Taking his change, Meteo stuffed the clean bills into his front pocket, and then eased the van away from the window.

Back out on Old 301; heading North, Meteo said, "I gotta tell you, Pana, those bills of yours? I've never been one to pass funny money, but those things are more beautiful than the real deal—legitimate fine art."

Swallowing a big bite of his double-cheese, LJ said, "They *were*, that's for damned sure, but that deal is over with." Shifting to face Sebo in the back seat, LJ said, "You want some fries, man?" He held the box out and it was close enough that Sebo could smell the crispy hot fries inside but he waved them off. "No thanks."

"Suit yourself, but you're missin' out." Twisting back to look through the windshield of the van, LJ stuffed in a few more fries before he grabbed another big bite of his burger. Sebo just watched while his gut rolled and twisted, and even with the van's AC on full blast, he could feel sweat soaking though his tee-shirt. He saw LJ wolf down his burger like it was the best thing the guy had ever eaten in his life—watched Meteo eat his like it was a raw oyster.

Sebo figured one solid punch to the left side of LJ's head would be easy enough from his angle. Sebo could picture it in his mind as clearly as he was seeing LJ slop down the last of his greasy burger. One punch, and he'd take LJ down, but one shot from the pistol would end it. Not LJ's miniature nine though, because LJ would be out cold. Sebo knew he'd buy it from the BFG Meteo was packing.

* * *

From the Shell station on the opposite side of the street from the burger joint, Pablo watched LJ's van turn onto the highway. He slipped his phone out from his jacket pocket, thumbed off a brief text to signal Justin, and to let him know the van was heading his way.

From a side street four blocks away, Justin glanced at Pablo's text before he and the rest of the crew spotted the van passing by. They rolled out to join northbound traffic, Pablo's intention being to kick over his Softail, join up with the other five bikers and do his part to deliver to LJ some much-deserved payback. He figured a couple hours is all it would take and he'd be back at work and nobody'd get wise.

Pablo still had his phone in his hand when it buzzed from an incoming call. He took a look at the screen, and the name of the caller made his face screw up—his plans, too. Pablo shut his bike down and lifted the phone to his ear. "Hey Chief, that was some kind of breakout—you got a real badass streak in you, man. How you doing anyways?"

Bill was perched on the tailgate of an ambulance with his phone to his ear and surrounded by first responders. A female paramedic worked to dress the graze on his upper arm. "Where are you?" Bill said.

"Nowhere special—just out on my bike."

"Why? Shouldn't you be helping out Jerome back at the tire store?"

"No problem, Chief—Jerome gave me the afternoon off."

"The hell he did—I just spoke to him." Antiseptic hit raw flesh and Bill winced at the pain; the woman apologized. "Pablo, listen up, you helped me out and I appreciate it, but I just watched one parolee get hauled back into lockup today. I don't want to see you go down too."

Still with his face screwed up like he was in pain, Pablo said, "I hear you, Chief."

"If you were really hearing me? You'd already have your ass back at work."

Pablo's face straightened out. "Look, Chief," he said, "I gotta tell you something—I just had eyes on Little Junior. It wasn't more than three minutes ago. Motherfucker just went through a drive-thru, now he's heading north on Old 301."

"What's he driving?"

"Nineteen ninety-eight Chevy club van, white."

"Good to know—I'll pass it on to the proper authorities; now get your ass back to work."

Thirty-Seven

I've been looking forward to this all day...

Pablo listened as he sat on his Softail, then he said, "Yeah, sure, Chief, I'll go back to work, okay? But you gotta know something else."

"What's that?"

"Sebo's in the van with LJ and another guy I've never seen before."

"I'm sorry to hear that—Sebo's the reason you and I are even talking. What else?"

"There's another parole officer tailing LJ."

"How on earth would you know? Who is he?"

"Drives a dark blue Crown Victoria interceptor, right?"

"That would be Freddy." Bill paused a moment. "Hey, Pablo, is he alone?"

"No, there's a woman with him."

"Shit," Bill said. "Look, you've been a real help, Pablo, and I mean that, but you gotta do me one more big favor."

"Name it, Chief."

"Go back to work."

* * *

"We grew ourselves a tail, Pana." LJ leaned forward and clicked off the van's radio. Smokey Robinson and The Miracles, "Everybody's Gotta Pay Some Dues,"got cut off mid-track, and LJ said, "Local cops or Feds?"

Checking his mirrors again, Meteo said, "Looks like local."

LJ eyed his side view. "You sure, man? 'Cause I don't see nothin'."

Sebo listened from the back seat while he took in a long breath, let it out slow. He didn't turn around, didn't look for himself. He just sat quiet and thought about how he might get out of this deal without getting shot.

"Look again, Pana—four cars back, see that dark blue Crown Vic? It's been in the same spot since we left the drive-thru—pork in a plain wrapper."

LJ looked again, but this time he smiled. "That asshole's nothing to worry about—you can ignore him."

"Heat's turned up, Pana," Meteo said. "Feds were all over your Impala back there; can't ignore the Feds." Meteo didn't hear anything back from LJ right away so he glanced across, and said, "We have to ditch this van." LJ was already pointing at where he wanted to go next. "Over there, you see that?" He said. "Head for that carwash."

* * *

"Yeah, I see the van; too, it matches up with the APB," FBI Special Agent Carson said and pointed. "Looks like it's in line for that carwash." She heard Martinez let out a groan as he made a pass along the street in front and then circled around back. "We have what we need; I say we go make the arrest," she said.

"Based on Freddy's word? And if he's wrong?"

"Local cops put out an APB," Carson answered. "They know something."

"They know what Freddy knows—we get one shot at this." Martinez spun the wheel of the Tahoe and rounded the next corner. He glanced back in the direction of the van, and the carwash. "And who waits in line to get their car washed when they're on the run, anyway?"

Carson looked over at the van again as it idled in line to enter the carwash, looking like every other vehicle that was waiting. She said, "You're forgetting Jackie Brown—she made a positive I.D."

"The high school sweetheart?"

"She never said she fucked him," Carson corrected. "She only said they went to the same school."

"She didn't have to."

Carson glared at him. "What the hell's that supposed to mean?"

"Forget it," Martinez said, and pointing at the carwash, "Look, I know every one of LJ's businesses, and that carwash isn't one of them—nothing about him being here makes any sense to me."

"If you think the witnesses are full of shit," Carson cut in, "then let's stop that van and find out—I'm sick of holding back—and for what? Because you're worried about striking out again? If we have a chance at nailing this fucker then we have to take it."

* * *

"I don't like getting wet with my clothes on," Meteo said. He steered the van onto the automated track, and LJ said, "You're the one who wanted to lose the van." Sebo felt the jerking motion when the clamps took hold and the van was pulled forward into a maw of spinning brushes. Spray pounded against the van's roof and Sebo was once more eyeing the door until he caught sight of Meteo's SIG. Meteo had the gun in his hand, waving the .357's barrel in little circles as he spoke, had it aimed in Sebo's direction. "We all go out through my door," he said.

FBI Special Agent Martinez watched the van disappear into the tunnel of spinning brushes. "We'll take 'em at the exit," he said. He swung the Tahoe around in the middle of the street and headed back in the opposite direction. Carson was already checking her weapon. He said, "You might get your hair wet."

She chuckled. "Fuck that shit—I've been looking forward to this all day."

With lights flashing, Martinez cut through traffic, maneuvering smoothly around a pack of five bikers in the process and entered the parking lot of the carwash. The Tahoe skidded to a stop just as the van's front bumper rolled out from beneath the dryers. Carson was the first one out. Martinez, weapon raised and ready, approached the driver's side, while Carson went for the front passenger door shouting, "FBI!"

Thirty-Eight

I could move these all day...

"No, man," Pablo said, "I can't, it's not gonna work for me." He was sitting on his bike, engine off and he hadn't yet moved from the Shell station's gas pumps; listening to Justin complain.

"How long have we all been keeping our mouths shut, taking the guy's crap, and getting next to nothing back for it? We're the muscle, we're the guys who do the heavy lifting and without us?" Justin said. "Where's that leave LJ? Who's he gonna lean on? Those two old fucking wrestlers? That big dumb fuck Sebo? That guy's been LJ's dog since we were kids, man—I say fuck him too. What you said before was the straight true—this is our chance to even up."

"Not about that; it's like I said—I'm on paper. My parole officer's got me up a tree. I got no options here. I'm sorry."

"What happened to you? When you called me up I was like, rock and roll baby! Kick-ass! Pablo's back! So, what is it now? You go all pussy on us?"

"You say whatever you want, I got no control over that, but what I do have control over? Not going back to jail, and I *do not* want to go back to jail."

* * *

Back behind the wheel of his Bronco, Bill was driving north on Old 301. After two rings through his earpiece, the call picked up and Bill said, "Freddy, hey, it's Bill. Where are you?"

"Heading north on 9th—almost to the Green Bridge."

"Elaine's with you, right? Let me speak to her." Freddy turned off his handsfree, handed his phone over to Elaine, and she said, "Bill? How are you?" Did you get hurt? I'm so sorry we weren't able to check up on you but—"

"I'm fine, thanks for asking. Hey look, uh, what's going on? What are you two doing?"

Elaine glanced over at Freddy behind the wheel and made a kind of screwy face at him. He nodded back, motioned for her to keep talking, and she said, "We are still tailing LJ."

"What are you doing that for?" Bill said. "This is a police matter, Elaine—a serious one, too."

"You're damned right about that. This *is* a serious matter—and so far? We seem to be the only ones taking it seriously."

"Elaine, the FBI are handling this—so let them handle it, okay?"

"We already tried helping those bozos and you know what? We just saw them blow a perfectly good chance at busting LJ—it's not happening again, uh-uh, no way. We're keeping up this tail."

"Let me speak to Freddy, please," Bill said.

Elaine dropped the phone on the front seat as Freddy flipped his handsfree back on. "Elaine's right, Bill," Freddy said. "The FBI let us down—we're on our own."

"That's ridiculous—what's that FBI agent's number? You were assisting them, am I right? You still got the guy's number?"

* * *

LJ tapped at the eight-way seat adjustments, then wriggled his butt some more in the quilted leather before he said, "I don't know what you got against Kias, Meteo. This is a pretty sweet ride."

"It has no class," Meteo said. "Let's just leave it at that."

Still checking out features, LJ said, "but look at this thing? It's got satellite navigation, parking assist—voice control?" He looked over at Meteo again. "I could move these all day. I don't know what you were complaining about."

Meteo let out a grunt, said, "That Impala of yours rolled off the line in Detroit back in 1960. That was fifty-seven years ago, Pana, and up until those *putos* wrecked her? She was still a classy ride. Where do you think this Kia will be in fifty-seven years?"

"Recycled into a toaster or something—I don't know. What does it matter?"

"It's about craftsmanship—pride." Meteo drummed his fingers against the Kia's leather-wrapped steering wheel. He took in a long breath as he translated his next thought from Spanish to English, and then said, "It's about building something that will last. Real men built that beautiful Impala. This car was built by faceless robots in West Point, Georgia. Took them all of about eight hours to do it, too—start to finish—it has no soul. Besides, these things cost me a lot. Half of them are hybrids. Hybrids are worthless in Venezuela—nobody wants one. Gas, hybrid—in a dark parking lot they both look the same. My boosters can never tell them apart."

Meteo checked the rear-view, locked eyes with Sebo. "You're a man who appreciates the classics, am I right?"

"Absolutely," Sebo answered. "Nothing beats Detroit steel."

Meteo nodded his agreement, but then he held Sebo's gaze for a couple more seconds. "You hear something?" Sebo nodded. "It's the guy in the trunk—been going on since we left the carwash."

"I guess he's not happy we stole his nice new car," LJ said, and lifting the man's wallet from the center console, "so who do we have here anyways?" He flipped it open, "Robert Fullberton...age 47..." Along with the wallet's cash, LJ slipped out a business card. "Says here the guy's an accountant."

"It was his fate," Meteo said. "But that said, attacking a man from behind is always the best option, but once the decision is made, you have to make it stick."

"You're right." LJ said, "I apologize—I should've hit him harder."

* * *

"This is FBI Special Agent Martinez speaking—Identify yourself."

From over the speaker inside the Tahoe came a clipped response. "Officer Bill Mazurek—Manatee County corrections—I have information to pass on."

Martinez let out a sigh and glanced over at Agent Carson. She shrugged before mouthing the words, *Who is that?* Looking back at the road, Martinez said, "Officer Mazurek, I don't believe we've met. How did you get this number?"

"Is that important?" Bill said. "I called to tell you one of our officers is currently tailing Little Junior; latest position puts LJ crossing the Green Bridge, heading north into Palmetto. The officer is requesting the FBI's assistance."

"I doubt that," Martinez answered.

"Why on earth would you?"

"We located LJ's vehicle abandoned at a carwash."

"That's my understanding too," Bill said. "But our officer happened to be on scene at the time. He witnessed LJ and two other individuals switch vehicles. Now they're driving a four-door, red, late model Kia sedan." Glancing back at Carson again, Martinez saw her sneer—mouth the words; *Barney Fife…* Martinez flashed a grin, said, "Why am I not speaking to Freddy then?"

"It was my idea to call you, not his—"

"Why?"

"I don't think he likes you—hey? Am I wasting my time here? Or would you like to make an arrest today?"

"Maybe I should come find you first?"

"Thirty-two fifty, Ninth Street East."

"What's that?" Martinez said, and Bill answered, "My current location—but it would be more productive if you arrested Little Junior."

Thirty-Nine

Well, you did say to make it big enough to fit the old lady...

"Mendoza Road?" Freddy said.

"I don't know for sure if it was Mendoza road," Elaine responded. "I just think it *might've* been Mendoza Road."

"Not much out that way but orange groves and cows."

"And chickens," Elaine said. "I never knew Little Junior all that well—even in school he was no good, but I did know his sister Lorette—she was a nice girl."

"You lost me."

"Just listen to what I'm saying. It was a long time ago, know what I mean? If I talk it out I'll remember it better."

"So what's the connection with Lorette?"

"LJ's sister? I remember she married this rich Cuban right after high school, and his family owned this big horse farm east of Palmetto."

"Now you really lost me."

"Just listen to me; I also remember hearing that the horse farm turned into a chicken farm after Lorette's husband inherited it."

"Does he still own it?"

"As far as I know, and it was a fancy place, too."

Freddy looked up and saw the next traffic light blink from yellow to red—saw the Kia sedan roll right on through. "Fuck!" Freddy shouted. "We just lost 'em."

"Hang on, just be quiet," Elaine said, and Freddy, still huffing out his frustration as he braked six cars back from the red light, and watched the Kia sedan disappear from his view. Then he felt a gentle pat on his arm. "It's not the end of the world, okay?" Elaine said. "I just remembered something important."

* * *

"Homeland Security?" Bill said. "Wait just a minute, this is a local crime, committed by a local criminal."

The lone, county sheriff's deputy let out a sympathetic sigh. He was lean, with a teenager's face and a military haircut, thumbs hooked to his gun-belt as he relaxed against his green and white parked in front of a Circle-K just off 9th Street. This after Bill had flagged him down. The deputy said, "Look, I'm really sorry, Bill. This kind of shit drives me nuts, but after that fiasco that went down earlier today? The FBI's got us locked down hard. They've taken full command—our hands are tied."

Bill stood in front of his Bronco, the painkillers wearing off and his arm starting to remind him that he had a fresh wound from a 9mm bullet. And while the young deputy's explanation made perfect sense to him, Bill still found it puzzling given the circumstances. With his left hand rubbing unconsciously at his right shoulder; the one that got tagged, Bill said, "I appreciate you letting me beef about this, deputy, I know you're busy." Bill took in a breath, let his left hand drop back to his hip. "Maybe I'm not making myself understood." He locked eyes with the young cop. "What I'm concerned about is the safety of my fellow officers."

Bill caught a nod of agreement from the uniformed deputy, so he continued. "I'm also concerned that they may be operating outside of their jurisdiction." With his eyes still held on the deputy's, Bill said, "does that information help you out at all?"

"Yes sir," the young deputy responded. "I believe it does."

* * *

From a truck-stop at the intersection of Memphis Road and South Tamiami Trail, a lone biker observed a red, four-door Kia sedan pass him by. Phone in hand, he called Justin. "Hey, you were right—looks like they're going out to the chicken farm."

"Keep track of the car," Justin said. "I'll call the guys and let 'em know. We'll catch up to you."

"Hold on," said the biker. "Where the hell's Pablo anyway? I thought he was supposed to be with me?"

"Pablo bailed."

"No shit? What the fuck?"

"Forget him. Keep track of LJ."

* * *

After he shut down the backhoe, Hatchet-Man leaned out from the machine's open-framed cab and called down to his partner Sling-Blade. "Now that, my friend, is one big fucking hole." Hatchet-Man, congratulating himself on his accomplishment, climbed down to stand beside his partner. The pair stared down from the edge of the enormous hole, and Hatchet-Man said, "LJ's gonna like this; you wait."

"Don't have to wait long," Sling-Blade said. "I see a car coming."

His hands on his hips, Hatchet-Man shifted his weight from left to right as he eyed a car he didn't recognize. It was bumping along toward them at low speed on the incoming dirt road; a red Kia sedan. "Must've had a change in plan," remarked Sling-Blade. Meanwhile, Hatchet-Man was shaking his head in disgust. "Shit!" he growled. "You telling me we dug that goddamned hole for nothing?"

The red Kia sedan rolled to a stop about twenty feet back from the edge of the hole and from where the two wrestlers stood together.

Meteo clicked off the engine but remained behind the wheel. LJ opened his door and got out. Sebo started to open his door too, when, from the driver's seat, Meteo shifted to face him. Raising a hand up in front of Sebo, Meteo said, "Sit tight." Meteo's command had hardly left his mouth before Sebo watched the guy look past him; the man's eyes narrowing to form two lifeless dark slits. Meteo then quickly shifted away from Sebo and stretched across the center console to shout out through the opened passenger door. "You have a runner, Pana! He's going like a gazelle!"

Through his rear passenger window, Sebo looked out to see LJ draw his weapon and then race out of view. Sebo then twisted to see out though the back, but what he saw instead was the Kia's raised trunk lid. Three shots followed.

Sebo winced at the sounds, but then he looked back to see Meteo still sitting behind the wheel and softly laughing at the small spectacle. "If LJ had hit that guy harder," Meteo commented, "he wouldn't've had to run him down like that; he could've just shot the guy in the trunk instead." Then Meteo looked right at Sebo. "Okay, Señor Millionario, now you can get out."

Under the bright intensity of the punishing Florida sun, LJ slipped his small nine back into its holster, and then rubbed his hands together as if he were cold. He turned away from the man he'd just shot, the man's body now lying face down in a heavily grazed cow pasture and a little more than ten yards from the trunk of his own car. LJ, spinning back on his heel as if what he'd just done meant nothing to him, walked back to face Hatchet-Man and Sling-Blade. He reached the edge of the hole where the two old wrestlers stood and said, "How are you two guys doing today anyway?"

"Could be better," Hatchet-Man said.

"Why on earth is that?" LJ responded. He stepped over to the edge of the gaping hole and peered down into its streaked wet swaths of gray and black loam. "Looks to me like, for once at least, you both put in an honest day's work." Letting his eyes settle on Hatchet-Man again, he smiled, said, "I'm proud of you two guys."

Hatchet-Man took a step closer to the edge and looked down. "Well, you did say to make it big enough to fit the old lady."

"Did I say that?"

"You sure did," Sling-Blade chimed in, while Hatchet-Man added, "Yeah, well, we just figured, you know, because you always like to call the Impala, 'the old lady.'"

"Sometimes," LJ said. "Other times I liked to call her my beautiful darling, and on occasion, a worthless bitch when she broke down and cost me money." LJ turned to face the two wrestlers. "I will say this about her; I would never put that car into some muddy hole dug by two dumb fucks such as yourselves."

Hatchet-Man glared back at LJ. "What's this about?"

LJ reached behind him, came back out with his compact nine, and said, "This is about tying up loose ends."

Forty

They weren't interested in utilizing our local expertise to its fullest potential…

From the driveway of *Increasing Joy Ministries*, the Crown Vic idling low and the AC blowing cold, Freddy had a straight forward view out through his car's windshield, and in an easterly direction down Mendoza Road's twin lanes of scorching asphalt. The corner of Oakhurst Road was directly behind him. Each side of Mendoza was lined with barbed wire stock fencing, thick green grass, and bearded oaks that swayed out from either side.

Elaine was listening in on the conversation while Freddy spoke into his phone. "Yes sir…" Freddy said. "I understand sir… If you don't mind me asking? Uh, how did you know to call me?" Elaine overheard a man's voice come back. "We are worthy of these United States' trust and confidence for a reason, officer—we get the job done."

Freddy ended the call and Elaine said, "Now who in the hell was that?"

"The Secret Service," Freddy answered.

"Why on earth would the Secret Service be calling you? Aren't they supposed to be guarding the president or something?"

"That's what most people think," said Freddy. "But their main job is hunting down counterfeiters."

Elaine let out a brief gasp before Freddy heard her whisper, "Oh my Lord…"

Freddy nodded, said, "That's right—fucking Alfonzo Lanzano."

"He was locked in the trunk with Bill."

"He was printing up funny money for LJ."

"Hang on," Elaine said. "Bill mentioned that Lanzano had set fire to one of LJ's trailers. He said LJ had beat the guy up pretty bad because of it too. Bill didn't know why at the time, and I didn't think it was that important either, but that must've been where Lanzano had his print shop."

Freddy felt the revelation sink in and his anger take hold; he slammed his fist down onto the dash of his own car. "I knew it!" Elaine leaned away and covered her ears as Freddy shouted, "Night watchman? Seriously? I should've known that little shit was up to something."

"Hold that thought," Elaine interrupted. Lifting her phone, she eyed the screen. "I have a call from Bill."

From the passenger seat of the deputy's cruiser, Bill said, "where are you guys?"

"Mendoza Road," Elaine said.

"I don't even wanna ask."

"This is serious, Bill. We tailed LJ out here and now we think we know where he is."

From over the Bluetooth inside the cruiser, Bill said, "That's great news. Have you made the FBI aware of this? I'm sure Special Agent Martinez would like to know where LJ is." Bill glanced over at the young deputy sitting behind the wheel of the cruiser and caught him cracking a smile.

"We gave up on the FBI; they weren't interested in utilizing our local expertise to its fullest potential, so we're now working with the Secret Service instead," Elaine said.

"What?" Bill looked over at the deputy again just to affirm what he thought he'd just heard. He briefly held the deputy's eye contact, and still speaking into his phone, said, "Elaine? The Secret Service arrested Alfonzo Lanzano earlier today—they already have who they were after in custody."

"They don't have everybody," Elaine snapped back. "We happen to know that Lanzano was printing his counterfeit cash for LJ, and we also know where LJ is, so yes—we are currently assisting the United States Secret Service."

A groan of frustration left Bill's lips before he said, "What's your exact location?" Without a word, the deputy quickly slipped a pen out from his shirt pocket and passed it over. Taking the pen and then a post-it pad from the cruiser's center console, Bill began scribbling, repeating back the words, "Increasing Joy Ministries." Bill copied down the address as Elaine read it off to him. "Do me a favor please," he said, "stay right there. I'm riding with a Sheriff's deputy. We're on our way."

Bill ended his call but he was still staring at the writing on the post-it and trying to think. The deputy said, "How fast do you want to get out there?"

Bill looked up, flashed a grin, and said, "How fast can you go?"

Forty-One

Bill's not going to like this one bit…

Justin picked up the outline of Freddy's Crown Vic through the ape-hangers of his wishbone hardtail. He signaled to the rest of his crew—four bikers minus Pablo. Elaine was still listening to Freddy complain about missing signals when the raucous rumble of Harleys extinguished their conversation.

Deafening bike revs surrounded the Crown Vic as the five bikers rode in close and then circled Elaine and Freddy's view. Elaine reached inside her purse and put her hand on her .38 revolver.

Justin rolled to a stop next to the car's driver-side window. From inside, Freddy only saw a large, heavily scarred fist decorated with oversized rings reach out and rap against his window glass.

"Don't open it." Elaine ordered, but Freddy already had his badge out. "Why not?" He said.

"Because they all work for LJ," Elaine answered. "They're a bunch of dangerous motherfuckers, just like Sebo."

"I'm not afraid of these clowns." Freddy held up his badge as he powered down his window. "You're inhibiting a police investigation," Freddy said. "Move along."

Justin withdrew his fist before folding his thick, bare, ink-saturated arms, across his leather vest. Flat-faced, he stared down at Freddy and just waited. Still holding up his badge and trying to sound tough, Freddy repeated, "Police business—I'm ordering you to leave now."

Justin smiled at him, said, "That badge doesn't mean shit. You're not a real cop; you're just a fucking parole officer."

Freddy raised his voice. "I will place you under arrest if you don't leave immediately."

Justin chuckled at him from the saddle of his Harley before he unfolded his arms and then proceeded to hold his thick fists out in Freddy's face, so close as to be nearly touching the guy's nose. The two fists held out side by side in an open invitation, and Justin said, "Go ahead and try." Justin was grinning at Freddy's pallid expression when the barrel of a Colt Cobra snub-nose came into view, hammer cocked and a woman's finger on the trigger. Justin quickly withdrew, while Elaine, leaning across Freddy's lap, stared back at the biker and held her aim. "You respect this badge, motherfucker?"

* * *

A rolling disco but without the siren, the deputy's cruiser slipped past late afternoon traffic without effort. Bill was back on his phone. "I apologize…" he said. "You're right; I should've called… I didn't want you worrying." He listened some more to his wife complain before Bill said, "That's why I hate this social media stuff—nobody has any decency anymore; they're too busy drawing attention to themselves."

209

The deputy continued to maneuver through traffic until a slowdown briefly halted his progress. Bill put his phone away. "Facebook," Bill said. "Can you believe that? My wife found out what happened when she saw a picture of me getting patched up on Facebook."

"I won't let my kids near that stuff," the deputy responded before he glanced Bill's way and said, "If it's any consolation? I wouldn't have called my wife either—no need for both of us to be suffering."

* * *

From inside the Crown Vic, Freddy and Elaine each watched as the five bikers left them behind and rode off to disappear down Mendoza Road. Freddy already had his car in gear, and Elaine said, "You think they're heading for the chicken farm?"

Freddy pulled out from the driveway of the church. "Only one way to find out," he said.

And then Elaine, hesitant, added, "Bill's not going to like this one bit."

"Bill's not assisting the Secret Service."

Freddy followed in the biker's path, driving east on Mendoza, a bone straight rural road as flat, dull, and featureless as they come, but it was easy enough to keep the bikers in view from a safe distance.

Freddy drove for only another mile before a cluster of five brake lights briefly flashed in the distance, Elaine and Freddy watching as the bikes rolled to the left in unison and out of sight. Freddy continued on until he reached the spot where the bikers had made their turn. He slowed, and then pulled off onto the opposite shoulder.

Elaine squinted against the glare as she peered through Freddy's window at a rusted pipe gate in faded green, but with the top and bottom rows long ago painted over in white. The gate hung across a jagged finger of dirt that pointed into a nothingness of thick, sub-tropical pine scrub. Remnants of dust left by the bikers still slowly swirled up into the humidity. "This is it," she said. "I remember that gate."

"You sure?" Freddy asked, cautious. "It could be a decoy; they could be trying to get us lost out there."

"I'm sure," Elaine said. "This place hasn't changed in twenty years."

Freddy shifted the Crown Vic into park, and said, "I guess we should wait here for the Secret Service to show up." Looking around, Elaine said, "Uh huh, that would be the correct thing to do, but there's no telling when that'll be." Freddy studied her vague expression for a few more seconds before he said, "Yeah, so we sit tight, then—wait for back up."

And Elaine, with a soft nod, said, "That is if you think we'd be dropping the ball, I mean, after all we've been through so far." Freddy flashed a thin smile before he turned back from the window and shifted the idling car into gear. Glancing her way, he said, "You sure you're ready for this?"

Elaine already had her pistol out, inspecting it one last time. "Yeah," she said. "Let's go."

Forty-Two

The two best guys I had...

The young deputy had shut down his cruiser's strobes miles ago—no need out this far. "There's the church," Bill said and, pointing at the sign out front, he read off the name, "Increasing Joy Ministries." They slowed for the turn and Bill was already frowning at the fact that the place was completely deserted.

The green and white cruiser rolled to a stop in front of the church. The deputy took one look around and said, "What would you like to do now?" He glanced Bill's way, not waiting for a response, before he added, "You know those two officers pretty well?" Bill nodded—didn't say anything. Resting his elbows on the steering wheel and rubbing at his forehead, the deputy said, "Would they be stupid enough to go after a guy like LJ on their own?"

"I'd like to think not," said Bill.

And with that response he heard the deputy let out a long sigh. "I'm going to have to call this in."

"Yeah," Bill answered. "I know you do."

The deputy was already reaching for his radio when Bill saw him freeze mid-motion. "What is it?" Bill said, and, catching the deputy's stern expression, Bill watched as the young uniform stared up into his rear-view. Bill twisted back to see what was behind them and spotted the grill of a large, black SUV. "That would be either the FBI or the Secret Service," Bill said. He turned back to see the young deputy smiling, and Bill said, "You still wanna call this in?"

The deputy placed the radio receiver back in its holder. "Better hold off for now," he answered. "Maybe we just got lucky; maybe the cavalry's already showed up."

* * *

"I hate fighting cocks," Freddy said as the Crown Vic bumped along the dirt road that ran past a dozen rows of low-roofed barns, each one filled with hundreds of cages.

"I hear you," Elaine added as she peered out through her window at the warehoused roosters. "But there's nothing illegal about breeding these things." Elaine turned her attention back to the road ahead before she suddenly sat up straight and pointed. "Up there on the left," she said. "See where the road gets better? That way leads to the main house."

A half a mile further on, as they drove along a smooth white path of crushed shell dug from an ancient seabed, Elaine looked out as they entered a circular driveway paved with native travertine. Framed by manicured landscaping, the driveway even had a bubbling fountain at its center. "Nice looking place," Freddy said. "You don't expect to find something like this way out here, that's for sure." He rolled to a stop in front of a mul-tistoried, Mediterranean-styled villa. "Are you sure we're in the right place? You said you were out here just the one time, right?"

213

"That's right."

"For a barbecue?"

"It was for Lorette's bridal shower."

"How can you remember? I mean, it was almost twenty years ago, right?"

"Don't remind me," Elaine said, "I feel plenty old enough—know what I mean?" Elaine let out a little huff before looking out at the stucco mansion in front of her. "You ever get invited to a rich person's house before?" She looked back at Freddy. "Because believe me, you will remember every damned detail about all the stuff they have that you don't."

* * *

"That's a top-notch man you got there, Pana," Meteo spoke above the roar of the backhoe, now with Sebo at the controls. LJ was listening as he stood beside Meteo. The pair were standing only a couple of paces back from the edge of the gaping hole that resembled something like a meteor crater, or the point where a small jet had plummeted to its demise with all on board. Meteo folded his arms and waited for LJ to say something smart, but the only thing that came out of guy's mouth was a low grunt. Then LJ cleared his throat. "The two best guys I had are lying at the bottom of that fucking hole."

"You ever have to shoot your own dog before?"

"Never owned one."

"That's right," Meteo said, with a knowing grin. "You like owning people instead." Leaving LJ's side, he took a couple steps forward and peered down into the hole. He watched as the bucket tipped back and another load of dirt spilled out over the three bodies lying at the bottom, those of Hatchet-Man and Sling-Blade being the most visible. The old backhoe's diesel rumbled up loud as its hydraulics whined, the combination doing a good job of drowning out other sounds.

For Sebo the noise was a comfort, along with the familiarity of the machine's control levers that moved so automatically in his hands. A familiarity he now clung to as if it were the only thing keeping him alive. The painful knot in his gut still rolled tight as a feeling he'd never experienced shuddered through his entire body—he'd never been on the losing end with LJ before.

The heavy machine's vibration almost masking his trembling hands as any idea of getting out of this situation while still breathing seemed to be evaporating fast. Sebo swung the boom back from the hole and then positioned the bucket to pick up another load of dirt. A bright glint shining off polished chrome caught his attention. He looked up.

* * *

"If I was a betting man, my money'd be on the woman." Bill smiled at the young deputy's observation as he stood beside him. The two men were now leaning against the green and white's sunbaked outer skin, the afternoon's heat bearing down and radiating up at them from the surrounding asphalt. In response, Bill's brow was dripping and his fresh wound was burning right along with it. Both he and the deputy watched closely as FBI Special Agent Martinez loudly argued, toe-to-toe, with Secret Service Special Agent Margit Spencer. The parking lot of *Increasing Joy Ministries* was now filled to near capacity with over-sized, black SUVs, and an idled, FBI SWAT team who stood by and sweltered inside their full tactical.

"I demand to know how you tracked us," Agent Spencer shouted, her voice coming off strong and not nearly as shrill as one might expect.

215

Martinez appeared to be listening but in reality, he was mostly just staring down at her, his thick arms folded, and with his thick head, atop his thick neck, tilted toward her. She took a breath and he found an opening; he didn't hesitate to bellow back into the woman's face. "That would be FBI privileged information," he sneered. "Way above your pay-grade."

From their vantage point beside the patrol car, the young Sheriff's deputy leaned in close and whispered into Bill's ear. "She's small, but that doesn't mean a thing; she kind of reminds me of my wife." Bill could only shake his head at the confrontation unfolding in front of him. He reached up and dabbed at his sweaty forehead with a soggy paper napkin, straightened away from the car and said, "Okay you people, I've seen enough." Bill stepped directly to where the pair of bickering Feds were still facing off.

With both hands lifted out from his sides, palms open, Bill first waved his left hand near Agent Martinez, then his right in front of Agent Spencer. Martinez was the first to react. "Who the fuck are you?" He shouted. Bill dropped his hands to his sides, took in an exhausted breath, and said, "Bill Mazurek. We spoke on the phone earlier. I'm a peace officer with the Manatee County Department of Corrections."

Martinez pointed in the direction of the parked cruiser, and barked, "Is that right? Well, Officer, you were a lot more help when you were standing over there with your mouth shut." Still pointing at the green and white cruiser, Martinez said, "I don't see you moving? If you like, I can have my men assist, so you can get back where you belong—which is out of my fucking face."

Bill folded his arms across his chest, planted his feet, and watched as agent Martinez's grizzled face turned beet-red, while one of the veins in his neck throbbed, but Bill didn't give him a chance to speak. "Would you like to make some arrests today, agent Martinez?"

"I would," Martinez answered. "I can start with you."

Nodding his agreement, Bill said, "Yes you could. But I'm referring to arrests that will reflect positively toward your performance in the field." Bill watched as Martinez's expression froze ever so briefly, but he was already on to his next task. Bill turned away from agent Martinez and shifted his attention to Agent Spencer instead. "You would also like to wrap this up today—am I right, ma'am?"

Bill read Special Agent Spencer's reaction, saw her anger slightly soften. She first nodded her agreement, but then added, "As soon as we establish my agency's jurisdiction." With that, Martinez leaned in toward her and pointed his finger in her face. "You got your counterfeiter—*your day is wrapped*." Without missing a beat, Spencer reached up and moved Martinez's finger out of her way. "I have the printer," she said. "But I'm not leaving without his boss—my warrant covers me."

Bill unfolded his arms and lifted his hands again. "Does it matter to either of you that two law enforcement officers are up against LJ alone, right now, and without backup, while you two stand here and argue over turf?"

Forty-Three

Speak English…

With her badge visibly clipped to her belt, Elaine briefly straightened her outfit before she cleared her throat, reached up, and then pushed the polished brass bell button next to the mansion's ornately carved, mahogany front door. As she and Freddy waited, a razor-like chorus from thousands of cicadas buzzed in the trees nearby. "You think they have a maid?" Freddy asked, swiveling from left to right as he stood beside Elaine.

"I would imagine," Elaine answered. "I'm just hoping somebody's home."

A minute or two passed by before the large door slowly swung open and a still strikingly beautiful, if not older, Lorette appeared. "Elaine?" She said, looking confused. "What are you doing here?"

* * *

Sebo recognized Justin's Harley. He'd recognized the other four riders too. It was easy enough from his higher vantage point inside the cab of the backhoe—the sight was a relief.

Sebo eyed the approaching bikers as he kept the bucket in motion. All five rolled toward him with their legs down to steady themselves as they bumped along the dirt road; still some distance away but closing. The backhoe's control levers moved smoothly in Sebo's hands as he maneuvered the bucket and picked up another load of dirt. He swung the bucket back over the hole, and that's when he caught a glimpse of Meteo and LJ still talking. They were just standing casually, side by side, and not paying much attention to anything other than their ongoing conversation, the roar of the backhoe's mechanics still masking the rumble of Harleys.

Shifting levers, Sebo tipped the bucket and another load of sandy-gray earth spilled out over the two wrestler's bodies, which were now nearly covered except for the two large men's feet and hands. Sebo's stomach was still rolling hard as he retracted the bucket's arm, and the growing sound of the bike's engines rose above the din.

At the distinct rumble of approaching Harleys, Meteo was the first to draw his weapon. "Hold up," LJ ordered, lifting his hands to block Meteo. "That's my crew."

Still gripping his pistol, Meteo said, "You called them? You ordered them to come here?"

"Not exactly," LJ said, and now Meteo was pointing his pistol at LJ. "What, *exactly* are they doing here then?"

The bikes each rolled up to the opposite side of the hole from where Meteo and LJ were standing, forming a line within twenty feet of the edge. Justin was the first to shut down his bike and dismount. The others all followed.

Meteo turned toward Sebo, and, gesturing with his pistol, signaled for him to shut down the backhoe. Sebo saw Meteo but shifted his attention toward Justin instead. The two men made eye contact, and inside those brief few seconds, Justin, ever so slightly shook his head—*No...*

* * *

"Are we in agreement then?" Bill said as he held eye contact with FBI Special Agent Martinez. Bill then stood by as Martinez briefly scanned across the weary faces of his fellow agents, men and women who had yet to see even an ounce of real action that day but were already exhausted due to a string of tedious delays and the oppressive heat. Martinez made the call. "Yeah," he said, shifting his attention to his Secret Service counterpart. "We'll work together then."

"And?" Bill insisted, while still staring at Martinez.

"Okay then," Martinez relented. "Agent Spencer runs the joint operation—but on the ground? My team will be on point." Audible sighs of relief rippled across the field of the assembled agents. Bill offered his hand to agent Martinez. "You made a good call," Bill said. "A tough call, but a good one."

Martinez gripped Bill's hand, but then he stepped in close, and whispered into Bill's ear. "If she blows this, I'll have your badge—and your pension."

* * *

"Do you like this house?" Elaine said, with her hands on her hips, and her feet planted. She held Lorette's eye contact but didn't give the woman a chance to respond. "Because, at this very moment, *your* brother is somewhere on *your* property committing multiple felonies."

Freddy took another step back from the two women, kept his mouth shut. Elaine relaxed a bit, and, cocking an ample hip to one side, she leaned in closer to Lorette's arrogant sneer, and said, "This is the way it's going to be; you can either cooperate

with us and *keep* this house, or you can keep that rich-bitch atti-
tude of yours and lose everything in the court-ordered, asset forfeiture—which I can guarantee will happen. What's it gonna
be?"

With a huff, Lorette slipped her perfectly manicured nails
into the pocket of her designer dress and retrieved her iPhone.
She pointed it at Elaine. "I have very good lawyers," she said. "I
don't *have* to do or say anything."

"No, you don't," Elaine replied. "You have that right, but
you have to ask yourself if you really want to take that risk—
knowing what you know, that is."

Elaine took in a breath and stared back at Lorette, waited…
Then she saw the woman hit the speed-dial on her phone.
Lorette held the phone to her ear and spoke in rapid Spanish.
Elaine loudly cleared her throat, and waving a finger in Lorette's
face, she said, "Speak English."

Forty-Four

Into the bottom of the hole...

H is hands still on the levers, Sebo stopped the bucket's movement at a point that left it suspended above the muddy chasm. Meteo shouted up at Sebo from the edge, "Shut it down!" He could hear Meteo well enough, but Sebo's hands didn't move. He glanced again at Justin, caught a slight grin this time, the two men making brief eye contact before Sebo looked back at Meteo, and Sebo could see that the man had changed position. Meteo was now standing only arm's length from LJ, his gun gripped tight, and LJ's face oddly frozen; the barrel of Meteo's SIG .357 shoved against LJ's right temple. "Shut that fucking thing down!" Meteo repeated.

From the opposite side of the gaping hole, a round of laughter rose up as the five bikers each drew their own guns. "Go ahead and shoot that son of a bitch!" Justin ordered. "That's why we came out here, man. You'd be saving us some bullets."

Meteo hesitated a few more seconds before he shifted the .357 away from LJ's temple, and instead, pointed it directly at Sebo. "Do you know what this man is worth?" Meteo shouted across the hole at the bikers.

"About two licks off a rat's ass," Justin responded. His four biker compatriots chuckled along in agreement, until one of them said, "He's been pretty worthless ever since he fell off that radio tower." An even louder round of laughter followed, but Sebo never heard it. His focus, and his complete attention, being firmly in the grip of the gun that was being pointed directly at him.

The backhoe's open-framed cab offering a clear line of sight and no real protection. Sebo's vision narrowed around the barrel of Meteo's gun; his next breath stalled out and stuck inside his throat. His mind fuzzed into a numbing haze, but his hands were still on the levers. The empty bucket was still poised above the hole, and the backhoe's diesel still rattled along. Sebo saw something move. It was an odd sort of motion that didn't register but only one thing about it mattered; whatever it was, it caused Meteo to lower his pistol and look away.

Sebo sucked down hard on a desperate breath and leaned forward to glimpse LJ tumbling down into the bottom of the hole, scrambling in panic over the partially covered corpses—desperate for cover. Next, Sebo caught sight of Meteo aiming his pistol downward into the hole. Sebo heard the sound of hydraulic pumps winding up, and the bikers' increasing laughter, felt his hands shift the levers and watched as the bucket dropped.

Shifting his stance to gain a better position, Meteo, without hesitation, fired two quick rounds across the hole and straight into the group of still laughing bikers. Caught off guard, the biker's reaction consisted of a chaotic and imprecise barrage of return fire, but by now, their delay had already cost them one of their own...

* * *

"This number, right here," Elaine said, as she held her phone up for Lorette to see, and pointing at the entry on her contacts list, Elaine repeated, "United States Secret Service—Special Agent Margit Spencer—you see it?" Lorette stared at the screen a moment before she tapped the number into her own phone.

"What do I say?" She asked as she lifted the phone to her ear.

"You tell Agent Spencer that you are cooperating with the local authorities, and that you know your brother is currently on your property, and that you also know exactly where he is on your property."

"Then what?"

"Then you'll tell the Secret Service whatever else you know about LJ's criminal activities," Elaine said. "And if you're smart? You won't hold nothin' back." Elaine stood by as Lorette began to speak to Agent Spencer, she and Freddy listening with satisfaction to a conversation long overdue. It was Freddy who was the first to pick up the sounds of distant gunfire.

Forty-Five

You better not be fucking with me…

From behind the wheel of his black Tahoe, FBI Special Agent Martinez steered with one hand as he maneuvered down a thin, rough dirt track. His free hand gripped a radio receiver, while his vehicle thrashed through thickets of palmetto and was whipped by branches and overgrowth. Meanwhile, Agent Carson, strapped in tight and trying to hold on, watched as loosened boughs of Spanish moss piled up across the vehicle's hood. "Repeat that last transmission," Martinez shouted into the receiver. "Repeat!"

"We're hearing live fire—multiple shots fired."

"There's a split in the road coming up," said Agent Carson. "Maybe this one will take us to where the action is."

* * *

Meteo ducked behind the heavy steel arm of the backhoe that rose up from the hole like the trunk of some rusted, yellow tree; a tree that stood between himself and the bikers. Meteo waited for a clear shot at his opponents—perhaps two seconds going by before he aimed, squeezed off three more rounds, and clipped another one of Justin's guys. The fallen man shrieked in pain while his buddies rushed to drag him clear of the line of fire. Meteo took advantage of the distraction and ran for better cover near the treads of the backhoe before he turned, and fired back with two more rounds…

Sebo's hands were no longer on the control levers. Instead, they covered his head as he attempted to crouch down inside the backhoe's small cab, the bulk of his body squeezed as far down as possible beside the cab's cracked and worn, black vinyl seat. A loud *Ping! Ping! Ping!* Sounding off as bullets struck the backhoe's outer metal skin, the sharp clangs piercing his ears with a series of painful jolts, before he heard Meteo shouting at him again. "Sebo! Move the backhoe! Reverse the fucking backhoe! Do it and I will protect you!"

"From what?" Sebo shouted back. "*You?*"

"Move the backhoe you big, dumb fuck!"

With that, a flash of anger ignited inside Sebo's mind, anger that for so long had only smoldered beneath a blanket of fear. Now it suddenly sparked and crackled, and with it, an energy surged through his body. Sebo took hold of his rage, and the world around him slowed—everything became quiet. The only sounds that registered were his own breathing, and his own heart pounding inside his chest.

Moving as if driven by some other force, something outside himself, Sebo pushed upright. He felt his right-hand grip against the greasy metal frame of the backhoe, felt his left hand against the vinyl seat as he briefly peered down at his target, and then jumped. Like a machine throttled at full, and out of control, he landed right on top of Meteo.

Knocked down but mobile, Meteo shoved his pistol into Sebo's chest and mashed the trigger. The only sensation Sebo felt in return was an empty *Click*. What Meteo received in response was Sebo's tightly clinched southpaw making hard contact with the side of his head.

* * *

The young deputy's green and white cruiser idled smoothly as it sat alone in the empty parking lot of *Increasing Joy Ministries*. The car's AC was blowing hard and cold, its interior as silent as the empty church in front of them, and neither he, nor Bill, minded the boredom. Both men were doing exactly as ordered by Special Agent Spencer, which was to wait, watch, and monitor from their assigned position.

A few minutes later Bill was on his phone again. "So you're both still in front of the main house then?" He said, as the deputy listened in. "Elaine, hey—" Bill paused a moment. He held the phone away from his ear as Elaine's voice rose to a shrill crescendo, becoming clearly audible—the deputy chuckled. "She all right?" he said. Bill nodded his response before he brought the phone back to his ear. "Look, don't worry about it—you hear me? I'm just happy to hear you two were out of the line of fire."

Bill listened some more. "You did good, you know that, right?" Bill said. "I owe you an apology; you were right about LJ all along." Bill let out a sigh, said, "So how's Freddy holding up?" Bill listened to Elaine's response, then chuckled. "That car of his is some kind of tank, isn't it?" Bill tipped his chin down as he continued to listen. "Yeah, I hear you—it's like I said; our side of the fence isn't so bad when you give it a chance. I've had all the excitement I care to tolerate—I like the dull days."

* * *

With his hands clasped tightly behind his head, Sebo dropped to his knees while a blur of black SWAT uniforms, weapons held at the ready, closed in around him. "FBI! FBI! Hands behind your head! FBI!" In his haze, the reality that he was going down again hadn't fully registered until somebody's knee drove hard into his back. Sebo fell forward and his face was shoved into the dirt, his arms were jerked back behind him and the cuffs went on tight.

Someone pulled Sebo back up onto his knees, and it gave him a chance to look around. What he saw in those brief few moments was a lot of SWAT: guys in heavy black tactical with fully automatic weapons. He saw Meteo face down, being frisked and cuffed. All total Sebo could see at least twenty more cops standing around. On the other side of the hole he spotted Justin, disarmed and on his knees, just like he was, along with two other members of his gang, while two more lay prone and immobile.

"Where's LJ?"

Sebo heard the question that had been shouted into his ear, but before he could answer, FBI Special Agent Martinez bent down, grabbed the back of his head, and yelled even louder, "Where's Little Junior?" Sebo spoke softly, while Agent Martinez, listening close, said, "Are you fucking with me?" Sebo repeated his answer, and Martinez hissed out a response, "You better not be fucking with me."

Martinez straightened before ordering one of his men into the cab of the still-idling backhoe. Striding to the edge of the hole, Martinez stopped and looked down at the partially covered bodies, and the backhoe's bucket that rested inverted on top of them. "Raise it up!" Martinez shouted and signaling to his men. "Let's see what else is under there." Sebo heard the diesel rev and the hydraulics whine; then he heard a series of high-pitched shrieks when LJ emerged from beneath the bucket.

Martinez stared down at LJ, and the two men made eye contact. "FBI!" Martinez shouted. "Hands behind your head! You're under arrest."

Forty-Six

You really know how to hurt a guy…

leven months later. Secret Service Special Agent Margit Spencer handed over her sidearm, then signed herself into the visitor log of the Petersburg, medium security Federal Correctional Institution in Prince George County, Virginia. "What's with the box?" The guard said as he shuffled his hands around inside. With his search completed, he snapped the lid closed and handed the plastic container over to Agent Spencer. "You sure you know what you're doing, ma'am?"

Agent Spencer paused briefly to stare back at the guard; she offered a reassuring nod before taking the box back. "Is my prisoner ready?" She asked.

"Sure is, ma'am," the guard responded. "Got you set up down the hall—a private interrogation room just like you requested. I'll have one of my guys escort you."

Once inside the brightly lit, but windowless room, Agent Spencer left her escort standing in the hallway as she closed the door behind her. "Mr. Lanzano," she said. "How are you today?" Alfi looked up from the table he was chained to, offering a slight smile when he made eye contact with Agent Spencer, and lifting his cuffed hands in her direction, he said, "I've been better."

"I don't doubt that, Mr. Lanzano."

Alfi's eyes followed her trim figure as she passed from the door to where he sat. He liked how she was neatly dressed in a nice suit but with a tailored skirt instead of the usual, boring pants, and low heels that still looked stylish, in his opinion. He held his eyes on her as she stepped over to the table and then stood in front of him carrying a black plastic storage container. It was slightly larger than a standard shoebox, and she had it tucked under her left arm.

Agent Spencer set the box down in front of Alfi. "I could use your help, Mr. Lanzano."

"What can you offer me in return?" Alfi said.

He studied her delicate features as he enjoyed the moment. Agent Spencer, her head tilted slightly to one side, raised an eyebrow. "You don't mince words, Mr. Lanzano, so neither will I—let's get down to business, shall we?" She opened the box and then tipped it toward him. He peeked inside, and smiled.

"Ah," he said with a wider smile this time. "So you wish to give me a little test?"

Agent Spencer nodded her agreement. "You're pretty smart."

"If I were a bit smarter." Alfi said with a sigh. "I wouldn't be here."

He leaned forward to study the contents of the box, and lifting his cuffed hands from the table, Alfi tugged at the long, thin chain attached to them; raking it through a slot cut into the table's center with a kind of rolling, rattling noise. The chain continued to clatter as Alfi began poking around inside the plastic container. "You have a lot of fake bills in here," he said.

"Is that so?"

Alfi looked up at her. Still holding his sly grin, he winked at her. "You have many different kinds of fakes in here—the work of many other printers."

"Show me."

Alfi dipped his slender hands back into the box and began lifting out the bills one by one. First briefly turning each of them over in his hands, he then pressed each one carefully between his fingertips and then examined the bill more closely before passing judgment. "Fake," he said. "This one as well."

Agent Spencer stood in front of the table with her arms folded and watched as Alfi quickly sorted through the entire contents of a box that held a nominal, eighty-thousand dollars' worth of marked, counterfeit cash. Notes of various denominations that had, at various times, been seized by her agency. None it being the standard, inkjet, or copy machine run-offs; this box held the best of the best. Halfway through, Alfi let out a sigh as he lifted out one of his own twenties. "Seriously?" He said, and still holding her eye contact. "You really know how to hurt a guy."

"How's that?" she said.

"You mix *my* work with all these other sub-standard guys."

"Sub-standard?" She chuckled. "Are you kidding me? You're looking at the past ten years of our toughest cases." She watched Alfi lift out another twenty, and looking it over carefully, he said, "This one's pretty good." He held the bill up to the light. "Let me guess… this was done by that Canadian printer, am I right?"

Eyeing the way the bill was marked, Agent Spencer nodded her agreement, while Alfi, still examining his counterpart's craftsmanship, said, "There's still a lot of his work floating around out there, you know."

She nodded again, then said, "And yours as well. What else can you show me?"

Pawing around the box's interior some more, and with the long thin chain attached to his cuffs clattering through the slot in the table, Alfi lifted out another of the marked bills, and looking at it closely, he said, "This one is very special."

"How's that?" She said as Alfi first held the twenty-dollar bill up directly in front of her, then said, "Because this one is actually real." Agent Spencer let a brief smile appear, and said, "Let me ask you one more thing."

With a shrug, Alfi said, "if it pleases you, madam. I have lots of time; ask me whatever you like."

With a smirk, Agent Spencer unfolded her arms and then took a step closer to the table. She leaned in toward Alfi's face, and said, "Would you like a job, Mr. Lanzano?"

"Does this job get me out of here?"

"On a trial basis; you'll be closely supervised, and you'll be wearing an ankle bracelet of course; your movements will be tracked."

Alfi showed a thin smile. "Do I get my own apartment?"

"If you can prove yourself," Agent Spencer responded. "Yes, I can arrange that."

"Will I still be deported back to Italy?"

"Not if you follow the rules of the agreement."

"So, my girlfriend can come too?" Alfi said, his eyes brightening a bit, something Spencer picked up on.

"That would be up to her, Mr. Lanzano."

The chain attached to his cuffs clattered against the table as Alfi relaxed back into his chair. He took in a long breath, and returning eye contact with Agent Spencer, said, "I accept your offer."

Forty-Seven

A man of leisure…

With the car up on the lift, Pablo walked beneath it for a closer look at the undercarriage. "You're one tough old bitch…" he mumbled aloud as he moved methodically from the front axle to the rear differential, shining a small flashlight up into the car's greasy recesses along the way, and mentally compiling the list of the parts he'd be needing.

"Hey, Pablo."

Clicking off the light, Pablo returned it to the front pocket of his coveralls before he pivoted to see his former parole officer standing in front of him. "Hola, Chief!" Pablo said. "Que pasa?"

"Muy bien, gracias," Bill said.

Pablo quickly wiped his hands with a rag, and then offered one of them to Bill. "It's been, what? Six months since you signed me off? I wasn't expecting to see you, man. What can I do for you?"

After briefly grasping Pablo's outstretched hand, Bill said, "Is the boss around?"

"Sure thing," Pablo answered, "he's back in the office." Pablo was about to point Bill in the right direction, but he noticed Bill was staring up at the car sitting on the lift. Eyeing Bill's expression, Pablo said, "I feel your vibe, Chief." Looking up at the car again, he added, "She kind of gives me the willies too."

"It's worse than that," Bill said. "But to each his own, right?" Pablo nodded his agreement before pointing past Bill's left shoulder. "Hey, look there, here he comes." Bill turned around and caught sight of Sebo's over-sized frame moving toward him at a brisk walk. "Bill!" Sebo called out. "Aren't you supposed to be retired?" Shaking Sebo's hand, Bill said, "You're right—which reminds me; how's Freddy been treating you? Everything going okay?"

"Yeah," Sebo answered. "I'm doing all right; still have another year left on paper, but I got no complaints." Looking around the well-equipped, custom car garage, Bill replied, "If I owned a place like this? I wouldn't have any complaints either."

"I have you to thank for it," Sebo said, but Bill only shook his head before staring up at his former parolee. "I was doing my job, remember? I seem to recall you thanking me after the judge handed down his verdict—so there's nothing more to be said on the subject." Then Bill pointed up at the vintage, 1960 Impala sitting on the lift. "But I gotta ask—what, in hell, possessed you to go and buy this piece of junk?"

Sebo shifted toward the battered Impala with a look of admiration. "She finally came up for sale at the police auction yard, and I was like, hey man, why not?" Sebo looked back at Bill. "We're a custom, rebuild shop—why not give the old girl another chance?"

236

"Speaking of giving an old car another chance…" Bill twisted to point at the parking lot behind him, and at his vintage, two-tone Bronco. "Now that I'm a man of leisure," he said. "I was thinking of fixing up my old rig; make it nice again so my wife will stop complaining about it sitting in our driveway."

Sebo smiled, said, "You bet—we can handle that."

* * *

Late afternoon heat shimmered off the freshly painted hood of a 1959 Chevrolet pickup. Once a rusted hulk, it'd been rescued from a dairy barn in Myakka City four months prior. Now the old truck was rolling like new again. Sebo was taking it out for a test drive, and along a familiar route down Old Highway 301. He caught the light at Cortez Road and turned east, the windows rolled down on account of the pickup's air-conditioning being a work in progress. Humid heat rose up from the asphalt and the meager amount of air flowing into the truck left the two-seater cab feeling like a rolling sauna; Sebo needed something cold.

"And that's seven dollars in change," Shelly said, before smiling back at the elderly woman in front of her. "You have a nice day, ma'am." Shelly had just closed the cash drawer when a bright glint of sunlit chrome caught her attention.

She looked up and took a moment to admire the gleaming, cherry-red vintage pickup that had just rolled to a stop in front of the pumps. A stippled tingle ran from her neck to the small of her back when she saw Sebo step out, and then straighten beside the truck; a blend of shocked surprise and excitement that she hoped wouldn't show.

He had his eyes on her when he entered the store, but he didn't say anything at first. He just walked up to the two big plastic tubs of slushy ice sitting on floor stands in front of the register. Sebo stood for a moment as he stared down at the cans floating around in the ice.

"If you're looking for a cold one," Shelly said, "you've come to the right place."

Sebo gazed at her and smiled. "What if I'm in the mood for something hot?"

She flashed a knowing grin. "Yeah, sure," she answered, and with a gesture toward the back of the store, said, "coffee machine's just over there."

With that, Sebo let out a sigh. "Look... uh..."

Forty-Eight

He was on all the cable networks…

S he was lying across his chest when the music stopped. Sebo didn't want her to move, because he liked how her breasts felt against his skin. When she sat up, he watched her push the sheets out of the way. Then he watched her swing her bare legs down to the carpet. She stood and he kept watching her as she tiptoed over to her old-fashioned stereo, naked and moving as if she wasn't.

She bent over and gently lifted the needle, and then removed the vinyl LP from the turntable. She slipped it back into its cardboard sleeve and returned it to a shelf thick with dozens of albums. It was like a little dance, and he was digging it. Then she started thumbing through more LPs.

"You have a big music collection," Sebo said. "You get all those yourself?"

"No," she said, still fingering through the stacks. "Not all of them anyway; these were mostly my dad's."

He folded his arms behind his head, leaned back against her pillows, and her old-styled brass headboard, kept watching as she placed another record on her turntable, the pleasant haze from their last spliff floating through his head and coloring the air inside the small room. Sebo could hear muffled voices through the complex's thin walls, and the noise from a TV filtering in from the unit next door. "What are you playing this time?" Sebo asked.

"Herbie Hancock," she answered without looking at him. She delicately set the needle inside the vinyl disc's first groove. "This album's called, 'Empyrean Isles.'" The music started and she spun back to face him. "What do you think?"

"I missed you."

She flashed a little grin as the album's first track, "One Finger Snap," picked up tempo. "You wanna fuck?" she said.

"Again?" He chuckled. "You never get tired."

"Nope."

She stepped toward him before slipping back into bed as if the sheets were water, and she was swimming in them. She wriggled back up beside him, said, "You like jazz?"

"Is that what this is?"

She giggled. "Yeah... you like it?"

Sebo put his arm around her. "Sure, it's all right."

Then she got quiet, and he was just holding her. He was listening to the music when she said, "You worried about breaking parole?"

She pushed herself away, then up into a little-mermaid kind of position. She stared back at him. "We have a prior association—we're not allowed to be together."

"Wasn't really thinking about it," Sebo said. He watched the way her breasts moved when she reached up and pulled her hair back behind her ears.

"I'm pretty worried about it," she said.

"This your first time on paper?"

She nodded. "I had no idea how much it sucks, either—I can't even leave the county."

"Tell me about it."

"You don't even think about it at first, but the other day I wanted to go to the beach with some friends out on Siesta Key—"

"And Siesta's in Sarasota County." Sebo grinned. "There's all kind of ways to fuck with people."

"Yeah there is." She paused a moment. "Did you see LJ's trial on TruTV?"

Sebo just shook his head. "Nope, I didn't see any of it. I'd already cut my deal with the Secret Service; they fast-tracked me right through to sentencing. Feds were really pissed about it, too."

"I was a state's witness—the FBI put me on the stand to testify."

"You were on TV?" He smiled. "If I'd known that I would've watched it."

"Thanks, but, it wasn't like, CNN, or anything big like that, and I was so-stupid-nervous. I don't even remember seeing the cameras. I think I was up there for like, not even ten minutes. The FBI was a lot more interested in that biker guy Justin's testimony—he'd cut a deal too. He was on the stand for two whole days. I remember the prosecutor making a big deal out of LJ's Venezuela connection." She rolled around and then crossed her legs in front of her but kept talking as she did it. "That guy Meteo wasn't just running the car-theft ring with LJ; he was wanted by Interpol for human trafficking. He ended up getting 25 years."

"Martinez must've jizzed over that one," Sebo said.

"He really wanted me in jail too."

Sebo's face hardened. "Bullshit—what for?"

"Process crimes," she said. "Agent Martinez had the prosecutor spin me up; they wanted ten years hard time, but the judge gave me two years' probation instead."

"Martinez…" Sebo let out a groan. "Such a fucking prick. When the Feds took me down? I was compliant, man, I wasn't about to get in their face, but Martinez just *had* to punch me a few times."

"He made national news," Shelly said. "He was on CNN. He was on all the cable networks—kept calling LJ, 'a cold-blooded killer' and 'the *black* mafia boss of Bradenton, Florida.'"

With a smirk of disgust, Sebo said, "Is that right?"

"That's right," Shelly said. "I didn't think they were allowed to say stuff like that on TV anymore, but I guess they figured they needed the ratings." Letting out a long sigh, she looked up at Sebo. "I was really happy when I heard you didn't go back to jail."

He smiled at her. "I was glad you didn't either."

"Thanks," she said. "I was pretty scared." Her expression went blank for a moment, then she said, "Hey, uh, you know, for a while there, they were showing your mugshot on TV a lot."

"Tell me about it," Sebo said. "I still get media people sniffing around the shop. I let Pablo talk to 'em—I honestly think they don't know the difference."

She giggled. "Good idea…"

He watched her face change. "What?" he said, and she kinda shrugged.

"Well…" She tilted her head, scrunched up her shoulders some more. "What's it like? You know…"

"Mostly it's weird," he said. "I mean, I'm still just an ex-con, but now people treat me totally different, and I know it's all bullshit, so I just stick around the people I know."

"I heard they took a lot of your money back."

Sebo laughed. "Yeah, they did—fucking FBI tried to take all of it, but my lawyer fought 'em off."

"No shit? Who's your lawyer?"

"Joe Crest."

"The guy from the trunk?"

"That's him."

"He testified at LJ's trial," she said. "So, he's really that good, huh? It must've been fate, I mean, you meeting him like you did."

"Yeah, I guess, but he couldn't fight off everybody, you know? Between the IRS, the court judgment, the prison system suing me for restitution—my legal fees. Seems like everybody's been into my pocket. You know Crest charges $1200.00 bucks an hour?"

"No shit?"

"I wish I'd known that when I locked him in the trunk of LJ's Impala; I would've negotiated." She giggled, and Sebo shrugged. "I got no complaints; he turned out to be a really good lawyer—he's been helping me organize everything. I got the shop, it's paid for, and I still got about a third of the lottery money left—even if I can't leave the county for another year. It's all good."

She was still in the nude when he kissed her goodbye. He slipped his hands down her back, pulled her in close but she gently pushed him away. "We can't do this again," she said.

"It was worth it to me."

"Me too," she said. "But next time we get together? We both have to be clear of this shit." She looked up at him. "You promise?"

"Yeah…" he said. "I promise."

Forty-Nine

What you are asking will be expensive...

"What in the hell are you doing here?" Elaine said.

Bill stopped in his tracks and stared back at her. "That's the greeting I get?"

Elaine let out a huff as she looked back down at her paperwork. "I just thought you'd be on a cruise to the Bahamas or something." Shuffling through the papers on her desk, she said, "The last thing I'd be doing is hanging around this place."

Holding up a file folder, Bill said, "Came across some more stuff for Freddy—figured I'd better drop it off."

Glancing up from her desk again, Elaine said, "He's out on rounds."

Bill twisted toward Freddy's desk and dropped the file on top of it. Turning back to face her, he said, "You'll let him know I was here then, right?"

Without looking up, Elaine answered, "Yeah, sure."

A brief sigh escaped Bill as he lifted his hands to his waist. He studied her a moment more then he said, "Anything else I should know?"

She stared back up at him. "I just miss having you around, that's all."

"You got a funny way of showing it."

"Look," Elaine said, and pointing her pen at Bill. "This is a shitty job, in a shitty place, and not all of us got it as good as you do."

Bill stared back at her. "What happened?"

She let her hand drop back to the desk. "I received a call this morning from that snitch of yours."

"You mean, Trudy?"

"That's the one."

"What'd she say?"

Tapping the pen against the stack of reports on her desk, Elaine paused a moment, then, "She says she saw Sebo hanging around her complex the other night."

"And?"

"And, there's only one person Sebo knows who lives over there," said Elaine. "*And*, that person also happens to be on paper, *and*, she has a prior association with Sebo, *and*, if what Trudy says is true, then this girl is about to fuck up her life in a very serious way."

"And you don't want to tell Freddy about it."

Leaning forward on her elbows, Elaine rubbed at her face, and sighed out, "You know how he is."

"Are you asking for my help?"

Elaine stared back at Bill. "You know how I feel about Sebo, okay? Having money won't change a man like that—he will always be a hard-core banger. That guy doesn't deserve a single penny of what he has." She paused, took in a long breath, let it out before she said, "But, he did save your life."

* * *

"¿Estás seguro de esto, mi amor?" Lorette held her eyes on her husband as she leaned back against the sofa's plush cushions. "My brother is on death row because of him. What do you think?"

"We are to blame as well, or do you not remember that part?"

"It wasn't supposed to turn out like this—they promised."

"Who promised? The FBI? They lie as a normal course of doing their business. We knew there would be risk, but I still feel we made the right choice."

Lorette sat up straight, then pointed at her husband. "That man is out there walking around, living his life with millions of dollars, while my brother waits for death—Sebo has to pay for what he did."

"What you are asking will be expensive—"

"He's your uncle, isn't he?"

"In matters such as this," her husband replied, "there is no family discount."

Fifty

This is not good news…

"Are you sure that's my Bronco?" Bill asked. He stood on the floor of Sebo's custom rebuild shop next to Pablo, scratching at the back of his head while he stared at the fully stripped out, and naked steel chassis of his 1971, Ford four-by-four. The hunk of metal was resting atop of a rolling floor stand. Bill took a few steps closer and briefly looked it over before he asked, "Where's the rest of it?"

"Don't sweat it, Chief," said Pablo. "She looks pretty ugly right now, but wait until you see her painted up. We're gonna take her back to the original factory spec—Bahama Blue and Pure White. She'll look like she just rolled off the showroom floor; you're gonna love it."

"I don't doubt it," Bill said. "But where's the rest?"

With a chuckle, Pablo answered, "The seats are out at the upholsterer's shop, new carpet's on order. I got your 302V8 on a stand right over there…" Pablo pointed over at the engine sitting in a distant corner of the shop before he looked back at Bill. "What would really dress her up would be some alloy wheels, and a nice, fat set of BFG-all-terrains, what do you say?"

"I think I'll have to consult with my wife first."

"Sure thing, Chief."

Still looking around, Bill said, "So where's the boss?"

"He's out back blasting the paint off of that old Impala."

Across the shop's main floor, Bill walked past the perfectly polished, cherry-red '59 Chevy pickup, and then a faded Porsche Speedster in desperate need of attention. He banked left after the Speedster, and, as instructed, headed down a central hallway before he took an L-turn, also to the left. Next, Bill passed the doorway to Sebo's office, before exiting the building through a rear door on the right.

Bill pushed open the shop's rear door to bright sun and the sight of LJ's old ride. The confrontation was almost as shocking to him as his Bronco had been. The car was hardly recognizable. It was parked on a heavy tarpaulin with its wheels and tires covered. Every bit of glass had been removed, along with every piece of chrome, and the entirety of its interior accouterments. Bill wondered if that had included the contents of the glovebox.

The noise from an industrial-quality, dustless blaster filled the whole of the closely fenced-in lot. Bill observed for a few seconds as Sebo stood over the car's hood, making synchronized passes with a carefully aimed nozzle. The machine was pumping out a high-powered slurry of water and micro-abrasive media. The process steadily sheared away layers of old paint like blowing leaves off a driveway. Bill stepped closer and waved at the tall figure wearing coveralls, goggles, and a face mask.

Spotting Bill, Sebo shut off the machine, and Bill said, "Sorry to interrupt your work, but, we need to talk about you and your friend Shelly."

Inside the main garage, Pablo was back at work rebuilding the 302's carburetor when he caught sight of a pearl-white Escalade pulling into one of the parking slots out front. Straightening up from the work bench, Pablo squinted through the glare. The guy getting out of the shiny-new SUV was older, gray-haired, average height, and heavy-set. He was wearing thick glasses, dark loafers with white socks, a light button-down shirt untucked, and tan Bermuda shorts. The guy looked like a standard customer, and just like a million other, well-off retirees who populated the Suncoast.

"What can I do for you?" Pablo said as the man strolled into the garage. The old man stopped a few feet away; didn't say anything, until Pablo heard him let out a brief groan, kind of quiet and to himself. A few more seconds of silence passed before he and Pablo's eyes met, and the old man finally said, "¿de donde eres?"

"I was born in Miami," Pablo said, but recognizing the man's accent he added, "Pero, mi familia vino de La Habana."

"This is not good news," the old man grumbled, and Pablo could now hear him cursing rapidly in Spanish.

"What the fuck's your problem?" Pablo said. "You got Alzheimer's, or something? You want to talk business, or what? I got work to do." Then Pablo saw the revolver. It had appeared so easily, and it was so small that the old man's thick hand nearly hid it from view. A nothing kind of gun—cheap. From the pen-sized barrel, Pablo knew it had to be target caliber—a .22 perhaps. That the tiny revolver could be a danger to him didn't even register. Pablo snorted in the guy's face. "You're driving a Cadillac old man—what the fuck kind of joke is this?"

"Me disculpo," the old man said. "I am the Iceman— the wet guy. Nothing personal, it's just my job."

Fifty-One

What details can you give me?

"Elaine did you a huge favor, Sebo, and she certainly didn't need to; she could've turned Freddy loose on you both. You know that, right?"

Nodding his agreement, Sebo said, "I really appreciate you telling me like this, Bill. It won't happen again."

"The only reason I'm still standing here, and even speaking with you right now is because I believe that you're being honest with me." Bill took in a breath, sighed it out. "If we're clear, then there's just one more thing I need from you."

"Name it."

"I need you to prove that I just did the right thing."

Before Sebo could say anything further, Bill held up his hand. "Did you just hear that?"

Sebo listened a moment. "I got nothing—what was it?"

Heading for the rear door of the building, Bill said, "I hope it was nothing."

* * *

251

The old hitman took a step back, and then another look around the deserted shop. After a further brief scan of the walls and corners, he was satisfied the place was devoid of security cameras, so he leaned over Pablo's body and popped two more rounds into his skull; the tiny, small-caliber pistol's report hardly rising to the level of a kid's toy. The old man smiled at the sensation it gave him—he liked his work. He could see his victim's blood spreading out in a slowly expanding halo around Pablo's head and across the shop's floor, and he knew the job was done. "Mírate, hombre muerto," he said. "Y fue un anciano quien te derribó."

He stuffed the small pistol back into his front pocket and returned to his car.

The Cadillac's interior was soaked in late-day heat, and the heavy, chemical smell that only a new car has. He turned over the engine and the AC came on strong. The old hitman leaned back against the leather as he plucked a perfectly starched and monogrammed handkerchief from his front shirt pocket. He mopped his dripping brow, and along with his own sweat, the pristine cloth absorbed a stray droplet of Pablo's blood. Glancing at the bloodstain, the fancy handkerchief was then unceremoniously tossed to the floor as he used the car's voice control to make a call.

Reversing out from the parking slot, the old man then drove off like nothing had happened. It was Lorrett's voice on the other end of the call. "It's all done," the old man said. "Do you hear me?"

"Yes."

"Good, don't say anything else."

* * *

With the shop's twin garage bays opened wide to full sun, the dark outline of Pablo's body could've been anything—until it wasn't. Sebo pushed past Bill. "You don't know who's out there," Bill called out. He hung back in the hallway and watched Sebo sprint toward the crumpled figure on the floor. Bill hesitated for one, perhaps two seconds. "Ah fuck it," he said, before he ran to catch up.

Sebo was already kneeling beside Pablo's body by the time Bill reached him, but Bill's eyes were already elsewhere, searching the parking lot beyond the twin garage bays. Bill caught the glint of perfect, pearl paint. "You know anybody with a brand new Cadillac Escalade?" Bill said.

Sebo glanced up—*angry*. "What?" He shouted. "Fuck you, Bill—Pablo's dead, man!"

Striding outside for a better look just as the Escalade entered the street in front of him and drove off, Bill was already reaching for his phone.

"You calling 911?" Sebo shouted. "Get an ambulance!"

"I'd rather get Pablo's killer," Bill said, and with his phone up to his ear, he waited.

A half-mile away, in a green and white, cruising the east side of town, the personal phone of a young, Manatee County Sheriff's deputy buzzed inside his shirt pocket. He slipped it out and glanced at the screen before pulling over.

"Officer Mazurek, how in the hell have you been?"

"Retired," Bill said. "But something serious just happened—I need your help."

"How serious?"

"Homicide."

"What details can you give me?"

"Location, perp's vehicle description, and a partial plate."

"That's a good start—feed it to me fast, please sir."

Fifty-Two

Just some geezer picking up his Metamucil…

L ate afternoon sunlight shimmered across the Gulf of Mexico and bathed the upper veranda of a cypress-clad, Longboat Key beach house. The intense light formed a golden glow around Lorette's body as she moved in her sheer cabana dress. From inside the home, her husband Raúl watched from the sofa. He was enjoying the view—all of it. "Come sit, my love," he said. "He's a professional—you have nothing to worry about." She turned toward him just as the shiny gold iPhone clutched inside her hand began to purr. Lifting the phone, she stared at the screen, smiled. She put the phone to her ear.

Her husband didn't move from the sofa; he was still admiring the outline of her body framed against the light. "Yes," he heard her say. She lowered the phone and stared at Raúl. "Is that it?"

"That's it," her husband said, and pushing himself upright from the sofa. "You won't hear another word from him—ever."

"What about the payoff?"

"I will handle it; you'll do nothing." He stood and then strolled across polished marble to a glass-topped dining table, and to a brown paper bag sitting rolled at the top. "I know my uncle," he said, and opening the bag, "he will want to pick up the money from me personally." Raúl glanced back at her and read her face. "No, my love, he won't be coming here. He'll want to pick up the cash at some gas station, or a payphone."

"A payphone?" She said with a smirk.

He chuckled softly. "Yes, well, the man is over seventy years old." Raúl peeked into the bag. "Twenty thousand dollars in crisp twenties," he said. "Exactly what he asked for."

Lorette moved in to stand beside Raúl. "Won't he know it's counterfeit?"

Raúl shrugged and then closed the bag. "No. This stuff's too good—he's half blind anyway. Besides, it'll be gone almost as soon as he gets his hands on it. He'll take a high-roller suite at the Hard-Rock, live large for a couple of days, blow it all on hookers and the horses."

A ringtone by Rihanna began to play. Raúl reached into his pocket, answered his phone, and said, "Sí, tío, te escucho."

* * *

From the rear seat of a county patrol unit, Sebo winced at the cuffs chaffing his wrists. He'd been crammed inside the back of the cruiser with his hands clamped tight behind him for the past half an hour. Through the closed window, he watched as Bill stood about twenty feet away, and in the midst of an intense meeting with two uniforms and one cop in plain clothes. The officers conversed with Bill for another few minutes before one of the uniforms finally turned toward the cruiser.

He opened the door and pulled Sebo out of the car. "Officer Mazurek just vouched for you." He removed the cuffs before spinning Sebo back around to face him. "It's provisional, of course."

Under the fog of his shock, and his disbelief, Sebo rubbed at his aching wrists as he stood near the police car and stared back at Pablo's body. By now It'd been covered over with a sheet of yellow plastic, but Sebo could just make out Pablo's left hand, and the edge of the pool of blood that had formed around it. The parking lot of his shop was now jammed with three county patrol units, two unmarked vehicles, a fire truck, and an ambulance. All of them lit up, and the traffic out front at a standstill because of it. Then he saw Bill.

"You all right?" Bill said, and all Sebo could do in response was to croak out something indistinguishable. "I understand," Bill said. "Hey, uh, look… they've got an APB out for the Escalade; whoever did this can't be far. I expect they'll be making an arrest pretty quick."

* * *

With two freshly made, Publix deli-subs in hand, one beef meatball, the other Mojo roasted pork, Officer Mark Hall, of the Longboat Key PD, married, saltwater fly-fishing nut, three kids, oldest in eighth grade, strode across the lavishly landscaped parking lot of the Bay Isles Shopping Plaza; an upscale retail development located just off Gulf of Mexico Drive, and about midway up the Key from New Pass, and the bridge to Saint Armand's. Along his path, officer Hall passed by two Mercedes, a Porsche GT, a handful of Cadillacs, a couple of BMWs, and one Bentley, before he reached for the passenger-side door-handle of his standard, blue and white patrol unit.

Officer Hall folded himself into the car's front seat, handing the bag with the two subs over to his partner who sat behind the wheel. The entire operation taking place with one smooth motion. "Nice and hot," Hall said.

"Fuck yeah," answered his partner. "My wife's been on this gluten-free, vegan kick lately—says she's trying to detoxify my system." He unwrapped his meatball sub, took in its warm, spicy aroma. "I've never felt so starved in my entire life."

The two blue uniforms were just finishing their subs when Hall noticed a pearl-white Escalade swing in from off the main drag. Gulping down the last bite of his Mojo-pork, Hall garbled between his chewing, "Any updates on that APB?"

"You mean the homicide?" Hall's partner answered. He was busy looking down at his chest and rubbing at the tomato sauce stain on the front of his uniform with a paper napkin. Without looking up, he said, "Far as I know, it's still active."

Officer Hall crumpled up the sub's paper wrapper and stuffed it back into the plastic bag. "We should check it out then," he said.

A few clicks on the notebook computer attached to the dash, and Hall came up with the police report and the partial plate: "Echo-niner-five," he called out, as his partner squinted through a pair of binoculars, and Hall said, "Can you see it?"

"Yeah… kinda… Oh, wait." He chuckled, lowered his binoculars, and then passed them over to Hall. "Here, check this out." Hall took the lenses and then focused them on the Escalade. The high-dollar SUV had taken a slot nose-in. It was parked on the far side of the lot and beneath the shade of a large Banyan tree.

Framed inside the binoculars, Officer Hall observed as a pudgy, older guy wearing an untucked short-sleeved button down, Bermuda shorts, and loafers with white socks, turned to close his driver's side door and then stand beside his Cadillac. "I see what you mean," answered Hall. "Just some geezer picking up his Metamucil."

Hall was about to put the spy-glasses away when a dark gray Audi sedan slipped in beside the Escalade. Officer Hall kept looking instead, and observed as a younger guy—late thirties, sharply dressed, slim, short dark hair—straightened into view from the driver's side of the Audi. The man then moved around to the rear of his car holding a rolled-up, brown paper sack in his left hand. Officer Mark Hall saw him briefly shake hands with the geezer in the loafers. "Something's up." Hall said. "I'm going over there and talk to this guy."

"You think I should call it in?" His partner responded.

Hall popped open his door, and then stepped outside of the cruiser. "Yeah, go ahead," he answered. "I'm sure it's nothing, but better cover our bases." Hall then glanced back just before he closed the door. "Keep an eye out, will ya?"

"Sure thing."

Fifty-Three

Step away from the bag…

"What the hell happened?" Elaine said. She held her phone to her ear as she stood up straight beside her desk. Freddy listening in nearby; both peace officers had been getting ready to pack it in for the day when Bill's call came in from the garage.

"They're still looking for the Cadillac," Bill said. "All I'm saying is, just keep an eye out, because whoever did this is a real pro."

After ending the call, Bill slipped his phone back into his pocket before he felt himself forced to look again at what was in front of him. By this time the crime scene had been fully surveyed. It'd been photographed from a dozen different angles, and the scant amount of evidence it yielded had been collected and catalogued. Pablo's body was on its way to the county morgue, and what Bill was watching was a group of three firemen armed with high-pressure hoses hurriedly washing down the floor of the garage. They were using a heavy amount of chlorine bleach, and the smell was strong. In hazmat coveralls, they formed a tightening circle around a foaming slurry of oxidized human blood and disinfecting chemical agent; swiftly herding the rapidly shrinking puddle of stained liquid into a large drain at the center of the garage floor. Sebo was watching too.

"You should go home," Bill said. He watched Sebo shrug in response before the guy pointed at the cinderblock building that housed his custom car garage. "I am home," Sebo answered. "You're looking at it."

* * *

"What's in the bag?"

Raúl smiled politely in response to the police officer's question, but he didn't say anything. He'd already handed the sack of counterfeit cash over to his uncle by the time they'd each noticed the uniformed cop approaching. He and his uncle were now standing side by side and in between the Audi and the Cadillac. As far as Raúl was concerned, the bag no longer belonged to him; his uncle being his elder, he felt he no longer held a place in the proceeding conversation.

Since Officer Mark Hall wasn't getting an answer out of the younger guy, Hall next turned to the old man. "You mind showing me what's in the bag, sir?"

"Sí señor," the man said softly.

Hall was waiting for old Mr. Loafers and white socks to open up the bag, or better yet, to hand it over. Instead, Hall watched as the old man turned and handed the bag back to the younger guy. Officer Hall heard the old man mutter something in Spanish. "What's going on?" Hall said, and with one hand now resting on his ready sidearm. "Hand over the bag, sir."

Raúl set the bag down on the hood of his Audi A8 and then lifted both of his hands. "Please sir," Raúl said. "My uncle doesn't speak English well, he doesn't mean you any harm. He just didn't understand you."

"Step away from the bag," Hall ordered, and now he was standing in-between the two men, his sidearm was in his hand, and he was pointing it directly at Raúl.

"Yes, of course, officer," Responded Raúl. And still with his hands in the air, his open palms facing the city cop, he took two generous steps away from the bag. Raúl's back was now up against the driver's side of his uncle's Escalade, just ahead of the front wheel well and near the front bumper. He watched as the blue uniform stepped over to the rumpled paper bag sitting on the hood of his Audi.

Officer Mark Hall, 38, father of three, still held his fully loaded Glock in his right hand when he opened up the paper bag with his left and looked inside.

From the left side of Raúl's line of sight, he caught sudden movement from his uncle—the old man jerking a small revolver from the front pocket of his Bermuda shorts. Raúl then looked on, as his uncle, the legendary *Iceman*, lunged forward with the dexterity of a man half his age, stepping up behind the distracted officer as if the man wasn't an armed cop at all, but some schmuck on the street who deserved it, and just like that—popped off two quick caps into the base of the cop's skull.

Officer Mark Hall's partner had just finished busily rubbing, once again, at the tomato stain on the front of his uniform when he looked up to see that both of the vehicles—the Escalade and the Audi sedan—were gone.

* * *

Funny Money

Raúl sat in the driver's seat of his Audi A8, while, in his rear-view mirror, he watched two automated garage doors roll down behind him. He took in a deep breath and then let it out slowly before he finally opened his door and stepped out from his car. His uncle's Escalade now parked in the space next to his Audi, and with the old man already standing outside of his SUV; holding on to a battered canvas duffle bag with one hand, while he gripped the paper bag filled with $20,000 dollars' worth of counterfeit cash in the other.

Raúl noticed his uncle had a much more youthful-looking face that told him the guy was still juicing off of his latest kill. The two men now stood facing each other in a four-car garage that filled the ground-level footprint of the beach house. A space that held two more vehicles: Lorrette's Mercedes convertible, and his Porsche 911.

"I'll take the Porsche," his uncle said, but Raúl shook his head, and instead, tried to hand him the keys to the silver, E-Class. "It's an automatic," said Raúl. "Not as flashy, and easier to drive."

Waving a liver-spotted hand as if in disgust, the old man said, "I would rather take the Porsche."

"You'll take the Mercedes." Raúl reached out and grabbed ahold of his uncle's hand. He stuffed the keys to the E-Class inside it, and then said, "I'll take care of your Cadillac."

"But…" Raúl saw his uncle's face change, older again, and more pleading. "It's brand new," his uncle said.

"You should have thought of that before you used it for a job." Raúl felt a bit guilty at killing his uncle's buzz. "Lo siento," he said.

"I'm sorry too," the old man replied. "And I'm sorry you had me kill one of our own; it's not right to do such things..."

The old hitman's nephew's face froze, and with a hard stare back at his uncle, Raúl said, "What the hell are you babbling about, old man?"

Fifty-Four

Target lives at the back of the shop...

"I'm going inside for a beer—you want one?" Sebo said. Bill thought about it for a moment, then said, "Yeah, sure, I could use one." Inside a windowless room located in the back of the custom car shop, Sebo had the fridge open. Not a normal fridge either, Bill noticed, but one of those extra wide, high-end gourmet models.

"Can or bottle?"

"I'll take a bottle, please," Bill answered. He had his back to Sebo and was looking around, standing in the center of the auto shop's back room—small being the main thought that came to mind. A doorway off one side led to a closet-sized bathroom, while, above Bill's head, he noticed the place was lit only by a single, overhead florescent light.

Bill puzzled over the four blank block walls before he took a seat on a black leather fold-out couch. He noticed a side table stacked with car magazines. There was a sink, and a microwave that sat on a countertop next to a toaster oven. At the sound of Sebo opening a bottle, Bill turned to look, and with his cold beer in hand, Bill thanked him—still eyeing the guy's homemade prison cell, Bill said, "You live here all the time?"

"Yeah," Sebo said, as he cracked open a tallboy. Bill took a swig from his bottle of beer, and then looked on as Sebo drained the oversized can dry in what appeared to him like one swallow. "Why?" Bill asked, and without missing a beat, "I mean…" Sebo crushed the empty can inside his fist and tossed it into the trash beside the sink. "You mean, why live like this?"

"It does strike me as odd," Bill said. "Why not buy a real house? You can certainly afford one, right?"

"Sure," Sebo answered. "But, I guess I just want to keep things simple."

* * *

Four blocks away, the old Iceman sat behind the wheel of Lorrette's E-Class and waited for the light to change at the intersection of 53rd Avenue and 9th Street East. It was nearing dusk by now, almost dark. He was still raging over the fact that he'd killed the wrong man—the embarrassment of it. The shame he'd brought upon himself, and in the eyes of his favorite nephew of all people—he had never made a mistake before. Not in forty years' worth of professional hits—never once had he failed on a contract.

The light changed, and the Iceman took a left. He knew the shop was three blocks down on the right; he'd memorized the location the week before the job. He'd mapped out the surrounding buildings, the immediate escape routes, and all of the adjacent streets, days ahead of the hit. He knew the next turn would be a side street that ran past the shop's rear gate, and he knew the gate would be padlocked.

Raúl had passed on specific details about the target; big guy, fit, close cropped hair, scruffy beard, muscled, no visible tattoos, but only one particular fact stood out to the Iceman at this very moment; target lives at the back of the shop…

* * *

Bill finished off the last of his beer. He'd been doing a lot of listening for the several minutes that he and Sebo had been alone together, which was mostly how he'd made his living for the previous thirty years. He'd figured out early on in his career that everybody, always, *wanted* to talk. The trick was not getting in the way of that natural impulse. People were more apt to speak freely in relaxed situations where they didn't feel threatened—like over a beer. Bill's phone began buzzing in his pocket. He set his empty bottle down on the counter. "I have a call coming in," Bill said, and pulling out his phone. "Mind if I take this?"

"Reception's better out in the garage," Said Sebo.

Sebo'd been honest about that part too. Bill wasn't able to hear the young deputy's voice clearly until he reached the center of the garage.

"Evening, Officer Mazurek. You have any information for us yet?"

"I do," Bill said. "But it's not what you think. How close are you?"

"I'm three minutes away. You're not getting anything from this guy then, huh?"

"I've been getting a lot of information from him, but none of it heads in the direction that you guys want it to go."

"It needs to go somewhere," the deputy responded. "Because just about an hour ago, this thing got a hell of a lot more serious."

"How's that?" Bill said.

"There's been a second homicide," answered the deputy. "A Longboat Key police officer took two shots to the back of the head—same .22 caliber rounds, same Cadillac Escalade. It took place in the parking lot of the Bay of Isles Shopping Center."

"Longboat Key?" Bill questioned. "Why on earth would the perp be way out there?"

"We suspect he was picking up his payment. The officer's partner was nearby; he didn't see it happen, but here's the important part; we have a description of the shooter."

Fifty-Five

He picked up an odd sort of hissing sound…

The trunk lid of the Mercedes E-Class convertible rose softly at the touch of a button. The Iceman reached inside and unzipped the battered, canvas duffle bag that sat next to his brown paper sack full of cash. The duffle contained two more .22 caliber revolvers with filed numbers, an extra box of ammunition, lock picking tools, a black-box code grabber for getting past security systems, and a set of bolt-cutters.

As much as he abhorred having to resort to manual labor, at least the chain with the padlock attached cut like butter; the old man hardly needed to exert much effort in the process. As the chain fell away, he grinned at the ease of it… *mierda barata…*

* * *

"I'm still not convinced," Bill said into his phone. "But Pablo did have a few old enemies—small-time thugs, mostly…"

"Mostly, but not all, is that right?" The deputy clarified.

"Correct," Bill confirmed. "But none of those leftovers would be driving an Escalade, and they aren't in a league to be doing business out on Longboat Key. Knowing what I know

now, LJ would be my number one suspect at this point, but we all know his alibi."

The young deputy said, "Look, I'm coming up on your location right now. How about I stop by and the three of us sit down and talk about this some more."

"Absolutely," Bill said. "We'll both be right here. Sebo keeps a place at the back of the shop; I'll have him unlock the rear gate for you."

Ending the call, Bill stuffed his phone back into his pocket. It was at this moment he realized that, while he'd been speaking with the deputy, he'd inadvertently walked to the center of the garage for a better signal. He glanced down briefly at his Clarks; the tips of which were next to the drain in the floor. Bill stared down at polished concrete that bore no trace of what had taken place there only hours before, and it gave him a chill like nothing else ever had.

* * *

As he swung onto the side street that ran past the shop's rear perimeter fence, the headlights of the deputy's cruiser illuminated the eight-foot-high chain link now off to his left. On the right, and from his angle, he could just make out the sparse block outline of a marine engine repair. At the end of the street, a single sodium vapor burned atop a utility pole. No trees. No sidewalks. No residential houses. Just two weed-choked strips of sandy ground located on either side of a narrow, nothing of a street, in an industrial zone on the east side of town. The Mercedes stood out.

The young Sheriff's deputy eased his patrol car to a stop only a few feet off the rear bumper of the fancy convertible. His

headlamps shined bright against the German import's silver metallic finish, the pure white light reflecting off of the parked car's
tail lamps, and its Mote Marine Lab vanity plate decorated with
a coral reef motif. He called in the plate and it came back
clean—no unpaid tickets or outstanding warrants. The car's reg-
istration popped up a big red flag though, even if the flag didn't
come so much from the database, as from the deputy's own
gut... *Longboat Key*...

* * *

Bill turned back to where he'd left Sebo, walking past the
bare-naked shell of his Bronco, then the cherry-red pickup, and
the sad little Porsche, but it was a noise that caught his attention. Bill was halfway down the hallway when he'd heard it. The
noise being a sort of *snap!* Not so much loud, as it was crisp, and
sharp... Bill had only covered another step or two of the hallway
before he heard the noise again, and this time it was clear to him
what it was, because he'd heard a similar sound earlier that
day—when somebody shot Pablo.

* * *

The rear gate had been left open just as Bill had said it
would be, but something wasn't right. Reaching down, the
young Sheriff's deputy lifted up the chain that hung from the
half-opened gate. He shined his flashlight against it, and on a
dangling link at one end that he could clearly see had been
freshly cut. A fully closed padlock was still attached to the opposite end. The deputy drew his sidearm and then pushed his way
through the opening.

He was striding toward the shop's rear door when the deputy heard what sounded like a muffled crash—the sound

stopped him in his tracks. Reaching for his radio, the deputy called for backup.

* * *

Bill, motionless inside the narrow hallway; his heart pounding up inside his throat and sweat forming over his brow, forced in a shallow breath as he stood and waited—unsure. The thought of his wife flashed through his head, and the thought of turning back did too. It was the sound of a thunderous crash that finally moved him forward.

Bill covered the last few feet of the narrow hallway until he reached the spot where it took a corner bend to the left. He sucked down another nervous breath, and then risked a peek. Bill caught a quick glimpse of Sebo's open doorway, and farther down on the opposite side, the second door that led outside to the shop's rear lot. Bill knew the armed Sheriff's deputy had to be close by. He was reaching for his phone to find out just how close, when he picked up an odd sort of hissing sound, along with what seemed like someone groaning.

"Bill? You out there, man?"

"Yeah," Bill called back. The sound of Sebo's voice startled him into breathing again. "Are you okay?"

"I think so," said Sebo, "You got the cops coming, right?"

"Yes, I do."

Bill stepped into the doorway and looked down. What he saw was an old man lying crushed beneath Sebo's giant side-by-side refrigerator. The huge appliance had landed facing away from the door. A dozen hissing tallboy cans of beer, and a dozen more brown bottles lay scattered across the floor as a result. The split cans, and busted bottles, forming a foamy puddle.

The whitish froth expanded across the floor and mingled with the dying old man's own blood.

Bill's phone began to buzz inside his pocket, and near enough to that same time, someone started shouting from outside, and pounding on the shop's rear door: "Open up! Police!"

Fifty-Six

Your wife must be happy about your accomplishment…

The young Sheriff's deputy stepped down hard on the old man's right wrist as if he were pinning down a venomous snake. He slipped an evidence bag over the .22 caliber revolver still clutched inside the guy's hand, and carefully took it away— the gun's hammer had been cocked.

Bill was looking at Sebo. "Your arm's bleeding," he said, and patting his own right shoulder. "Take it from me, that's gonna start hurting like hell in a few minutes. You better get it looked at."

It was late by the time Bill pulled into his own driveway with his wife's Prius. She'd been waiting up for him, but she wasn't angry; she was just glad to finally have him home.

A week later Elaine was watching from her desk as Bill walked past with yet another brown, cardboard file box in his arms. "Is that the last of it?" she said. "Didn't anyone ever tell you to leave work at the office?"

Bill set the box down in a corner of the room and next to several others. He straightened, stretched out his sore back, and then turned to face her. "No," he said, catching a breath. "Not really, but I wish somebody had." He thumbed back over his shoulder at the stacks of deactivated files. "There was thirty years' worth of crap piled up in my garage—took a lot of nagging, but I finally got it cleaned out."

"Your wife must be happy about your accomplishment."

"She wants to sell and have us move to a condo next to a golf course."

"You know how fucking *white* that is?" Elaine said. "I thought I taught you better than that."

"What about Tiger Woods?" Bill responded, and Elaine rolled her eyes. She pointed at him. "It was all those white girls who messed up that man's life—you do not want me going down that road." Instead, she spun her laptop to face Bill. "You see this one yet?"

Bill eyed *The Drudge Report* headline, and an accompanying photo splashed across the screen: *"Infamous Cuban Hit Man Permanently On Ice."* Bill bent down for a better look. "Yep," he said. "That's the guy, but he was a lot younger when that picture was taken."

"That's it?" Elaine said. "You helped to blow open one of the biggest cases in county history—one that took down a Cuban mafia boss, of all people, and all you got to say about it is—*'Yep?'* She let out a huff. "You should have more to say then that—you should be proud."

Bill was still looking at the screen. "From my perspective it was more like plain old bad luck—being in the wrong place at the wrong time."

Elaine flashed a smile, and then she added, "Did you know that the Sheriff's department recovered $20,000 dollars' worth of counterfeit twenty-dollar bills from the trunk of Lorette's

Mercedes convertible?" Bill did know, he'd heard this one a few times over already, but he let Elaine say it again anyway, because he knew how much joy it brought her.

"LJ and his print shop—I always knew that little Italian prick was back at it."

Bill spun around, waved, "Hey Freddy, when did you get here?"

"Just now," Freddy answered, and stepping over to eye Elaine's laptop screen, he said, "I'll never get tired of looking at that, I already took a screen shot and saved it." Freddy looked back at Bill. "I'm putting together a collection for my Facebook page."

"Must be some women out there who go for that sort of thing," Bill said.

"You bet there are," Freddy answered. "They like holding my badge."

"Shut the fuck up," Elaine said. "Unless you have anything at all to say that is even remotely interesting—just shut. The fuck. Up."

"Okay," Freddy responded. "How's this? I know Lanzano's out of prison—can you believe that shit?"

"Where'd you hear that?" Bill said.

"Probably from his love interest at the Secret Service," Elaine answered.

"Margit's just a friend," Freddy snapped back.

Elaine, titling her head at him, "Uh huh… whatever you say—*fanboy*."

Fifty-Seven

First full day of freedom…

S ebo stretched his arm out as far as he could reach and then tipped his iPhone forward for a better view. "How about now?" he said. "Does it look okay? What do you think?"

Alfi's voice came back loud and clear over FaceTime. "Yes," he said. "I think the black t-shirt was a nice choice, and the sport jacket is a good fit." Sebo wriggled some more inside the blazer, and Alfi chuckled, he said, "Women always enjoy seeing a man who is dressed well, but you must take control of what you wear, it has to be a part of you, and this is the secret— this is what they will find attractive."

"Whatever you say, man." Sebo drew the phone in closer to his face. "When are you coming back down here anyway?"

"Soon, I hope," Alfi said. "Work's been crazy."

Sebo caught the motion as a young woman's face entered the screen; she had long dark hair and a bright smile. "Hi Sebo," she said.

"Hey Angie."

She waved back before slipping her slender arms around her lover's neck. "Alfi's gotta go now."

Alfi only smiled…

Outside, in the front parking lot of his shop, Sebo sunk down into the open cockpit of a now fully restored, 1957 Porsche Type 2 Speedster. He turned the key and the car's four-cam, Carrera engine rumbled to life. It was only a ten-minute drive from his shop over to her apartment.

"I like what you're wearing," Shelly said, the girl giggling with glee as she popped open the little Porsche's passenger side door. She lowered herself down into the leather seat, and in the process, offered Sebo a full view of her short little dress and strappy heels. She leaned over and kissed him. "I'm starved," Shelly said. "Where do you wanna eat?"

"It's your first full day of freedom, Babe," Sebo said. "So, I got something special planned." Shifting the Porsche into first, he glanced her way. "It's this place out by the beach called 'Euphemia Haye.'"

Shelly gasped. "No shit? You're kidding me, right? You know how expensive that place is?"

"It's a big night," said Sebo. He steered the vintage roadster back out onto the street. "I got something to show you first, though."

From the east side of Bradenton, Sebo took the modern, six-lane, new Highway 301 south toward University Parkway. The air was thick and warm and he never thought it would be possible to feel this good: driving south across Manatee County, in a car like this, and with everything around him bathed in a golden evening light, and the wind rushing in as it twisted around her blond hair. Then she realized where they were. "You ready?" Sebo shouted above the roar of the Speedster, and just as the car crossed the county line into Sarasota, Shelly screamed out at the top of her lungs—"Oh my god! I can't believe this!"

Twenty minutes later they were cruising past the glittering shops and eateries of St. Armand's Circle, but to Shelly it might as well have been Paris, or any of a thousand other exotic places she dreamed of seeing.

The Speedster crossed over the bridge at New Pass, and then onto Longboat Key. Only a few minutes later and Sebo was steering the vintage Porsche through a wrought iron gate, and then down a driveway paved in antique brick. "Where are we going?" Shelly said. "This looks like somebody's house."

They pulled up in front of a four-car garage—the first level of a two-story beach house. Sebo shut down the car and then he looked at her. "Here we are."

Shelly giggled, then she caught herself. "Wait... What did you do?"

He opened his door and climbed out from the Speedster. Shelly was still sitting in the car, still looking around, hesitant... "You gonna just sit there?" Said Sebo. "Or you want to come take a look at my new place?"

"What?" Shelly burst into shrieking laughter as she stood up inside the convertible. She then vaulted out from the car and proceeded to stick a perfect landing without even bothering to open her door.

Sebo was already at the top of the stairs and fumbling with the keys. He shouted down to her, "You coming?"

Inside, he thought for sure she would want to see the whole house, but Shelly bypassed it all—the designer-decorated living room, the modern kitchen, the baths and bedrooms, none of it appealed to her like the view. He stood back and watched as she strolled out onto the upper veranda. "You like it?" He said.

She gazed out at the powder-white beach below, and the gulf at sunset. "I can't believe this is real," Shelly gasped. "You actually bought this place? It had to have cost a fortune."

"I got it at auction a couple of months ago," Sebo said, as he strolled out to join her. "My attorney recommended it, so it's like an investment—right?" He slipped his arms around her waist and pulled her in close. "After two years of living inside a garage, I figured it was time to have a real home." Shelly reached for his neck, wrapping her arms around him, she squeezed tight before she relaxed again, and now he could feel her little fingers playing with the back of his hair, and the movement of her body as she giggled softly.

"Isn't that sweet?"

Shelly looked first. She opened her mouth but nothing came out. She could only stare at the stranger standing near the sofa—clean cut, slim, average build, dark suit, dark hair. Sebo was looking too. "Who the hell are you?"

The guy held his thin smile and said nothing.

"What the fuck?" Sebo said. He left Shelly standing on the veranda and took a couple of steps toward the guy. "This is my house." Sebo barked. "You can't just come in here."

The guy unbuttoned his jacket, showed the gun. Sebo stopped cold. "What do you want?" he said, gesturing toward the interior of the house. "You want any of this stuff, man? Just take it."

"I am here to take something," the stranger said. "But it's not your stuff." He drew his weapon—a personal favorite: a Walther P22, mounted with a suppressor, and loaded with hollow point, *stinger* rounds. A weapon most would consider to be something of a joke—a cheap target pistol. But he knew better, because he'd learned from the best...

He waved the slender gun in Shelly's direction. "Go sit on the couch." She took a few tentative steps but kept her eyes on Sebo.

"It's okay," the stranger assured her, his gentle voice dropping to a near whisper as he spoke. "I have no argument with you, pretty girl—go sit, please." Sebo nodded to her, and so she left the veranda. Sebo held his eyes on her as Shelly stepped from the honed cypress onto the interior marble floor, and then onto the rug near the sofa. Sebo never heard the gun go off.

Drawing back his freshly discharged weapon, the hitman glanced down only briefly at the girl's crumpled little body. There was hardly any blood at all, and he was pleased with the hit—a single round to the back of the girl's head as she walked past him. It was smooth, and quick, and *quiet*... He was still feeling the pure pleasure of it—like a perfect *amuse-bouche*... He turned to see the reaction from his main target of the evening, and the expression on the man's face was classic—a moment he never grew tired of seeing, because it was always so real, *so authentic*...

Sebo was still standing and staring, his eyes fixed on Shelly. Only a single second before she'd been looking right at him, and a second later she simply folded onto the rug beneath her without uttering a single sound. She had fallen slightly onto her right side, and her blond hair now covered her face; he couldn't move. He couldn't speak. He could only look at her.

"Do you know whose house this is?"

Sebo heard the guy say something, but he was too stunned to comprehend the words. "What?" He said.

"Do you *know* whose house this is?"

"I… I don't know what you mean?"

"You bought this house at an auction that took place sixty-two days ago."

Sebo nodded.

"I was there; I was watching you. I've been watching you for a long time, and you're boring as all hell—you know that? What the fuck's wrong with you anyway? You won so many millions of dollars—so what if you were on paper? You could've been out chasing pussy, you could've been doing a lot of things—why on earth would you live in that crappy garage?"

"I don't know…"

"I can tell you—it's because winning the lottery is the shittiest way possible to get rich, that's why. A machine picked some numbers, and they happened to be the same one's printed on a little paper in your hand—everybody knows who you are, and everybody knows that nobody ever deserves money like that— it's poison. That's why it ruins your life."

Inside the blur of his shock, Sebo caught a shadowed movement just before the cold sensation of hard metal pressed into the side of his head, and the soft voice of the dark stranger whispered into his ear.

"My father didn't deserve to die the way that he did…"

* * *

Satisfied with his work, the young hitman removed the silencer from his pistol and then slipped it into his inside jacket pocket. He wiped down his weapon and then placed the pistol inside Sebo's lifeless left hand. He was careful to close the house back up before he left. Locking the upper French doors of the veranda from the outside, he took the stairs down to the beach, and then walked back around to the front through the landscaping.

Then he noticed the car... *Por la gracia de Dios...*

The beautiful Speedster's engine turned over smoothly. He shifted the Porsche into gear and drove away.

Epilogue

Do the right thing...

"Can you get the door, honey?" Bill's wife had just stepped from the shower, hardly wrapped in a towel when she heard another knock on their condo's front door. "Bill?" she called out. "Are you getting the door?"

"I got it," Bill answered back. He glanced again at the half-cleaned, fresh grouper lying in his kitchen sink. He quickly rinsed the fish scales from his hands and called back to his wife. "On my way." Wiping his hands with a dishtowel, Bill went for the door and opened it.

Joe Crest looked back at Bill. "You smell like fish."

Bill was still wiping his hands with the towel. "Is that right?" he said. "Well, you smell like trouble. What's going on?" Bill stepped back and allowed Crest into his new home.

Crest, glancing around at the neatly furnished town house, said, "I would've called, but your number's out of service."

"I'm retired," Bill said, and dropping the dish towel on a side table; his hands now on his hips, he added, "so, what's this about?" Reading the expression on Crest's face, Bill said, "It *is* trouble, isn't it? What happened?" Crest slipped a folded set of documents out from his jacket and handed them to Bill.

"Depends, on how you look at it I guess."

Bill unfolded Sebo's Will and read down the first page. "What the hell?" Bill looked back at Crest. "Why me? Didn't he have any family? Any friends he'd rather leave it to?"

"Just you," answered Crest.

"Are you sure about that? He was a young man," Bill said.

"He made his wishes more than clear, and just to let you know, he had no known siblings, his father's somewhere out there in the great unknown, and his mother was killed in an armed robbery ten years ago. You were his PO, didn't you ever read his file?"

Bill, flipping through the pages, said, "I had a forty-hour work week and around seventy parolees to monitor at any given time; didn't leave me much of an opportunity to get to know these guys."

Crest eyed Bill for a moment, then said, "So now the ball's in your court, Officer Mazurek. How do you want to play this?"

"I don't." Bill handed the documents back to Crest. "I don't want anything to do with it—news I got said it was a murder/suicide. I don't wanna get anywhere near something like that."

"That was the initial report," answered Crest. "But I hired an investigator; he thinks it may have been a professional hit—I've convinced the police to reopen the case."

"Then I definitely don't want any part of it."

"Shouldn't your wife have a say in this?"

"She'd agree with me," Bill said. "But as soon as she's out of the shower she can tell you herself. What the hell possessed this guy to leave me 56 million dollars? Who does that?"

"I guess he figured you would be the one guy he could trust to find a good use for the money—do the right thing."

Bill let out a sigh. "So, what's the right thing? What am I supposed to do about this?"

Crest handed the documents back to Bill, said, "Look, why don't you think on it? My card's clipped to the top. Take your time, stew on it with your wife and give me a call—we can discuss your options."

Author's Note

Greetings Dear Reader

Did you enjoy the ride? I would like to know your opinion—
please leave a written review, be careful to avoid spoilers, but
express your thoughts and feelings, because, hearing from you
means a lot to me. If you would like to learn more about my
other books, or read interviews, visit my website at:
www.trschumer.com.

With gratitude, T. R.

Acknowledgements

This story lurked in the farthest corner of my mind for twelve long years before it finally made its way out and onto the page. Mostly it sat ignored and unattended, but every so often it would stubbornly bubble to the surface, and as often as I outlined the idea, started it, researched it, wrote short story versions of it; the results just never felt right. As it turned out, what I'd needed all along was more experience, and also, I needed distance.

Once this story's engine finally kicked over, there was no stopping it. A very special thank you goes to my friend Leslie Bass, for arranging the interviews, and for imparting her own knowledge and experience from her years as a Manatee County Peace Officer. My sincere gratitude also goes to Judy McLauchlin, for encouraging me when you did; you were my first pitch. It was back when the idea was in its infancy, and your response, "Tell me more about Sebastian," would resonate for years to come. I would also like to express my gratitude to Eugene Page, and for all of those nights we spent covering late night crime for the Bradenton Herald, the Sarasota Herald Tribune, and documenting crime scenes for the Manatee County Sheriff's Department, it was a long time ago to be sure, but "thank you" has no statute of limitations.

Also by T. R. Schumer

The Fearless Trilogy

Death Catch

Drone Catch

SEAL Catch

Other books

HUM

About the Author

T. R. SCHUMER is an Amazon bestselling author, 2018 indieBRAG Medallion Honoree and a 2017 Self-Publishing Review Book Awards Finalist. She is also an instrument rated pilot, sailor, scuba diver, and world traveler who has visited more than 90 countries. A fourth generation Florida native and graduate of the University of South Florida, she once copiloted a single-engine aircraft around the world, and is now in the much slower process of sailing around the world. She currently lives aboard a sailboat with her husband somewhere in Southeast Asia. You can visit her at www.trschumer.com